MALFUNCTION JUNCTION

MALFUNCTION JUNCTION

Memphis Stories of Stops, Starts, Wrong Turns, & Dead Ends

EDITED BY APRIL JONES

*Cover Design by Justin Siebert &
Daniel Reece*

MWJ

A Memphis Writers Junt

Copyright © 2021 by MWJ Publishing

First paperback edition January 2022

Book design by Justin Siebert and Daniel Reece

ISBN 978-0-578-33773-9 (paperback)   .

CONTENTS

CHAPTER 1

Null and Void

Rae Harding

In Morrow's opinion, if an employee is on time, they're late. And if they're late, they don't have respect for the job. So when the new suppression specialist was not at the Memphis Pyramid Arena upon Morrow's arrival, he had the guy pegged. *Don't let us keep you. It's only the end of mankind we're trying to prevent. No worries.*

The security officers arrived half an hour ago. The weather was fine—no flight delays. No major wrecks on Interstate 40. With nothing to excuse the new recruit's absence, Morrow was convinced this would be a long ten hours of taking up the slack.

It wasn't like a second suppression specialist was needed; Morrow had enough experience to handle the situation on his own. Besides, possessing the heart scarab gave him the backup needed. But the Directors required two specialists, so two specialists there would be; if one agent is compromised, the other could prevent a breach.

Morrow had partnered with countless new agents in his twenty-five years at the Parapet—all of which had lacked the fundamental understanding of the vital role the Parapet played in keeping the world and all its dimensions intact. But once agents were shuddered to the core, once they witnessed firsthand how loosely woven the veil between chaos and order was, many would go insane—drooling, bathing-in-your-own-shit, knocking-your-head-into-walls, no-idea-what-your-name-is insane.

The others learned to never be late to the job again.

Three of the four security officers, happy-go-lucky, baby-faced, recruits returned from the bathroom. They chuckled amongst themselves as they meandered down the hall, more like a pack of fraternity brothers than newly met colleagues. Their grins disappeared under James's glare. As the senior officer, James knew better than to make friends on the job. He fell under a category of employee Morrow appreciated: the *I've-seen-some-shit* category. He was a tall, bald, black man with a stern expression plastered on his face. Folded across his chest were arms displaying a set of biceps as large as Morrow's head—if Morrow's head was swollen.

Once his crew's mirth died under the weight of his intimidation, James marched over to Morrow. "Where do you want us, sir?"

Where does one get shirts with sleeves that large? thought Morrow. He considered asking but decided against it.

"You have your directives." Morrow pretended to consult his clipboard. "Two at the door leading to the vault and two at the actual vault itself. I will man the Pyramid's interior perimeter throughout the remaining time. At 4:00 A.M. tomorrow, we will enter the vault, replace Specimen X-40 in the sarcophagus, and you can catch the next flight out of Memphis."

"What about the staff, sir?" asked one of the younger officers. Morrow sensed he was fresh out of the army. His brown hair was clean-cut, and there was a stiffness to his stance ingrained into the body of a freshly-minted soldier.

"There are none," said Morrow. "This building was shut down four years ago in 2004. Our presence has been explained by a required building inspection." Morrow examined his watch. "Since the other suppression specialist seems to be delayed, I'll escort you to the vault now."

The security officers nodded in agreement. Morrow glanced around one more time, grabbed a small cooler, and guided the Parapet security officers to the elevator. He punched in a code, and the lift traveled to a below-ground garage. A wave of cool air entered as the doors retreated. The concrete expanse was flooded with fluorescent light and eerily empty. Morrow led the way to a shadowy metal stairwell door, which he opened with a pass card.

Finally, they reached another door; this one fitted with a key code pad. Morrow pulled up the Parapet-issued camera feed app on his iPhone 3 to verify Specimen X-40 was contained. There, in the shadowed corner of the vault, was a humanoid. Dingy and disintegrating bandages draped its torso and limbs. It did not move, but it had become activated. Instead of the shriveled husk that usually stayed within the sarcophagus, here stood a creature with supple skin, muscles, and definition.

Morrow entered the thirteen-digit numerical string, and the door's pneumatic locks disengaged with a *woosh*.

"Wait here for me," James said to the officer with the crew cut.

The rest of them followed Morrow down a sloping corridor, bathed in red. The emergency lights had been triggered upon Specimen X-40's movement out of the sarcophagus fourteen hours ago. At the bottom of the passage was another door flanked by metal folding chairs. It was also outfitted with pneumatic locks and a keypad, but this one would not be opened until Specimen X-40 returned to its dormant state.

"Here ya go, fellas." Morrow set the cooler on the floor next to one of the chairs. "Nothing to it. Make yourself comfortable. Only two rules: don't fall asleep and don't knock on the vault door—it agitates the creature. In the highly unlikely event Specimen X-40 escapes the vault, I'm sorry to say, you'll probably end up killing each other." The two security officers' eyes widened; one gulped. Morrow loved rattling new employees. It ensured a level of reverence for the job. "Sandwiches and bottled water in the cooler. Good evening, gentlemen!"

Morrow smiled and made his way back up the passage, followed by James. He reentered the code in the keypad, and the locks disconnected.

Morrow turned to James and Crew Cut as the door closed. "Under no circumstances should you open this door again until time has expired. If it opens from the inside, shoot to kill."

James nodded.

Morrow nodded back. "I will monitor Specimen X-40 on the camera and check in with you every few hours. You can contact me on the walkie at any time."

"You got it," said James.

Morrow returned to the upper portion of the Pyramid with a warring debate in his mind. Would he yell at the new suppression specialist once he showed? Should he contact the local Directors if he didn't? He didn't need to war too long. In the lobby stood an expectant man, dressed in the Parapet issued uniform: black, polo shirt with the O.T. Marshall Architects logo embroidered in white on the sleeve. His hair and eyes matched—raven black—and his skin was rich sepia.

"There you are," said the man sauntering towards him, an affable smile stretched across his face. "Apologize for the delay. Westy's was a zoo." He held high a Styrofoam box. "Hungry? I was famished."

Morrow snuffed the flame of rage trying to ignite. It was unprofessional to lose your temper on a colleague, although he scoffed at the idea of calling his new partner such—he was a minimum of fifteen years Morrow's junior. Clearly, he had not yet experienced the kind of shit Morrow had while working at the Parapet.

The man offered a handshake. "Name's Amon Mohamed."

Morrow did not take Amon's hand. "Our instructions were to meet at eighteen hundred hours Central Standard Time. It's nearly twenty-one hundred hours. Nice of you to join us." If he was going to contain his wrath, a little passive-aggressive behavior was in order. "Thomas Morrow, Senior Suppression Specialist for the Memphis site. The security officers are in position."

"Great," said Amon, unfazed. "So, how shall we pass the time?"

"This isn't a playdate."

Amon chuckled. "Hey, man. I'm just playin' around a bit. No need to be uptight. Specimen X-40 is Stable."

"Specimen class Stable does not mean *not dangerous,*" scoffed Morrow. "How long have you been on the job?"

"First day in the field," said Amon.

Morrow folded his arms over his chest. "But you've been through training. Or did you sleep through it?"

"Man, are you going to be like this for the next seven or so hours?" Amon folded his arms to mirror Morrow. "Of course, Specimen X-40 is dangerous. All I'm saying is there is no way for it to escape, even if it left the vault."

"Apart from the implausible occurrence of getting its hands on Specimen P98, no."

"See? So lighten up," said Amon. And then, as an afterthought, "Specimen P98?"

Morrow stared blankly at Amon, processing the question before formulating another question. "Weren't you hired out of that reliquary area? You should know all the Specimens contained in the facility you work at."

Amon shrugged his shoulders. "Haven't toured all the sectors yet. Guess I better get on it."

Smug son of a bitch, thought Morrow.

"Nevertheless, it's in the file you received upon assignment to this site. Specimen P98 is a page from The Egyptian Book of the Dead. Touch it, and you spend your days on life support, staring into the void while a nurse changes your diapers. That is unless you get possessed by the entity inside the scroll."

Amon inhaled deeply, followed by a slow exhale. *I bet he does yoga,* thought Morrow, *A hippie-dippie yoga guy. Probably used to wear a man-bun.*

"You know," said Amon, "I think I do remember that one. But what does it have to do with Specimen X-40?"

Morrow sighed. "Because if that scroll were to ever meet with Specimen P98, it won't be up and about for twenty-four hours —it'll be up and about permanently."

"So? Even if he manages to escape the vault, he can't escape the pyramid."

"Theoretically, this is true," agreed Morrow, "But I don't leave anything to chance. The impossible can become possible. Then we'd be looking at a Moira scenario."

"I know what that is!" said Amon with the enthusiasm of a first-grader. "Mankind goes insane. World ends. Null and void."

Morrow smirked. "Give the boy a gold star."

"Gotta say, though. With all the crazy crap people do to each other in this world—doesn't sound like we need any help from a Specimen."

Cynicism flowed through Morrow's veins. He didn't say anything, but there was a half-second of appreciation for the like-minded sentiment. Morrow had questioned his efforts at the Parapet many times over the course of his career. So much work to keep mankind safe when every evening news story heralded another tale of violent and deadly crime.

"Well, now you've straightened me out," said Amon, "how shall we proceed with the evening?"

"We'll tour the facility and verify the Pyramid is structurally sound." Morrow lifted the tool bag off the ticket desk counter and retrieved a large flashlight for Amon.

"Wait," said Amon, taking the flashlight. "The city thinks we're here inspecting the building and our job for the next seven hours is to inspect the building?"

Morrow nodded, retrieved a two-way from the bag, and handed it over.

"Huh," said Amon as he accepted.

"Is there a problem?" Morrow pulled out his flashlight and set the bag back on the counter.

"It's just," began Amon, "with an organization as clandestine as the Parapet, I never figured my cover would actually be a part of my job. The Parapet isn't known for being very...truthful."

"Look, buddy. I know you're new, but there's something you need to realize. The world can't handle the truth."

"The Grays would disagree—"

"The Grays consists of a bunch of nut jobs who have spent too much time studying and not enough time in the field. Anomalous rights and normalization! Ha! They're so mixed up they see dimensional portals in each other's assholes."

Amon chuckled. "You're funny, Tom."

"Morrow. Just call me Morrow."

"Fine. Morrow it is."

"Shall we?" Morrow gestured to the dimly lit hallway surrounding the arena.

Amon turned on his flashlight. "What are we looking for?"

"Structural cracks. Stress fractures," said Morrow.

Amon scratched the back of his head. "What would it mean if we find one? Like, the mummy can get out?"

Morrow cut his eyes to Amon. "I'd prefer you refer to the anomaly as Specimen X-40."

Amon nodded.

Morrow continued. "Stress fractures may indicate a weakness in the dimensional shield surrounding the Pyramid. Due to the New Madrid fault line proximity, we may find several. Until my recommendation for seismic retrofitting is approved, it's the way it is."

"And when we find one?"

Morrow led Amon to a wall with a thin, dark vein branching slightly at the end. He ran the flashlight beam down the length and back to cover each branch.

"These flashlights are designed to detect even the slightest tear in the dimensional fabric. If it's hot, a blue glow will emanate through the crack, and it will need to be sealed with hieroglyphs A5 and A15 on the Gadiner List."

"As simple as that, eh?" asked Amon.

"As simple as that," Morrow echoed.

"I hear they might turn this place into a Bass Pro Shop," said Amon with a chuckle. "Can you imagine?"

"It's a good cover," said Morrow, matter-of-factly. "And it would give field agents more access without producing suspicion."

The two men meandered the hall, their flashlights swirling on opposite walls. The awkward silence was magnified by the resonance of their footsteps as they walked the empty corridors surrounding the arena. At one point, Amon played with the echo by tap-dancing or attempting to. *Jackass,* thought Morrow.

"Where are you from?" Morrow's curiosity had won out over his desire to maintain a degree of intimidation. He had to know where the Parapet managed to recruit this numbskull.

"Boston," said Amon.

"Really," Morrow said. "Whole life?"

"Pfft!" Amon rolled his eyes. "Have *you* lived in the same place your whole life?"

"No."

"Same," said Amon. "I've even lived in Memphis."

"Same," said Morrow.

Amon smiled. "No shit?"

Morrow nodded. "Went to college here. But that was thirty-something years ago. Only get by these parts now when Specimen X-40 activates."

"And how often has that happened?"

"Since being contained in Memphis? This is número dos." Morrow focused on a thin, black line on the right wall, but it was only the remains of a dusty spider web. "You?"

"Me, what?" asked Amon.

"You get back to Memphis? You got any family here?"

Amon shook his head. "No."

"And how did you get recruited into the Parapet?"

"Are you kidding me?" said Amon. "They basically kidnapped me. My life was going in one direction, but they swooped in and whisked me into their world of 'Conceal and Defend.'"

Amon had answered the question without answering the question. "I mean," said Morrow, "what were you *doing*?"

MALFUNCTION JUNCTION — 11

"Ohhhh. Logistics."

The conversation ended. Amon walked ahead and resumed swinging his flashlight's beam into corners.

Morrow was bewildered. Amon's veneration for the position he held was virtually nonexistent, yet the Parapet clearly saw something in him as they once did with Morrow when he was recruited as a civil engineering major.

"Let me ask you a question or two, Tom," said Amon, turning around. "If I may?"

Morrow nodded. "Morrow. Please."

"You have a family? Married? Kids?"

Morrow shook his head. "No."

He had no regrets. There had been several opportunities, but he had not wanted to bring children into a world existing on the edge of pandemonium.

"And have you had a containment breach on your watch?" asked Amon.

"No," said Morrow, trying not to sound offended or arrogant.

"Never?"

"Never."

Amon sighed. "Not even a little slip? Ah, well, don't feel left out. There's a first time for everything."

"Not for something like this," said Morrow. "I've cleaned up too many breaches caused by overconfident, cocky specialists who believe Specimen containment is trial and error. You know what a slip is at a containment facility? A goddamn mess is what. So, no, Amon, there won't be a first time for me. I don't allow mistakes. And if you're prone to making them, I suggest you get out of my way and let me do my job."

Amon raised his hands in surrender. "Hey, man! We're partners—"

"Partners? You're a mentee. You are a parasite, something I have to carry for the next six and a half hours. You're some twerp I have to deal with until you go back and tell your Acolyte-level buddies all about the hard-ass you got stuck with while baby-sitting a mummy. And your supervisors will send you on to the next case where you'll be late again and not take the Specimen seriously because your talents are underappreciated on any anomaly below Virulent class. Am I right?"

"Such hostility, Tom. You feeling all right?"

Morrow's heart pounded. He wanted to punch this punk in the face, but he had been reprimanded one too many times about his temper. The shrink suggested the job might be getting the best of him. She was right, of course. He had spent the beginning of this life blissfully oblivious to the monumental task the Parapet faced. But after discovering the one thing standing between madness and rationale in this world is the Parapet, the pressure is bound to get to you once in a while. Every day on the job was one day he could do his part to make sure the Parapet succeeded. But some days it seemed as if he was the only one taking the job seriously.

So when the Facilitators recruit yahoos like Amon, how can he be expected to keep his temper in check? Suppression specialists should be precise, meticulous, and ten steps ahead. Each Specimen needed to be put in a box, and each box needed a designer. The Parapet needed more designers like Morrow, not Amon.

"I'll tell you what," said Morrow, teeth gritting, "We'll cover more ground if we separate. You take the east and south planes.

I'll take the west and north. We'll meet back in the lobby at midnight and inspect the arena."

"Whatever you say, partner." Amon clicked his tongue, cocked his head to the side, gave a two-finger salute, and walked away.

Morrow fantasized about smacking his flashlight across Amon's head, the moment of impact so vivid he had to close his eyes. *A little break is in order,* he thought, *that will even me out.*

Morrow took out his phone and pulled up the camera feed from Specimen X-40's vault. There it stood, as it had been. No change.

Morrow considered the creature. *So much time spent petrified as a mummy, and it spends this day motionless, staring in the corner like a naughty child being punished.*

"You're a bad boy," said Morrow to the camera image on his phone, "But you're not in trouble. Let's keep it that way." He patted his chest where the scarab hung from the chain around his neck.

Two hours later, and Morrow still needed to let off steam. How had he allowed Amon to get under his skin? What did he care if the guy didn't take the job as seriously as he did? Surely when he began working for the Parapet twenty-five years ago, some senior specialist had the same thoughts about him. *Get a grip on yourself, Morrow. It's a class Stable. Do your job, and in four hours, you can put the bastard back in its box and head home.*

"Specialist Morrow!"

Crew Cut's boyish voice startled Morrow. He fumbled for the handheld transceiver. Static coming from the other end was like a scratchy record.

"Specialist Morrow?" said Crew Cut again. "This is Bradford. Do you copy?"

"I did not. Say again. Over." Morrow moved around, holding the two-way radio higher in an attempt to gain a better signal.

Screeching static "...officer...missing." *Screeching static* "...I repeat. Officer Johnson missing. Do you copy?"

Officer Johnson, thought Morrow. *James?*

Morrow pressed the call button. "Copy. I'm on my way."

"We heard an odd sound coming from the stairwell," said Bradford upon Morrow's arrival. "He went to investigate, and he never returned."

"How long ago was this?" asked Morrow.

"Half an hour."

"The stairwell I came from?" asked Morrow.

Bradford nodded.

Morrow checked the camera feed. There was no change with Specimen X-40. "I didn't see him on my way here."

Morrow studied Bradford's wide eyes as he began to speak, then stopped as if unsure or afraid. This was maddening for Morrow. First, the Parapet hires some hotshot moron, and now he discovers they hired a cowering boy? *What the hell?*

"Speak up, man!" Morrow commanded.

Bradford returned to himself half a second later. "It's just— the sound, sir. It...wasn't human."

This assignment just keeps getting better. Morrow exhales. "It's the building settling."

"No!" said Bradford. "It was...a moan."

"Look." Morrow shoved his iPhone into Bradford's vision, showing him Specimen X-40 in its vault. "This. This is our only concern at the moment. This Specimen has a Stable classification. It's not getting out unless someone lets it out, and since my partner and I are the ones with the code, you can rest assured it's there to stay. I'm sure Officer...James...I'm sure Officer Johnson will turn up any minute. He's probably in some secluded bathroom taking himself a peaceful shit. Now, if you'll excuse me, I have work that's a bit more complicated than standing guard at a secured door."

"Tom!"

Morrow spun. Amon was approaching, the same affable smile upon his face.

Morrow crossed to meet him. "What are you doing here?"

Amon held up his two-way. "I heard the call. Everything okay?"

A low and ghoulish howl exploded in Morrow's ears. He whirled around, but by the time he located the origin of the wail, it was too late. James appeared from around the corner wall and leapt onto Bradford's back. They tumbled to the floor, and Morrow watched in disbelief as James sunk his jaws into Officer-Right-Out-of-the-Army-Crew-Cut-Bradford's neck. He yanked violently, sending a spray of blood landing squarely on Morrow's shoes. Bradford twisted, miraculously wrenching James off, flinging the crazed officer onto the floor. A heartbeat later, Bradford pulled his pistol and opened fire. It took three shots for the boy to hit James between the eyes.

Morrow dashed over to Bradford, unable to process the turn of events. Bradford dropped his firearm and clutched his neck, holding pressure, but the blood seeped profusely between the boy's fingers. The damage had been done. Morrow grabbed his iPhone and dialed the number for the local Directors. Before the call connected, Bradford knocked the phone out of his hands, sending it crashing into the wall and dropping to the floor in pieces. His arms reached for Morrow. With eyes fixed, Bradford locked his blood-wet hands around Morrow's neck and squeezed.

Morrow punched and kicked ferociously, desperate to break Bradford's hold. He managed to wrestle Bradford to the ground but found himself rolled onto his back with Bradford straddling him. Blood gushed from his neck, spilling onto Morrow's face.

"Must die," said Bradford, his voice raspy. "All must die."

He's lost his mind. He's hallucinating. Can blood loss create such an immediate change? The boy actually *growled*. Morrow searched for sanity behind Bradford's eyes, but all he found was hate. Bursts of light exploded in Morrow's vision. *Not yet. I just need to last a bit longer.*

His feet slipped on the blood-slick floor, miraculously sliding the firearm in reach. His vision blurred; Bradford's hold was not easing up. Morrow stretched his fingers as his sight grew dark, finally reaching the pistol. With the last moment of consciousness Morrow could muster, his fingers climbed the grip until it nested in his palm. He brought the muzzle to Bradford's temple and pulled the trigger. The body tumbled like a felled tree.

Morrow gasped, rolling over into a puddle of blood. His ears rang from the gun blast.

"What the hell, Tom."

Morrow waited for his eyes to focus. Amon stood over him, expressionless.

"He...he tried to kill me."

"Um, I saw that," said Amon.

"And you...didn't...think to...stop him?" Each word was like a razor blade through his crushed windpipe. His skin pulsed, where moments earlier fingers were buried. Amon laced his arms under Morrow's armpits and pulled. Morrow slipped in the pools of blood on the floor before gaining sure footing.

"We...need to call...Directors..." said Morrow. "Something's not right."

"You think?" Sarcasm dripped from Amon's tone. "Perhaps we should check on the security officers in the corridor?"

Morrow shook his head. "Not a good idea. We need contingency units here. Give me your iPhone."

Amon retrieved his phone from his back pocket, unlocked it, and handed it to Morrow. Morrow dialed the hotline number, but nothing happened. He stared at the screen for a moment, tapped the red button to cancel the call, and then redialed. Nothing.

"No signal." Morrow's words were nothing but whispers.

"It's okay. I have something to show you top side. We'll check the signal there. Follow me."

Amon's conduct had changed drastically from the carefree suppression specialist hours ago. Morrow had to concede: the numbskull seemed to be handling the situation better than expected. In fact, of the two, Amon's demeanor was far calmer than Morrow's. As he followed his new partner back up the Pyramid, he tried to clear his foggy brain. The rapid change in Bradford and James had been horrifying. Horror he could handle. Not knowing the *cause* of the change was terrifying.

Morrow followed Amon to the east side of the Pyramid's first floor, where an old soda dispenser sat against the far wall. It appeared odd, there by itself, with no furniture or anything indicating it lived there before the Pyramid had been shut down. There wasn't even an outlet where the machine would have been plugged in.

"There," said Amon.

Morrow slowly approached the machine. A clearing of dust on the floor told Morrow it had been moved recently from its original position. He turned to Amon, who reassured him with a nod. Morrow pulled the machine back.

There behind the machine was a large opening in the wall. A vent cover stood sentinel next to the cavity, propped against the cinder block wall. *Vents are not breaches,* thought Morrow. His eyes rested on a faint light deep within. He hunched and entered the vent. Inside he could stand. It reminded him of a mirror image of the corridor leading to Specimen X-40's vault, but instead of red, the tunnel was blanketed in a gentle white, natural light. He walked further, reaching a ladder leading to a circular opening in the Pyramid. Perfectly framed in its center was the moon.

"That counts, right?"

Morrow whirled; he had not heard Amon follow through the vent. "You found this? Open?"

Amon nodded.

"It doesn't mean there's a breach," said Morrow, more to convince himself than Amon.

Amon aimed his flashlight up. A faint, electric blue haze illuminated the shaft leading out the Pyramid. Morrow exhaled in relief. Blue was good.

But the blue dissipated. Morrow grabbed the flashlight out of Amon's hands and shined it up the shaft again. Nothing. His heart fell to his stomach. The barrier was compromised. He swallowed hard. "Okay. That's why we're here. This is our job—to fix the box. Specimen X-40 is still secure in the vault. I saw it on the camera right before—" *Before James and Bradford lost their minds.* He couldn't say it aloud. "It can't escape. Not the vault, not the Pyramid, not my control. Damn the barrier."

"Control?"

Morrow pulled the chain around his neck and retrieved the scarab from the depths of his blood-soaked shirt. He brandished it in Amon's face. It had been carved from green nemehef stone, small for a heart scarab but still far heftier in comparison to its other scarab cousins.

"What's that?"

"A funerary scarab," said Morrow. "There is a spell etched on the flat side. It gives the bearer complete control of the entity. Specimen X-40 is not going anywhere while I have this."

"Why didn't I get one of those?" His voice was on the verge of a whine.

"Only one," said Morrow.

"You say Specimen X-40 can't escape," Amon began, "but maybe this vent was opened for someone to get in. Perhaps we are not alone. Perhaps someone is here to compromise the containment."

Morrow shook his head. "What good would it do? In three hours, Specimen X-40 will resume dormancy."

"Unless," said Amon. "He doesn't."

Morrow thought of Specimen P98, the scroll torn from the Book of the Dead. He couldn't move. Moving would mean he believed it possible Specimen P98 was there in the Pyramid. Moving meant he had a containment breach to stop. It couldn't happen. *Couldn't* happen. But even as he eviscerated the improbable scenarios, he knew it was conceivable. It wouldn't be the first time the Parapet had been infiltrated. It could have even been a member of the Grays, here to *save* Specimen X-40. Or one of Specimen P98's personas? Could one of them have escaped? No. Amon had been at that facility. He would have known. Besides, he had not been aware Specimen P98 existed, let alone what it *was*. And the local Directors would have included such an occurrence in the file.

But still...

"Try your phone again," Morrow ordered.

Amon dialed the number, held it to his ear, and showed Morrow the screen.

Call Failed.

"Let's go," said Morrow.

Arriving back at the gory scene turned Morrow's stomach. Bloody footprints, *his* bloody footprints, tracked around the bodies like a grotesque treasure map. Bradford's brain matter had splattered onto the walls like a tossed bucket of chum. James's eyes were open, still feral and spiteful. Morrow wanted to close them but couldn't bear the thought of touching the corpse.

This wasn't like Morrow. He had witnessed more death than he could count on both hands, and yet he was gripped by terror. He could not catch his breath. His hands were clammy and shaking. Was he going into shock? Or was Specimen X-40 to blame?

Opening the door to the corridor was against all procedures in this type of situation, but Morrow had to have answers. Without a phone, he could not contact the Directors. Nor could he visually verify via the camera Specimen X-40 was still contained. He couldn't let a breach happen on his watch. Protocols would have to be overridden. After all, their adherence would be detrimental to the restraint of Specimen X-40.

Morrow searched the floor for the firearm he dropped after shooting Bradford. It rested three feet from the body, a streak of blood from where Morrow pushed it away. It was sticky in his grip, so he wiped away as much of the gelatinous blood as possible. With shaky fingers, Morrow entered the thirteen-digit code, releasing the pneumatic locks.

Amon protested. "Hey, man! You sure about this?"

Morrow turn. "I have to verify the vault is closed. That's all. There's no other choice."

"Tom," said Amon. "As your partner, I'm asking you to follow protocol. Don't do something you'll regret."

"So you're staying here?" asked Morrow.

Amon hesitated. "Screw that."

With it settled, Morrow opened the door. The crimson passage was now nightmarish. There was utter stillness as they proceeded down. Morrow listened intently for signs of life. The officers, entirely unaware of the chaos unfolding above, could be playing gin rummy or eating the sandwiches he packed for them.

But there was silence. Only silence. He gripped the pistol tight in his right hand and held out his flashlight with his left.

"Hello?" Morrow's voice echoed back. "Officers?"

No reply. He glanced back at Amon, who dipped his chin slightly to urge Morrow forward. He advanced deliberately, heel-toe, down the passage, anxiety rising with every second of the continued silence. He quickened his pace, controlled at first, then frantic. He ultimately fell into a sprint, arriving on yet another death scene. A faint yet putrid, metallic smell rose from the blood slick floor. The walls were splashed in sanguine shadows. A body lay on the ground like a pile of boneless flesh.

From the corner by the vault door came heavy breathing. Before Morrow could aim the flashlight, something leapt onto him, knocking it out of his hand. He wrestled with the thing, but it punched him over and over. The pain barely registered in Morrow's brain, all survival instincts in full throttle. He quickly discovered the *thing* was another crazed officer. He lunged, teeth gnashing as Morrow blocked with his right arm. The officer's teeth sank into his flesh, and he screamed as the pain coursed up his shoulder and down his fingers. He reached for the fallen flashlight with his left hand and swung at the officer's head with all his might. The officer fell back. Morrow aimed the gun, using his left hand to steady his now damaged right arm, and fired.

The gunfire was deafening in the small space. Amon hovered over him. His lips moved, but Morrow could not make out the words. Amon's eyes darted back and forth between Morrow's face and abdomen. He lifted Morrow's shirt. It didn't take long for Morrow to look too.

"Fuck." It was the single word Morrow could utter. His abdomen was mutilated, blood gushing like a volcano. The crazed officer had inflicted substantial damage.

Amon jumped into action, ripping the shirt off of the dead officer and using it to plug the massive wound. "What do I do?"

There was a tremor in Morrow's hand as he tugged the chain and retrieved the heart scarab. Pain pulsed throughout his body in massive waves of electricity. With each undulation of agony, his breath exploded and his heart imploded. He pulled the scarab from around his neck and placed it in Amon's hand. "Open the vault," he said weakly. "Do you know the code?"

Amon nodded. "I don't know how Specimen X-40 is doing this, but if we open the vault, we are releasing him into the world. The Pyramid is compromised."

Morrow shook his head. "The heart scarab is the failsafe. You can stop Specimen X-40 with it. It must do as you command."

"Are you sure about this?"

"I'm not going...I...don't think...," Morrow couldn't finish. He wasn't ready to come to terms with his fate. "We have to stop it. Hurry."

Amon sprang up to the keypad and punched in the code. The pneumatic locks disengaged with a hiss. He knelt to recover the flashlight and gun before gently pushing the door inward.

Morrow managed to lift himself a bit, reclining on his elbows, biting through the pain. The rancid odor of decay and sour wafted up his nostrils. Amon aimed his flashlight into the corner. There it was—Specimen X-40 in person and not on a camera feed. But it was undeniably the same anomaly Morrow had monitored since his arrival in Memphis, standing motionless in the corner, wrapped haphazardly in rotting bandages.

Morrow's next thought was, *Why? The door is open? Why is it not attempting to escape?* Amon crept over and grabbed it by the shoulder. On contact, Specimen X-40 fell to the ground like a sack of potatoes. Dead, blue eyes stared at Morrow, blonde tendrils framing the youthful face. This was no Egyptian entity. This was no mummy humanoid. This was *human*.

The vault contained a decoy. Specimen X-40 had breached its confines. On Morrow's watch. The mummy was on the loose.

"I told you there's a first time for everything," said Amon in a calm tone, tossing the scarab up in the air and catching it.

Amon grinned, and in that instant, Morrow discovered the situation was far worse than he first imagined.

"You'll never escape," said Morrow. "You can't cross the Pyramid's barrier. And in a few hours, you'll become what you are inside—a dried-up, empty casing."

"It's true, I am powerless to circumvent the Pyramid's confines. Not without a key, of course—a way to punch a hole in time and space, to reconcile the blessed and the cursed, to rip the veil between the living and dead, to pop the bubble you call a barrier surrounding this pyramid. But you see, Tom, I've had millennia to design my escape. Where do I go when I lie in the sarcophagus?"

Morrow remained silent. His pulse accelerated. He was cold and weak from blood loss. The pain was turning into numbness all over this body. The first signs of shock were manifesting. He wouldn't have known what answer to give even if he could.

"The Void, Tom. He is in the Void. I had all the time in the world to find him, and I did. And we had all the time in the world to wait for a braggart new recruit with fatal curiosity to break procedures and touch Specimen P98." Amon produced the scroll from behind his back.

Morrow's hopes sank. Specimen X-40 would be active forever. Unless he could keep it contained in the vault, Specimen X-40 would infect anyone who saw it, anyone who heard it, anyone who came in contact with it and spread its vitriol faster than any plague on earth.

"Specimen P98 possessed the recruit."

Amon nodded. "From there, it was merely logistics. I told you I did logistics."

It wasn't enough. Morrow needed to identify when and where the fault occurred. *How did this box break?*

"I woke from my slumber and activated the alarm," it said, nudging the decoy's corpse with its foot. "He-Who-Is-In-The-Void used this body to volunteer as your new partner. Begged, more like it. 'Eager for fieldwork.' 'Desire to learn from the best.' Upon arrival in Memphis, *he* used the key entry codes to release me. I read the scroll and merged with He-Who-Is-In-The-Void. See? Logistics."

"But the camera feed. The Parapet is watching at this very moment," said Morrow.

"This is true, Tom. But *what* is it they are watching?"

Morrow stared vacantly.

"A loop, Tom. A loop. By the time my twenty-four hours have expired, I will be long gone, unleashing mankind's innate cruelty, giving you humans what you truly desire—oblivion."

"Why haven't you, then?" asked Morrow, his voice raspy. "Why are you still here? Why haven't I been affected?"

Specimen X-40 sauntered over and knelt. "You felt it. Deep. Underneath your skin. Ready to burst to the surface." It held the scarab for Morrow to view. "But this. It's protected you. Until now. I stayed because I needed this. I couldn't begin my devastation if you had the ability to stop me."

"Then why didn't you kill me? Why didn't you steal it?"

"Didn't you know? How could you, of all people, overlook such a crucial piece of the information? It's even in the file." Specimen X-40 clicked his tongue. "I couldn't take it from you. It had to be *given*. And I thank you for it."

"The Parapet will send—"

"The Parapet keeps shocking the heart of this world into beating again, no matter how many times it flatlines," said Specimen X-40. "Maybe the fucker deserves to rest in peace. Does anyone give that any consideration? Hmm?"

Morrow closed his eyes in resignation.

"Oh, Tom. Don't pout. You have spent a quarter of a century protecting this world, when in fact, your animosity towards mankind rivals mine at times."

Morrow's arms gave way. He grimaced at the pain as his body fell flat. Specimen X-40 stood, grabbed his arm, and dragged him into the room. Morrow groaned. He was powerless to fight it.

"I don't think you'll survive your injury, Tom, but certainly can't underestimate you either." Specimen X-40 yanked Morrow over to the sarcophagus. "You get to stay here, in the vault, with your partner." It gestured to the blonde corpse lying next to Morrow. "Get acquainted with each other."

Morrow wanted to leap to his feet and rush Specimen X-40. He wanted to take the gun and empty the magazine. But his body was dying. He was dying.

"Goodbye, Tom," said Specimen X-40. "It was a pleasure working with you. Now, if you'll excuse me. I have a world to throw into chaos one city at a time."

Specimen X-40 walked away and closed the door. The vault was engulfed in darkness. The world was about to end, and the only thing Morrow could do was give in to the blackness of the void.

CHAPTER 2

Stake and Eggs

Daniel Reece

No one deliberately plans to be in a Waffle House at 2 A.M. It's just one of those things that happens without a conscious decision being involved. Once you're there, you start to question all your recent life choices. Here I am, stirring my coffee mindlessly and waiting on my All-Star. I'm in my favorite booth by the front window facing the empty street. The glass is wet with condensation on the outside, soaked by a humid Memphis night. Through the window, I watch a green traffic light and the dull glow line of sodium streetlights casting amber framed shadows along Germantown Parkway. The world looks as abandoned as a zombie apocalypse, and occasionally a car will roll slowly by, like the dead stumble-walking in a dream.

You can feel the sleep of the weary world pulled over the city like a shroud. The night snores softly at this late hour with all the good people tucked into bed, dreaming their dreamy dreams and dreading the malaise the morning will bring. When dawn arrives, the streetlights flick off and that traffic light, so innocent and unassuming at this moment, will transform into the bane of every commuter's existence, to the point where their attitudes toward everyone else might be determined by whether they faced a green or red-eyed monster on any given morning.

Genny comes over and sets my order down in front of me, then goes back behind the counter to continue her crossword puzzle. I've been coming here in the dead of night about once a week for the last few years. I'm a regular and a decent tipper, so we got a good thing, Genny and me. However, this is not our routine. Usually, it's just me alone with my textbooks and hashbrowns. Tonight I'm waiting for Jasper to arrive.

The Waffle Weasel is empty, save for Dennis on the grill and waitress Genny, her with the deep, sunken eyes standing behind the counter. Dennis likes to joke that he is the only grill cook at this establishment not currently on probation. Genny always manages a smile even though I know she is parenting a two-year-old granddaughter and a live-in twenty-six-year-old son at home. The two-year-old is the mature one. What Genny wouldn't give for a bit of a break from this life. Genny would gladly take any bargain Jasper laid before her. She'd probably trade five years off her life for a weekend trip to Cancun if offered. Jasper would consider Genny low-hanging fruit, though.

Jasper made it clear to me his business model wasn't quantity but quality. He would only take someone like her out of a sense of boredom and probably call it a mercy. Jasper made no bones about being a snob. My mother would have called him highfalutin. My grandmother would have just called him a horse's ass. It gave me an immense sense of pleasure to force him to come back to this greasy spoon to complete our transaction.

The glass door opens with a slight tinkle from the small bell dangling over the entranceway. Jasper came in with his typical gravitas as though walking in slow motion. He was dressed in a black three-piece suit with a blood-red square perfectly tucked into his breast pocket. He reluctantly glided over to the booth and spilled into the seat across from me. He glanced down at the feast laid out before me with a disapproving shake of his head.

Scrambled eggs, bacon, two waffles, and hashbrowns all the way. Double. Genny came over, and Jasper ordered a cup of hot tea without bothering to look in her direction. She returned a moment later and set a fresh cup of hot water with a single tea bag and a small stainless steel water pitcher in front of him. She paused, and he sent her away with an unnecessary hand flourishment. Genny flashed me a dentured smile before retreating back to her counter.

I watched Jasper steeping his tea. I didn't think it was possible to steep tea with obvious disdain for humanity, but somehow he managed.

"Are you done considering my offer?" asked Jasper impatiently.

"Geez. Buy a girl a drink first," I said. "We haven't even had any foreplay."

Jasper rolled his eyes and said, "Stewart, when you become as old as I am, you learn to forgo the foreplay and get right to the good stuff, as it were."

I leaned back in the booth and said, "See, it's things like that which make me think I definitively shouldn't take you up on your offer."

"Things like what?" he asked as he grabbed the sugar dispenser and began to pour a continuous stream into his cup.

"Things like your insistence on calling me Stewart when everyone calls me Stu."

Jasper sighed and said, "I'm offering life everlasting to Stewart. If you wish to remain, Stu, then I suggest you go back to your family's farm and continue raising swine."

This was a not-so-subtle jab at me. One of the reasons I studied biochemistry was to convert my family's slaughter farm to soy farming. Looking down at the meat on my plate, I did not feel one ounce of hypocrisy. I planned to enjoy the pigs as much as I could while they lasted. As soon as I could make soy reasonably taste like bacon and could offer farms, like my family's, a sustainable alternative, I intended to put meat out of business.

"Why wouldja want a po' country boy like me din?" I asked, digging for my Haywood County roots which weren't that deep an excavation.

Jasper stirred his tea, nearly as thick as syrup with all the sugar he poured into it. "You have certain talents my kind would find useful. A thousand years ago, we would have simply made you our pet. But these days, we are trying to be more...diverse."

Now it was my turn to roll my eyes. "I'm so privileged that you would allow a commoner such as myself into the palace."

For someone who claimed to be immortal, Jasper was mighty impatient. "Were you able to pass my test?"

"Yes," I answered.

"Then come with me, and I'll show you delights your science will never be able to explain. You may even call it magic."

"*Magic is just science for people who don't understand science,*" I quoted.

"Funny," said Jasper, "Oppenheimer?"

"No. Princess Bubblegum." I could tell by the look on his face that Jasper was not a fan of *Adventure Time.*

"What is your answer then, man of reason?" asked Jasper.

I opened my mouth to say something, then I slowly closed it. I couldn't be reactionary. "My answer is that I need to piss," I said anticlimactically.

I got up and walked to the bathroom while Jasper continued to roll his eyes and sip his tea. Genny gave me a strange look, then nodded towards Jasper. I shrugged my shoulders. Dennis continued to scour the grill, looking at the clock overhead from time to time and as he calculated how long until his smoke break.

I entered the bathroom, which was clean. It was always clean, so I shouldn't have been surprised. It wasn't the bathroom that felt gritty. It was me. I stood at the urinal and unzipped my fly, barely aware of the slow trickle I was producing. I leaned forward and placed my head against the cool, white tile and closed my eyes, and tried to think how I found myself in this devil's bargain.

It was a week ago today when Jasper came into this same restaurant and slunk into the booth across from me. I always come here late at night when my roommate stumbles home from the bar with whatever fly decided to stumble home with him. I didn't begrudge my roommate, whose drunken dalliances were often brief and only occasionally conducted with an open door. Yes, I had been propositioned by an unsatisfied last call on more than one occasion, but only took up the mantle once. So I couldn't honestly pretend to be incorruptible to Jasper, and my standards were obviously not that high.

However, I couldn't study Bio Chem while my roommate was studying inebriated physiology. Besides, I think biscuits and gravy go well with botany.

"How would you like to live forever, Stewart?" was his opening line.

The scientific portion of my brain answered first. "Everything dies," I replied.

Jasper smiled, and when he did, I could see his slightly elongated canine teeth. I found this odd but not convincing. I knew a guy in my British Lit class who had a bifurcated tongue. Even he didn't sell the image as hard as Jasper with his expensive suit and deep red pocket square.

Jasper ordered his hot tea from Genny and said, "I used to think the same thing myself. I've seen everything die. Men and nations. I've seen how death spreads. Ships and cities burned to the ground to try to contain death. Bodies carted through the streets and piled together, my god boy, you've never smelled the rot. I was lying on a bed, burning fever and praying for death when my savior found me and asked me the very same question."

All the while Jasper performed his rant, he seized the dispenser and emptied a cascade of sugar into his tea, then stirred it with annoyingly slow deliberation.

"Are you a....?" I started to ask, but the loose grip upon the rational section of my brain refused to say the word.

"Pfff. Labels," said Jasper. "If it helps you wrap your head around the concept, then *yes*. Does that shock you?"

"No. I mean, I suppose you are insane. The cogent mind would ask for proof."

Jasper sighed and rolled his eyes. "Must I turn into a bat or perhaps a mist? Do you want me to find some star-eyed maiden and drink her like a Capri Sun? A small demonstration then." Jasper grabbed the steak knife from the table. My reaction was that he was about to jump across the booth and bury it in my chest. Instead, he slowly pushed the blade through his palm. There was almost no blood and what small fluid flowed from his wound was thick and black. The blade protruded from the opposite side of his hand. This, I might have argued, was an illusion, but when he removed the blade, I watched the blood draw itself back into the gaping hole while slowly sealing the wound until the hand appeared completely unharmed.

"I guess I can't argue with that." My cogent mind was telling me to run, but I settled back into my seat as my scientific curiosity took over. "Why me?"

"Why not you?" pondered Jasper.

"What's the catch?" I asked.

"Must there be a catch?" Jasper sighed with a rather calculated condescension.

"There's always a catch."

"You can't walk in the sun. It's pointless to love a human. Garlic burns like acid in your throat. These are pretty well-known downsides."

"I love garlic," I said. "What about food? Can I still eat at this Waffle House?"

Jasper rolled his eyes and said, "If your greatest desire is to suck the grease from the crevices of this hell hole then, by all means, you can spend the rest of eternity pining for the diabetes you can never acquire."

Genny overheard a bit of that diatribe and looked at me with a raised eyebrow. I gave her a shrug as if to remind her a little insanity is to be expected during the 2 A.M. Waffle House shift. While Jasper convinced me of his powers, he hadn't convinced me he was stable. I pierced my last piece of waffle dripping in butter and syrup and put it in my mouth to slowly savor it. I thought, *Who wouldn't want infinite waffles?*

"Suppose I say yes?" I asked. "What then?"

Jasper removed a notecard from his pocket and slid it across the table toward me. On it was the drawing of a molecule. It was something organic, complex, and I was intrigued. "A small test," said Jasper. "Can you create this?"

I looked it over and said, "It will take about a week."

"Then I will meet you in one week's time," said Jasper as he rose and headed for the door.

"I'll be here," I said. His back was to me, so I can't be sure he rolled his eyes, but I think we all know he did.

Jasper gave me too much time to think. It took me less than a day to replicate his little test. It wasn't easy, but I happen to be good at this stuff. However, unlike the people who created Sarin, I spent most of my time not asking *how* I was making it, but *why*? Once I realized the compound's purpose, the rest of my decisions fell into place rather easily.

I zipped up my pants, then reached into my jacket and brought out the wooden stake I had fashioned. I spent most of the week searching through vampire lore at the Ned R. McWherter Library, but I wouldn't characterize any of the reading I did as *research*. That would be an insult to research. There were few universals among the mythologies when it came to slaying the undead. There were two methods that seemed most acceptable, and a stake through the heart was one of them. However, the length of wood I bought for a buck off the scrap pile at Home Depot felt grossly inadequate.

I flushed the urinal then washed my hands, which were noticeably shaking. I placed the stake back in my jacket then checked myself in the mirror to make sure it was concealed. I waved my hand under the automated paper towel dispenser, grabbed the paper towel, dried my hands, and pitched it at the trash can. Swish. I took a deep breath, opened the bathroom door, and walked back toward the table.

I knew something was wrong immediately. It wasn't quiet, but there was a lack of movement and sound. I exited the short hallway and heard the flat top grill sizzling. I turned toward the kitchen area and saw Dennis slumped over, his face pressed against the grill surface. His white apron was stained with blood. I reeled back, drawing the stake from my jacket scanning the restaurant for Jasper.

My eyes came to rest on Genny, who was splayed out across the register. Her eyes were wide open, and the check spindle completely ran through one side of her neck until it protruded from the other side. I clenched my jaw as a wave of rage rose inside me.

I could have run at that moment, I suppose. The exit was right there and appeared unblocked. But I knew I wouldn't have made it halfway to my Toyota Prius before he was on me. I moved down the line towards the front of the restaurant, but all the booths appeared empty, and there was no sign of Jasper. I could feel his eyes on me, which reminded me of my dad looking at his prized hog after winning the county fair. Dad made me slaughter Mr. McFatty myself after he found out I named him.

Whether Jasper changed himself into a fog or a cat or if he was dangling from the ceiling, I couldn't tell for sure. I caught a glimpse of him in the window's distorted reflection, dropping down behind me like a bad horror movie, and just like an oversexed teen, I was painfully slow to react. I had just turned around when he struck me across the face, picked me up, and threw me against the glass window. The window did not shatter but cracked as my back slammed into it. I landed in the booth and scrambled quickly to my feet. I jabbed the stake out weakly. Again Jasper moved fast as thought and wrenched the stake from my hands, lacerating my skin as he ripped it from my feeble grip. My palms were nothing but blood and splinters.

Jasper laughed as he examined the stake. "You didn't even remove the sticker from where you bought this worthless piece of wood. Is it sacred ash, blessed with consecrated water? If not, I hope you kept the receipt, dear boy." He dropped the stake to the ground as he loomed over me.

"Why did you have to kill Genny and Dennis?" I asked.

"Isn't it obvious? I wanted to take my time killing you, and they were delaying my gratification. Were you even able to recreate my little molecule?"

"Easily. It's not quite perfected yet. I could tell it was a blood preservative."

"You figured it out, didn't you? Well, human blood can only be stored for 40 days without freezing it. Frozen blood is useless to my kind. You can't develop a mass market unless you have a reliable way to get the product to the consumer. Don't worry. When it's time, I plan to raise my livestock cruelty-free."

"You also can't start a war unless you can preserve rations," I pointed out.

"Clever boy, but that's the long game."

Jasper came towards me, his fangs bared and his eyes wild with fire. As he prepared to tear my throat out, I raised my bleeding hands in surrender and pleaded, "Can I ask one more question?"

Jasper smiled and backed a bit away. "If you must."

"I only found two reliable methods for killing your kind. One was the stake. The other was silver."

Jasper sighed again and said, "Yes. Those are both reliable methods. Do you have a gun loaded with silver bullets that I am unaware of?"

I shook my head, "Naw, *mane*. But I've got a Masters in Biochemistry from the University of Memphis."

For the first time, Jasper didn't sigh or shake his head at me with his typical there-there. In fact, rather than rolling his eyes, they widened in surprise. He took a step toward me then winced in pain. His face contorted, and he stumbled back a few steps as I stood up from the booth. For, perhaps, the first time in a hundred years, Jasper truly felt real fear. Once, he had been both burned at the stake and buried alive on the same day, but this was different.

"What have you done to me?" he said, spitting black blood from his mouth, which began to run down his chin.

"It wasn't easy to synthesize silver nitrate into something tasteless that would dissolve. Took all week to get it right, and I had no idea if it would work. You should lay off the sugar; that stuff will kill you." I shot him a smile.

The silver began to burn through Jasper from the inside out, like his stomach was full of lit kerosene. He howled as the fire burned through him. I felt a pang of guilt for the pain he was suffering --I thought the process would have been quicker. Then I saw Genny and Dennis laid out, and those feelings quickly dissipated. A slow burn built in Jasper's chest and began to turn his innards to ash. It spread to his arms and legs, and he was able to raise one hand to his face and watch it slowly crumble away. He tried to breathe in to let loose one final wail, but his lungs were already gone. He was unable to scream as his face began to crumble. I allowed myself the enjoyment of watching his slow deterioration. He stumbled forward and fell into me.

I closed my eyes as the ash rained down around me. My hair, face, and clothes were saturated with Jasper. Something hit me in the chest and then fell by my feet. I coughed a bit as I spat and tried to brush the ash from my shirt. On the floor at my feet was a dark and still-beating heart. This wasn't completely un-expected. I read in several books that sometimes the blackened heart remained. I thought to put it in a blender Eve 6 style, but the tradition was to bury it.

I used one of the laminated menus to push the heart into a Styrofoam to-go box and closed the lid, still feeling the slow pulse underneath. I was sorry I couldn't do anything more for

Genny and Dennis other than this small revenge. I walked outside into the parking lot, still trying to knock the dust of Jasper off my clothes and watching him float away on the wind. I made my way down towards the Wolf River. It wasn't easy in the dark, but I found a spot where the ground was moist. I dug a two-foot hole with my hands, piled dirt and leaves on top of the heart, then rolled a big stone over the grave to mark the spot.

As I walked back toward my Prius, I allowed myself a little chuckle. I liked my vampires just like my hashbrowns: scattered, smothered, and covered.

CHAPTER 3

Forever and Ever in Both Directions

Justin Siebert

– 1 –

Danny

The Greenline is my favorite place in the whole world.

It's basically an unending forest tunnel right in the heart of Memphis. Trees hang over each side of the paved trail like hands ready to clamp down on you, but they never do. It's so long I can run and run in either direction until my legs are jelly and it hurts to breathe and still not see where the path ends. If you take your bike and go really, really far, it becomes a bridge over a clouded, green swamp. After that, it opens up into a giant field like the scene in *Jurassic Park* where they first see the dinosaurs, except instead of dinosaurs, there are humongous metal towers that carry electricity. There's even a prison at the end, but Dad tells me not to stare at it when we bike past.

There are all kinds of people, too. Big people and little kids, running and walking, some biking in tight, funny clothes. I'm not allowed on it by myself, even though I turned six and a half last week. Our backyard connects right to the Greenline, so I've already been on it lots of times before with Dad and Mom— my older brother Tomás told me that big kids say "Mom," not "Mommy" like Nia does, but she's only three, and—

Thomp. Something hollow and rubbery smacks me upside the head, and I see our red kickball soaring up and up over our backyard fence. Tomás laughs, this big, booming guffaw like he's trying to announce to all of Memphis that there's something funny happening, and he's part of it. He always wants to be part of what's going on.

"Turd bucket," I say, soft enough to deny it but loud enough to feel tough.

"Qué dices?" Tomás asks, still laughing, circling around me as I try to look away.

"Nothing."

"You said something. Look at me!" He grabs my arm and pulls my head over to inspect where the ball hit me. Tomás's face gets all serious, but I know he's about to say some mean, stupid joke.

"The ball went over the fence, Danny, but look on the bright side: your big ol' cabeza is gonna be bright red enough to replace the kickball we just lost!"

More stupid laughs, even though his joke doesn't even make sense. My skin's too dark to turn that bright red. He rubs my head, making my curled hair go all wild.

"Vámos para la pelota, hermano!"

Pelota was one of the first Spanish words I learned to say, and I learned it from Tomás. It means "ball." Even though they can't speak it that good themselves, our parents made all of us learn some Spanish words. But they really made Tomás learn Spanish because they said it's part of his culture, which I think just means that his birth mom speaks Spanish. He's adopted. So am I, and so is Nia, which means that we grew in our birth moms' bellies, not Mom's belly.

"We can't go out past the fence without Mom."

"Sure we can," Tomás whispers, his voice low like he has a big secret that little kids aren't supposed to know. "I go out to the Greenline all the time."

"No, you don't."

"I do."

"No way."

"Yes way."

"I don't believe you."

Tomás looks through the house window to make sure Mom isn't watching. He walks over to the fence and stretches his arm up to unlatch our backyard fence gate, which leads to the Greenline.

"Come on," Tomás says, smiling ear to ear from behind the gate, "unless you're scared."

I frown. My head hurts, and Tomás is treating me like a little kid, but I'm not a little kid anymore, and I'm not going to act like one. I'm not going to cry.

"I'm not scared," I say.

"Attaboy."

I follow him through the gate and down five steps onto the Greenline. Tomás holds me back as a white woman on a bicycle flies past. She disappears down the paved path that stretches on forever and ever.

"Cuidado. Keep your eyes peeled, hermanito."

"You mean 'hermano'?"

"No, 'hermanito.' The 'ito' means you're just a little bucket of turds. Now go get the ball."

I search hard for any sign of red. On our side is just houses, but on the far side of the Greenline are lots of trees, like more than two hundred, I think. I follow Tomás as he searches.

"Donde estar," I say, practicing my Spanish, "la pelota rojo?"

"Roja."

"I said that."

"No, you didn't."

"On the left!" someone yells, a sweaty jogger running past us. "Hey, he looks like me!" I say, holding up my arm to Tomás to indicate my dark brown skin. I wait for a mean response from Tomás, but he just stares at me weird, sort of blank. After a second, he smiles and looks me in the eye, but he seems sad, and I didn't know a smile could be sad.

"That's pretty cool, Danny."

I sprint forward after the jogger and see a flash of color to my left, among the trees. There it is: the red ball.

"I found it, Tomás! Here it is!"

I leave the paved Greenline and bound down the dirt path, between trees that grow up like long, crooked fingers. The ground is a mush of wet leaves and sticks and slimy worms. I feel suddenly far away from Tomás, from home, and even far away from myself.

I reach down for the red—

"What are you looking for, Danny?"

What *am* I looking for? I know I'm searching for something, but there's nothing here. Instead, there is a person about Dad's age, who looks like Dad, but also looks like me and Tomás and Nia and Mom and everyone I can think of. Tomás always makes me feel stupid if I speak up when I don't understand something, so I clamp my mouth shut.

"Danny, I won't make you feel stupid. I am an Always Person, and Always People know all parts of your journey."

"An Always Person? Are you a good guy?"

The Always Person shakes their head.

"I'm neither good nor bad. I'm whatever you need me to be."

They smile, and their face stretches forever and ever in both directions all at once. When I look far left, they are a young girl, then a baby, like Nia. When I look far right, they are old, like a grandpa. I look in the middle and see a boy about Tomás's age.

"You want to be like your brother? Like me?" asks Tomás-the-Always-Person.

Do I? Tomás is smart and big and never scared and always very sure of himself and everything he says. I'm little and afraid of saying something stupid like a little kid.

"Yes."

"Do you know who you are?"

I am Danny, duh, but I don't think that's what they mean, so I shrug.

"You will know who you are," Tomás says, "more than I will ever know myself."

Tomás-the-Always-Person looks sad, like my brother Tomás had earlier when he smiled...

I turn away, to the right, but I still see Tomás still right in front of me. His face changes as I turn, his cheeks thinning, stubble sprouting on his chin and neck, lines spreading around his eyes. He's not as old as Dad, but he's older than the Tomás I know.

"Tomás?"

"Hermanito," he says, smiling through tears.

"What happened to you?"

"Todo bien, hermanito. Don't you worry about me."

I've never seen Tomás like this. I want to close my eyes, but I know it is important not to.

"Why are you sad, Tomás?"

"I'm not sad. No, no, but I need you to do something for me, see? I need your help. You know how you like to draw and paint pictures all the time? The kind Mom likes to put up on the fridge?"

I nod. Tomás-the-Always-Person taps himself on the chest.

"I want you to paint me. Not as I am now, but as I used to be. Paint me here in this place, where I can live forever. Before I lose my way. So I can be here with you and Nia, so I won't be alone. Can you do that for me, Danny?"

I'm shaking.

"Can you help me with this? Please, hermanito?"

"…"

"I need you to promise me."

"O…okay. I promise."

"Thanks, Danny. Hey, don't cry now. Don't be sad for me."

But my eyes are already wet as this Tomás kneels down and wraps his arms around me, holding me tight like Mommy and Daddy sometimes do, but the real Tomás never has.

"You have to know who you are, little bro. It's something I never really figured out. But you will. You're strong, you know that? I know you always looked up to me, but I look up to you too. Es cierto. Don't shake your head; I mean it. I gave you a hard time, crossed the line sometimes. But even after we stopped talking, I thought the world of you."

He pulls back, holding my shoulders, and looks me up and down.

"I love you, little bro."

I don't know what to say, and it hurts real bad to look at him, so I clamp my eyes shut. Someone pulls on my shoulder, and I stumble back a bit.

"Danny?"

I open my eyes. Tomás—the real one—frowns at me.

"Todo bien? Are you crying? You look like you saw a ghost or something. What happened?"

What had I seen? The whole thing feels forever ago, like trying to remember what being a little baby was like. But Tomás seems different now, strong on the outside and broken on the inside, someone I love but don't want to be.

"Here's the ball," I say, noticing the rubber kickball in my hand, though I can't remember picking it up.

He takes it, bounces it on his foot, then reaches out to grab it because he can't keep it in the air.

"Last one back's a turd bucket!" He tosses me the ball and laughs a big, happy laugh—a Tomás laugh—as he sprints back toward our house.

I know he'll win, but I don't mind anymore. I chase after him as hard as I can.

- 2 -

Tomás

"Tomás, para donde vas? Dijiste que cuidas a Nia y Danny esta noche."

I don't look at her as I put on my hoodie and unzip my backpack. Danny is old enough now to take care of himself and babysit Nia. Mom knows Nia is probably safer with responsible Danny anyway.

"Tomás?"

I pull the lighter and cigarettes from the back corner of my sock drawer. Before I throw them in the backpack, I hold them long enough to make sure she sees.

"Mírame, Tomás."

I sigh out loud, partly just to irritate her. She's standing in my doorway with one hand on her hip as I walk up to her, still refusing to look her in the eye.

"Que pasó hoy?"

"Let me through."

"Por fa, Tomás, mírame, díga—"

"God, Mom, just speak English."

She pauses, blinks, deflates. "Okay. You can talk to me. You can tell me what—"

I squeeze past her through the doorway, bumping her harder than I mean to, and she stumbles back against the doorframe.

"Jesus Christ, Tomás, what has gotten into you?"

When I look up at her, I don't know what words will force themselves out of my mouth. An apology, a string of curses, a plea for help, whatever I say will be something I regret. So I say nothing, instead letting the hatred in my stare—the only way I can truly communicate with her anymore—cut her open so she can maybe feel the tiniest fraction of the pain I feel every day.

"Please don't look at me that way," she says softly. Her face quivers. I wait for a tear, but I know she'd never let me see how much I hurt her, how much the pain I cause will ripple through the family. Danny will hear her crying in the bedroom and wonder if he is the problem. Little Nia will be sad because Mommy is sad. Dad will comfort her, trying to push from his mind the damning thought that maybe adopting me in the first place was a mistake. He'll hate himself for letting that messed up thought take root. Like the kudzu that has crept into our backyard, he'll pull it up and pull it up until it's all gone and live in sad denial that it might ever sprout up again, knowing deep down it will always come back, that he could never kill it completely.

"What's wrong?"

I spin. Danny stands there confused, his iPad in one hand, a drawing of a man with multiple heads staring from the screen. He got the iPad from our parents last Christmas, and I bought him this drawing app. He loves sketching unsettling portraits: babies, old geezers, all kinds of folks. He's like Rembrandt, but even more dark and depressing, making some really weird, artsy shit for a kid his age. You could frame his stuff up in a museum for people to ooh and ahh over; it's that good.

I cock my head to get a view of one of the faces on his drawing. It looks familiar, Latino, like an older version of myself.

Danny clicks the screen off as Nia runs into the room and wraps herself around his other arm. I soften my face, shake my head, and force a smile. "Nothing's wrong, hermanito." I tousle his hair with a smile, try to play it off, laugh like I did when I was Danny's age, but it falls flat. He doesn't believe me. He looks sad—not kid-sad, but sad like the way an old person's drawn-out face is tired and given-up, ready to face what he knows has been coming for a long time.

I turn back to Mom for a moment.

Then I leave, letting the back storm door bang against the frame.

The air is a crisp November chill that nobody ever thinks of when they think of Memphis. I pull my hood up, light a cigarette, and shoot Lucy a text as I step onto the Greenline.

I met Lucy almost a year ago when I was fifteen. I was walking just to get away, and it so happened she was biking for the same reason. The third time she passed, I asked if she was stalking me, and she responded, "Well, what if I am?" Turned out we had a lot in common. We both hated the same things, such as overbearing parents, pineapple on pizza, and that group of white private school cross country runners on the Greenline who wear shorts so damn short it looks like their dongs will poke out. But mostly, we're both loners, and loners don't have a lot of options when it comes to friends.

We aren't dating exactly. We made out a couple of times. Never sex, though we got close once, and I knew she wanted to go farther. I never told Jonathan or Rodrigo about any of that because guys don't say no to sex, especially with hot girls, and Lucy...well, she's pretty hot. I have enough of their bullshit to deal with without them calling me a fag.

"What the hell happened to you?" she says when she sees me walking toward her on the Greenline with a death stare on my face. I'm not hiding my emotions well.

"A fight."

"You don't look like it. You must've won."

She smirks but looks pissed when I don't respond.

"So what happened?"

I try to say the words, but all I can picture is Jonathan and Rodrigo laughing between classes this morning, speaking in patronizingly slow Spanish so the pocho could understand, making me feel like I always have to prove my Latino-ness, and knowing I can't. I'm not Latino enough for them, not Latino enough for my adoptive white parents, and not whitewashed enough for the white kids. Worst part is how it so easily gets under my skin through scars I've been bearing all my life.

"Alright, Tomás, you call me out here on this cold-ass day just to act all silent and emo? You know, I got better things to do than freeze my tits off if—"

"I don't know who I'm supposed to be."

I'm not walking anymore. I'm shaking. I crumple to the ground, hands on the pavement, frozen breath drifting from my lips. I bite my sleeve to stifle whatever is trying to come out.

Lucy looks at me like, *Oh, Jesus Christ, this is no longer normal. What the hell is happening to him?* I'm not someone who cries in front of people. I laugh things off, maybe get angry now and then, but never show this kind of weakness.

Lucy stammers out filler words. She's terrible at giving advice.

"...look, like, whatever happened, come on Tomás, please just stop this..."

I slam my fist onto the pavement, then cover my face with my hands as my body drains itself of any excess fluids through my eyes and nose.

"Maybe I should go...," she says, and another sob bursts out of me. "I don't know what to..." As she trails off, I feel her hand resting awkwardly on my shoulder. "Just please stop."

And I do. There doesn't seem to be anything left. I wipe the snot and tears from my face. Lucy starts to hug me, and I hold up a hand.

"I'm alright. That was weird. Not sure where that came from, but I'm straight now."

"Tomás, I don't think you're okay."

"I'm good. I promise."

She raises an eyebrow. "Okay. You tell yourself that. But I've seen panic attacks, and that came close."

I ignore her comment, and we continue walking in silence. A few bicyclists fly past.

"I'm sorry for freaking out back there."

"You said you didn't know who you were."

"I don't want to talk about it, Luce."

"I know what that's like."

"En serio, did you not hear me?"

"I got something that could help." She holds up a little bottle of pills and shakes it. "From my parents."

"Oxy? Like, oxycodeine or whatever?"

"OxyContin."

"What's the difference?"

She shrugs. I search her face to see if she is seriously suggesting this.

"You stole these from your dad, didn't you? I don't know, Lucy." But I do know. I know that saying no would hurt our relationship, but saying yes might destroy me, at least from what I've heard all my life.

"I know I was scared the first time too." She shrugs. "So it's cool if you don't want to do it. But it makes you feel…" She holds up the OK hand sign and makes a little click with her tongue.

"You know how I feel about that shit."

"Come on, you're just afraid to do it. Or are you afraid your rich, white, Christian parents are going to find out you got high on something other than Jesus? They do this shit too, you know."

I laugh too hard at that. "You don't know my parents then."

"I know they're rich. Everybody thinks of whores and the homeless dudes on street corners when they think of drugs, but rich people do way more. It's statistics and shit. Data. Look it up. And this is the specific shit rich people do, my little kemosabe."

"You also don't know that kemosabe is not a Spanish word."

"Don't care," she says, twisting off the child-proof cap and holding up a little pill. I know right away I'm going to give into the mischievous, demanding look she gives me, her eyes bright with a new experience she needs to share. I nod slightly, and she grabs my neck, bringing my lips down to hers. I let her drag me, stumbling playfully, into the woods off the far side of the Greenline. If it weren't cold enough to freeze off body parts out there, she'd probably have my clothes off by the time we fell to the ground.

"Okay. You ready?"

I don't respond. She pops the pill in her mouth. Then two more, washing them down with a swig from her water bottle.

She grins at me from ear to ear.

"Just one," I say. She puts two in my mouth. They slide down my dry throat, and I take a drink to help them along.

Time passes, and I focus on making out with Lucy. I focus on touching her body how I'm supposed to touch her body, lest she think me inexperienced, trying not to be too self-conscious the whole time. But I feel good. Lighter, like we will float away. Then, as my mind catches up with the moment, she is floating away. I reach out to her, but she is gone, and this high I'm experiencing for the first time evaporates.

Who am I? Who is Tomás?

I look around.

The trees form a wall. I stumble around them, blocked in every direction, trapped in a doorless room. I yell for help, but my words drift away like...

Someone has drifted away, but I can't remember who I was with.

Frantic, I run, trip, and come down on all fours in the cold, damp dirt. Leaves and forest debris cover my hands and knees. I wipe my hands on my pants and look up.

My mother is standing over me.

"Qué haces? Qué haces con tu vida?"

What am I doing with my life?

"You followed me out here? You're such a...!" I scream, then: "Sorry. Sorry, Mom, help me. I don't know where I am. Mom..."

"We've given you so much. Mama Rosa wanted more for you. And look at what you're doing to yourself! Mira a tu mismo! Smoking, taking pills."

"Who do you want me to be?" I yell. "What do you want me to do, huh? What do I need to do to be your perfect little adopted Hispanic child?"

Her lips curl downward in disgust. "You're not the son I thought..."

I turn to look away, to run, but my mother shifts, changes, until she isn't my mother anymore.

"Nia?" It's my sister Nereida, but older, even older than me. Her long hair is shaved on the sides and pulled back into a knot on the top. She's wearing a camo jacket over a plain, white tee and jeans.

"I couldn't take you with me," she says. "When I left home, I knew you needed to leave too, to get away from everything here, but your sorry ass was too far gone. I hope you like that shit you're shooting up your veins these days better than your own family. Your little brother and I looked up to you. What a joke. You think you look cool? You're a drug addict."

"I'm sorry," I choke out the words, not sure what I'm apologizing for, but knowing I'm screwing things up somehow. "I have to get...I have to leave here."

I turn, and little Danny is there, tears in his eyes. "What happened to you, Tomás? Why do you look like that?"

"Hermanito, I'm still me. I'm still your big bro." I reach my hand out, but he pulls away, repulsed by me.

I'm spinning now, Jonathan and Rodrigo laughing at my gringo accent, Dad shaking his head and wondering out loud if my adoption had been a mistake, Lucy flipping me off and telling me it isn't going to work out, that I'm too emotional, too unstable, that I cry too much, feel too much. I run and run, but there is no escaping this nightmare of people I've disappointed, me unable to meet their impossible expectations, and them unable to accept me for just being me.

I collapse to the ground, out of breath.

Mama Rosa stands before me.

"Tomás?"

My biological mother. She's older now, wrinkles beginning to show on her middle-aged skin. I haven't seen her since Christmas when we last video chatted. How is she so old? I say nothing. I just wait for her to speak, to tell me how I've let her down as well.

A single tear drops down her cheek, curving around her pained smile.

"Mi Tomásito."

I can't speak.

She repeats my name. "Tomásito. Mi querido. Mi hijo."

Her arms extend out to me, and I rise to meet her embrace. But I never feel it.

"The hell was that, dude?" Lucy's voice. She's slapping my face. "You had some kind of reaction. You okay?"

My head swims, but a feeling of relief washes over me, like waking up from a nightmare and realizing that none of the terrible stuff you just witnessed is real.

"Yeah, Luce. I'm good."

We lie there in the grass for God knows how long as the effects wear off. I had hallucinated—or dreamed?—about Mama Rosa, and her image keeps coming back to me. We Skyped with her on my last birthday, and we probably will again on Christmas, but I haven't seen her in person in maybe five years.

So I make a decision, a promise to myself. When Nia is older, I'm going to take her to go visit our birth mom.

"Okay," Lucy says, turning to me. Her cheeks rise in a smile. "You want to try it again?"

- 3 -
Nereida

After walking half an hour, I come to yet another road crossing, Waring Street this time. I stop, look around, shrug, push the crosswalk button, wait. This endless—and endlessly flat and boring—path stretches for over six miles from some random point on Tillman all the way to Shelby Farms Park.

I never understood what this place meant to Tomás and Danny. It's not like they were marathon runners or bicyclists. The only memory I have of the bikes Dad bought them is walking into the garage and seeing them slumped forlornly against the wall. But they both spent hours of their childhood on the Greenline, mostly without me. First, I was too young. Then, I was too female. They had their boy time while I helped Mom in the kitchen because I had a vagina, and as a vagina-haver, I had to do the things that only people with vaginas are supposed to do, like cooking and laundry and picking up after the penis-havers.

That makes me sound bitter. I'm really not. Despite all they did that made me feel ostracized, I see now that they always loved us. In some ways, my domestication was for the best. My girlfriend Hanna is brilliant and funny and strong, but she's no Anthony Bourdain. She's got his charisma and command of hyperbolic storytelling, without the depression and culinary skills. Also, she's hotter. And a woman.

Anyway, that's how I ended up a lesbian homemaker, which I've come to enjoy well enough. I was never the take-down-the-patriarchy kind of feminist, but more of a just-let-me-do-what-the-heck-I-want-in-peace variety. I want to be myself, not change the world.

At the moment, Hanna is stranded without our rental car, forced to awkwardly explain to my family why I left the funeral early. No goodbyes, no tears, no unnecessary words. I don't know what I would have said, anyway.

I left home the same way six years ago. It was early June after senior year, and Mom was planning out details of my life without much input from me. I was headed to Rhodes College on a pretty hefty academic scholarship because, one, I made the ACT my bitch, and, two, I'm Latinx, whereas the rest of the student body was uniformly not.

Rhodes was also fifteen minutes from my parents' house. I was a gay woman who spent her formative years vaguely hiding her sexuality from parents who knew but never acknowledged it save for the occasional offhand comment about loving the sinner but not the sin of same-sex relationships. The thought of staying another four years in Memphis made me feel like a caged bird finally set free, but with clipped wings that would never let me fly like I was made to do.

So I left. I flew.

I had secretly applied to Reed College in Portland. During my freshman year of high school, I read about the college in *Blue Like Jazz*, a Christian book of which my parents were quite skeptical. The author (a Christian) audited classes at Reed, which was decidedly not Christian, and had some very interesting experiences. I fell in love with the mythical place immediately. Two years later, I sent in my application using my friend's address so my parents wouldn't see any Reed mailings. One Google search and my parents would have disapproved of the college just like they disapproved of my gayness.

I felt bad about leaving and not saying goodbye. I never asked what it was like for them as they pieced it all together and realized I was gone for good. They blew up my phone with calls and texts, and I responded in the fewest number of words needed to let them know I was okay but wanted space. I cried a lot that first month. I was a naïve kid still, and my new freedom was its own lonely challenge.

I surfed couches for a few weeks using the phone app, and it turned out Portlanders love this kind of thing. That's how I met Hanna: sleeping on her hippy parents' couch the summer before college. Hanna was a sophomore at Reed, living on campus, and her parents wanted to have someone in the house after she moved out.

The following summer, I got a text from Mom asking me to come home for the summer. It wasn't an explicit apology, but it was something. I never returned the text.

I explored my sexuality with Hanna that year, but there was still another part of myself I needed to get to know. I bought a bus ticket from Portland to San Antonio and spent most of the journey reading and intermittently texting Tomás and checking my phone for a reply. I even called him the second day as I sat on a park bench in El Pueblo, this touristy historic district across the street from LA's Union Station, where I was killing time before catching an Amtrak train for the other half of the journey. I was eating taquitos in a "world famous" avocado sauce from a street vendor called Cielito Lindo. I looked up their website on my phone as I bit into the first taquito. It was all in English, except for the words muy auténtico. It was the perfect ironic metaphor for how I felt in that moment and how I'd felt for most of my life.

Along the streets, people sold trinkets of Mexican culture—serape blankets, Catholic crosses, brightly-painted guitars, fruits—from little tiendas sandwiched between restored historical buildings. What did a liberal, lesbian, feminist transplant from Memphis, now living in weird, white Portland, have in common with any of this?

My call to Tomás went straight to voicemail, which wasn't even set up, and that made me feel lonelier than anything else had up until that point.

The rest of the journey passed uneventfully. On the third day, I almost regretted traveling by bus and train instead of catching a flight like a normal person would have. But I hated convention, and this slower method of transportation made it less of a trip and more of a journey, a much sexier word, especially for a nineteen-year-old trying to find herself.

The hardest leg of the journey was the twenty-five-minute Lyft ride from San Antonio Station to Mamá Rosario's house in Dellcrest. It was a one-story brick home, modest but well-kept, especially for a single woman in her fifties who still worked for barely over minimum wage. I rang the doorbell. Nobody answered. I sat in one of her two plastic green lawn chairs and read my book.

It didn't feel quite right, sitting there alone. Without Tomás. When I was a little girl, he'd always tell me we would go visit her someday, just me and him. He made me promise over and over, pinky swear it and everything, that I'd go with him. But he never made the trip. There was always a job he couldn't take off from. He needed the money. Then he would lose the job, and somehow all the money he saved would be gone. We all knew where the money was going. And I knew our trip was never going to happen. I felt naïve for thinking this time might be any different.

Mostly, I missed my brother. I still do.

About an hour later, as the sun was setting, a gray car pulled into the driveway, spitting a few pieces of broken concrete from beneath a tire. Besides a few Skype sessions on a birthday or Christmas, I hadn't seen her since I was a kid, the last time my parents took Tomás and me down there to visit. I saw her worn eyes through the windshield. They widened, then her whole face changed.

I smiled.

I dropped my book onto the clover-covered lawn. There were tears in Mamá's eyes before she'd even made her way over to where I stood. "Mi Nereida querida!" she said, pulling me in for a tight hug. She stood me back to get a look at me. "Qué pasó con tu pelo lindo? Muy corto." She indicated my short hair, cropped to what my adoptive mom called "boy length" and wrapped in a red bandana. "Más fácil así," I lied, knowing both my mothers had that in common: girls should look a certain way. I shrugged. Rosa smiled and shuffled me inside to escape the Texas heat.

She apologized profusely for the house being a mess, although it wasn't, at least compared to Hanna's parents' comfortably messy house. I returned with an apology in mediocre Spanish for just showing up out of the blue.

She fixed a meal of fajitas that put those Californian taquitos to shame, speaking Spanish faster than I could quite keep up with, pausing to ask me questions about my life the past year. I explained, as best I could, about college and life in Portland. I left Hanna out.

"Pero, no diga nada a Mamá o Papá de esto o de Portland. Ellos no..." I searched for the Spanish word for approve, but settled for, "...a ellos no les gusta que me voy a Portland por asistir la Universidad."

She furrowed her brow in response to my request to not talk to my adoptive parents, then slowly nodded. "Bueno," she said, then kept cooking.

Eventually, as we ate the best Tex-Mex I'd had since the last time we visited, Mamá's face got serious. Lines wrinkled back from her eyes. "Y Tomás? Cómo está mi hijo?"

I looked down. My parents adopted Tomás thirty-two years ago, when Rosa was just twenty years old, recently kicked out of her family's house, and in an abusive relationship. When she found out she was pregnant, she broke it off with the guy and avoided her parents for the next seven months. My parents took

Tomás home with them a couple days after he was born, and they stayed in contact with Rosa, knowing that while closed adoptions make for great Lifetime movie storylines, open adoptions are much better for adopted children.

A few years later, my parents adopted Danny from the foster care system and assumed he would be their last. I was an accident of sorts. Rosa's second pregnancy came at a time in her life when things were still pretty unstable, and she wanted me to be with my brother Tomás. My parents agreed.

I told Rosa I hadn't been able to reach him, that I'd wanted him to come down and meet us here, that my soul needed the three of us to be together again, if only for a few days. I told her he had some issues holding down a job, that he'd gotten in with some people that did not have his best interests in mind. I told her that her boy needed her prayers. I'd mostly given up on appeals to the Almighty since moving away, but I knew it would mean something to her to hear she was needed. I didn't mention the drugs. I didn't mention that he looked more distant, more shriveled, in each successive selfie he uploaded to Facebook, his middle finger usually raised to the camera. I didn't mention the email my adoptive mom sent me earlier that year telling me to pray, saying he'd briefly come home to ask for money for drugs. I didn't say any of that.

I told her that Tomás loved her.

I told her he would be here if he could.

She smiled. It was the only time either of us mentioned my only biological brother that summer.

I planned to stay a few days with her, but the days turned into weeks. I learned more Spanish talking to her than I had in eighteen years with my adoptive parents and four years of high school Spanish classes. She brought me along to a friend's granddaughter's quinceañera. She taught me to cook frijoles de la olla, salsa in a molcajete, and her red enchilada sauce recipe. I was discovering a part of me that had been missing. Still, I never got to be fully myself with her. I never mentioned my relationship with Hanna, never even said her name. When Mamá asked about boys at college, indicating that I needed to find a good husband, I just said there were a lot of cute boys there, that I'd probably meet the right one eventually. I was still fragmented, compartmentalized. I suspect I might always feel that way.

I know it's how Tomás used to feel. I don't think that a summer spent at our birth mom's house would have saved him —I'm not that naïve anymore—but if I could change one thing about the past, I would have found a way to get him down to San Antonio to be with me and Mamá Rosario.

Five years after that summer, now a college grad still living in Oregon and still dating the best woman in the world, I'm back in Memphis.

The crosswalk light turns green.

On the other side of Waring Street, just over the hill, is the I Love Memphis mural, painted maybe a decade ago on an old railroad tunnel. It shows a family biking in front of a background of bright colors. By now, it's likely chipped, faded, whatever happens to outdoor art over time as it's exposed to the weather.

As I crest the hill, I see a young black man in a suit seated on a bench, facing a brand new mural that's been painted over the one I remember. Even though I've never seen it before, this new mural looks strangely familiar. The concrete wall is covered in faces, dozens of them. Old women, little kids, young men, black and brown and white and every shade in between. And yet, somehow, I see Tomás in every one of the faces.

"Danny, it's beautiful," I say, taking a seat next to him on the bench. I put my arm around him and pull him close. "You never told me you got to paint this."

"I wanted you to see it in person first," Danny says.

"You knew I'd be back. To Memphis, I mean."

"I suppose I did."

"How did you know I would come here, though? To the Greenline?"

"When I saw you leave the funeral, I had a feeling you'd come here searching. I needed some alone time too, and this is a good place to remember Tomás. We had some good times here on this long stretch of pavement."

He stares at the ground for a moment, then looks up to me.

"I know there's not much left for you here in this city, but I hoped this wouldn't be what it took to get you back."

I wipe some wetness from my eyes, and we sit in silence for a while.

"I shouldn't have left early," I say, not sure if I'm referring to leaving the funeral or to leaving my family all those years ago.

"We all grieve in our own way, Nia. No single right way to do it. Sometimes you need space to figure things out for yourself."

I sigh. "I can't stand watching Mom blame herself for what happened to him. She already blames herself enough for how I turned out."

"How you turned out? Seems like you're doing pretty well. You definitely make more than a lowly art teacher like myself."

"Someone's got to teach the childrens. Inspire future generations. Stamp out ignorance. You know."

"Something like that," Danny says. His lips curve up with the slightest hint of a smile. "Hanna seems pretty great."

"She is."

I nod, and Danny looks at me with squinted eyes.

"I watched that show Portlandia. People really like that up there?"

"Fred Armisan and Carrie Brownstein are actually Hanna's parents."

"Oh, is that right? How about that."

I chuckle, and it's the first time I've laughed since getting back to Memphis for the funeral two days ago. First time I've laughed with my brother in over six years. As my laughter changes into tears, it's the first time my brother and I have cried together as adults.

"I can't believe he's gone," I say between sobs. Danny places his hand on my back.

"I recognized him in the mural," I say after regaining my composure. "Right away. How did you do this? Each face is so different, but they're all him."

He shrugs. "I don't know. But Tomás could never really figure out who he was. It killed him that he couldn't be all the people others expected him to be. So I tried to paint that. I tried to paint Tomás, in all his forms, in all the ways he tried to be himself and never could. I finished it a few days before he died. I kept a promise I made to him years ago to immortalize him on the Greenline. You can feel him here with us, can't you?"

I smile, awkward and uncertain. "I'm not sure what I feel right now."

He looks at me for a moment, then stands, beckoning me with his hand.

"Come on. I need to show you something."

I follow him toward our parents' house, toward that place with so many beautiful and terrible memories, raucous laughter and unreasonable expectations, hopes of salvation and fallings from grace, unconditional love and love expressed in all the wrong ways, constricting and suffocating.

The trees crowd in on the path as we walk, their long branches needing a fresh trim, red berries smushing beneath the soles of our shoes. The path rises slightly uphill, giving the illusion of continuing on forever. Light passes sporadically between the branches like a strobe light, and a chilly breeze wafts its way past our shoulders. I shiver.

"You remember that time Tomás replaced all your Wheaties with Raisin Bran?" Danny asks, stepping off the Greenline and walking between trees.

"Just the bran. He took all the raisins out." I follow him, unsure about what he planned to show me in the middle of the forested area.

"Such a good prank."

"An obnoxious prank."

"You were eating huge spoonfuls, completely unaware that anything was out of the ordinary, couldn't even tell the difference!"

"I could tell."

"You had no idea! Eating away, wondering why we were laughing! You were just like, 'Whaaaat?'" Danny puts on a confused-face imitation of me, and I punch his arm, but I'm smiling and enjoying the retelling of the story.

"I was so mad," I say.

"You actually spit out the flakes of Raisin Bran when we said what we'd done. Stormed away, yelling for mom—"

"Who was in on the joke the whole time! I can't believe she let him do that."

"That was one of teenage Tomás's proudest moments," Danny says. "I wonder what he'd have to say about it if he were alive now."

We stop for a moment to look around. The trees are thinner here, but they're all we can see around us, and Memphis feels far away. It's hard to believe we're still in the middle of the city.

"I never understood your irrational hatred of Raisin Bran, Nia-Pia."

My skin flushes with warmth. That nickname...

That voice...

"Don't be scared," Danny says, placing a hand on my shoulder, but he's distant, like a memory.

"I'm sorry about a lot of things," Tomás's voice says, "but that prank is not one of them."

I turn and see this ghost of my oldest brother growing from a tiny babe to a toddling child to a brash teen who is far less sure and confident than he pretends to be.

"Are you surprised to see me, Nia-Pia?"

Impossibly, I'm not surprised at all. This feels more real than all the life I've lived up to this point.

"In a couple of years, you're going to come to your senses and finally shave that ridiculous goatee," I say.

"And disappoint all the girls? No way," he says, stroking his chin with a swagger he actually thinks he can pull off.

"Oh, please. You must not have looked in the mirror recently. That patchy baby hair on your face has got to go." Still, even as I give him a hard time, I actually do think he looks cool. He's my older brother; he had always defined "cool" for me and Danny.

Danny...

He was here with me, wasn't he?

I turn to look for him, and when I turn back, Tomás is a little boy.

"Hola, hermanita! Mira!" he yells, in a high-pitched, preadolescent voice. He is pushing one sleeve up and showing off his bicep, which is totally there if you have a vivid imagination.

"Wow, Tomás, so strong!"

And then he's slapping my arm, yelling, "You're it!" and sprinting away. I chase him, circling trees, stumbling over roots and branches, laughing and tackling him to the ground. He squeals as I tickle him...tickle my baby brother...who is my older brother. The thought gives me a strange sensation that something is off, like none of this is real.

"I shouldn't have left you behind," I say.

Little Tomás's face contorts into an over-exaggerated frown.

"What are you talking about, sis?"

I hear an echo of Danny's voice, explaining that this is Tomás from before I ever left. Danny's hand guides me, turning me around. Tomás's goatee fades first into a clean-shaven face, then into a scraggly beard. His face thins out, lines creasing deeper around his eyes and mouth. He lets himself slowly collapse to the ground, chest hunched over his knees, body trembling slightly.

I tell my body not to look away.

"You know, I don't blame you for leaving," he says, his voice coarse and frail. "You had to, needed to. I never blamed you."

"I called you. Texted and texted and called. So many times. Why didn't you answer?"

"Look at me, hermanita. What was I supposed to say? I'm fine, just biding time until the next hit, wondering and not caring if it's my last, the weather's nice here, and how are you?"

"I spent a whole summer with Mama Rosa. You were supposed to be there too."

"So?" He looks away, his mouth quivering.

"So? So, I wanted you to come see her, too. She asked about you."

"She gave us up."

"You know that's not true."

"Yeah, what's not true about it? Our real mom gave us up, Nia, and our other parents both suffocated us into being people we were not, and you're going to sit here and…"

I wrap myself around him and let my big brother cry into my shoulder. He feels so small.

"What Rosa did was selfless," I say. "She wanted the best for us. She always has. And Mom and Dad love us too. Sometimes that love was not what we needed, and sometimes it left wounds, but they were trying their best, trying to give us the best life we could have."

He nods. His shaking subsides for several moments, then comes back in shudders. He looks down at the holes in his arms, the bruising. "I think I went too far this time. Nia, are you there? I'm going to die here, alone, aren't I?"

I hug him tighter. "It's okay. I'm here with you. I'm right here."

"Tell..."

"It's okay. It's okay."

"Tell Mom and Dad I'm sorry."

"I will."

"And tell Mama Rosa 'te amo' for me. Tell her I'd be there with her if I could."

I think back to that summer I spent with her, to that moment she asked about her son with an intense, quiet hope. The sadness in her eyes. I think about what I said to her.

"I will, Tomás. I already have."

He nods, struggling to hold together a wavering smile.

"Thanks, Nia-Pia. Thanks, hermanito."

I notice Danny standing next to me again, and I squeeze his hand tight.

"I love you guys," Tomás continues. "Thanks for never giving up on me. I know I let you down. Over and over again. But now, I'll always be here for you when you need me."

Tomás smiles, looking like himself again. Danny and I watch him back away between the trees toward the Greenline's pavement, his arms spread wide, stretching and stretching, unfolding, flattening, forever and ever in both directions.

CHAPTER 4

Lashonda's Grace

Xia L. Cox

The humidity slapped me in the face like that money shot three days ago; I knew it was coming and still wasn't ready for it. My whole body felt just as sticky. I hate this city in the summer. The heat and humidity are too much for me to deal with. I don't know how everyone living here does it. I'd never been as happy to have moved away as the moment I first stepped outside of the airport.

Luckily my Uber was waiting on me. Unluckily, the car ride was just as hot inside as being outside. It was nice and cool when I first got in, but the guy's AC broke before we even left the airport. It was suddenly blowing out hot air, and he didn't know what to do about it. We had to resort to having the windows open the entire trip to the hotel. Driving on the interstate wasn't so bad, but as soon as we stopped at any red light on the streets, the heat became unbearable. It reminded me of the summer my great-grandfather died. The week after he passed were the hottest days this city's ever seen.

I was probably a bigger bitch than usual to the guy, but it's too hot for your AC to be breaking. In the moment, I knew he couldn't really help that, though. I tipped him all the same. He needed all the help he could get. As soon as I got out of his car, his back tire exploded.

Since I was only staying for the afternoon, I decided not to waste money at an expensive hotel. I would have loved to stay at The Peabody, just to be able to say I have, but the Holiday Inn across the street was good enough for taking a few showers and changing clothes. I was gonna be on the first flight back to LA as soon as the funeral was over.

There were still a few hours to kill before the funeral started. I checked in and put my bag in my room. I had packed light, bringing only one duffel bag. I made sure to tell the housekeeper to put in clean sheets when I saw one walking the halls. The shower mostly worked, I wasn't getting any cold water, and I made quick use of it. My clothes were soaked through in the brief time I'd been in the city, so I needed to wash all the sweat off. I brought a few outfits just to have something to choose from, but the way things were going, I might not have enough to last until I could get back home.

I slid into an off-white cotton open-back top, some daisy dukes, and my sky blue open-toe heels. The AC in my room stopped working sometime while I was taking a shower. If I had been in New York, there's a good chance I'd have walked outside topless, but I didn't have time to cuss out every other person I saw.

With a few hours to kill, I decided to prepare for the funeral while I still had time. It didn't take long to find a place to get a drink. The bar was empty aside from the bartender. The walls were plastered with photos and graffiti, and the ceiling was littered with toothpicks. The AC was on full blast and felt amazing, and that was all that mattered at the moment.

The bartender took one look at me and flashed the brightest smile I'd seen all year. That's one good thing about this place. I haven't seen a bartender in LA give a genuine smile while working once in the five years I've been there.

She was a tanned shortstack with dark brown hair put up in a side ponytail that hung over her left shoulder. She had the type of hips that made me jealous I couldn't put a baby in her myself. She was thick, like she grew up on grits and bacon every morning. I would've bet my life she knew how to make good cornbread. She had the type of motherly vibe that bred momma's boys. Most importantly, behind that smile, I could tell she didn't take no shit from anyone. My kinda woman.

"A dirty martini, please."

"Sure thing, shugg." Her voice sent a much-needed chill down my spine.

She put her hands in various places reaching for various things. She's been working here for a while. Smile everpresent, her eyes barely left me as she mixed my drink.

"Here you go, shugg."

Despite the heat, her friendly attitude was putting me in a better mood. "Thanks. Here, start a tab." She not so subtly ran her fingers across mine as she took my credit card. I was starting to think I might have misread her friendliness.

I took a sip of my martini. Heavenly. "I can only remember it being this hot once when I used to live here."

"You used to live here? Yea, it's a rough time to be back, especially the last few days. It's been hotter than hell, each day hotter than the last."

"Years ago. It's been about five years now. I'm only in town for a few hours . . ." I downed my martini in one motion. "I'm here for a funeral."

"Oh no, I'm so sorry to hear that." I didn't know if it was because she obviously wanted to get in my panties or because she was actually concerned, but the bartender leaned on the bar and grabbed my hands with her own. "It's gonna be okay, shugg. You'll get through this."

Without thinking, I squeezed her hand back. It was then I realized having to come back for the funeral might have been hitting me harder than I expected. "Can I get another?"

"Sure thing, shugg."

Thuwwwwmp. The bar door slammed open. "Fuck!" A man stormed in. It was my Uber driver. I could guess where this was going.

"What's wrong, Lex?" the bartender called out.

"Hey Whitney, yea, one of my tires exploded. And then the other three melted while I was replacing the blown one. Fuck this heat, man."

"I'm sorry, sweetie. You want a drink or just escaping the heat?" she said while sliding my martini towards me.

"Some water would be great. I'm gonna go back out after I calm down a bit." He took a look around the bar, and then our eyes met. "Oh hey, you're that girl. LaShonda, right? Thanks for the tip. That shit really helps, ya know?" He sat down next to me. "What are you drinking?"

My glass was empty. "A dirty martini."

"Salty's good in the summer."

"I love salty in every season."

"Get her another. And Joe's here, yea? Let me get lunch."

"Sure thing, sweetie." Whitney went to the back and gave a shout for Lex's order. She came back and mixed two more martinis for me. I finished the first one before she even got the olives in the second. They were finally starting to hit, so I sipped the second.

"You're really knocking 'em down, shugg."

"I'm not looking forward to this funeral. There's a reason I haven't been back in five years."

Lex's ears perked up. "Oh, you're a native? Gonna be in town for a while?" He straightened his back, puffed out his chest, and let me see that he was actually quite a bit taller than me.

"I'm heading back to LA the moment the funeral ends . . . but there's no telling what could happen before then."

"On a time limit, yea? Then I'll make the best of it. So who died? Someone close?"

"Lex!"

"What?"

"It's fine," I said. "I like men that know how to drill down to the good shit without wasting time." I took a deep breath. To my own surprise, I hesitated. "My great-grandmother died three days ago. She was ninety-seven. It wasn't a surprise or anything." That was the first time I had said those words, even to myself. I took another sip of my martini, though the urge to down it was strong.

Someone came out from the back with a double cheeseburger piled high with bacon and a basket overflowing with steaming hot fries. He was big and muscular, like he wrestled bears as a hobby. He wore tight-fitting jeans and a white t-shirt, tucked into his pants, that didn't have a single grease stain on it. He smelled like he lived in the kitchen and the frown on his face said he hated not being back there now. He set the food down in front of Lex with the force of a butterfly landing on a flower petal.

"Thanks, Joe. This is what I live for." Lex didn't waste any time digging into his food.

Joe gave a nod and hulked back to the kitchen. But not before pausing to give me a once over. He looked at Whitney and gave a sharp nod so short I might have imagined it. He used his forearm to wipe the sweat off his forehead and left without a word.

I realized I couldn't feel the AC anymore. The chill of my glass was the only thing keeping me cool. But only when the drink was fresh, so I ordered another. I ignored the glance Whitney and Lex shared between themselves. I've seen that look on my mom's face too many times to be bothered by it.

"Here ya go, shugg." Whitney set a glass of ice-cold water in front of me and my martini behind it. The concern in her eyes was too genuine for me to want to fight her over it. And it was slowly getting hotter. I finished off the water in two gulps and started sipping on my martini.

"You're really shaken up, huh? Y'all must've been close."

"My great-grandmother and I were a lot alike. She was basically a saggier, wiser version of me. No matter what stupid shit I did growing up, nothing surprised her and she always understood. She kept me from making some really dumb choices because she already lived those mistakes. She's the only person I've ever taken advice from because she's the only one that understood. She never judged me because she was me. She taught me everything I know. High-key bragging, my technique is so good because I had a master to teach me. There isn't a single time I can remember showing her something she didn't already know or hadn't done herself. Shit, sometimes she'd be surprised I took so long to ask her about it and then improve my game. And now . . . she always told me to live in the moment and for the future, but all I can think about are old memories. We'd roast marshmallows every afternoon in December. Mom would get pissed every New Year because she'd always let me drink a glass of champagne. Hah, she beat up the first boy that broke my heart. She only hit him once, but he was out cold. Summers were spent growing water-melons and peppers in her garden. I was the only other person that could handle eating the peppers with her, too spicy for any-one else. We barbecued every night without fail. She loved an open fire. At night she'd tell me all the wild stories about when she was younger. And sometimes, we'd sleep outside on really clear nights to stargaze. After many, many drinks I might get lucky enough to hear about the things she didn't get to try, like traveling the world or going to college. Heh, once she told me she wanted to try jumping into a volcano, just to see how hot it was. Knowing her, she'd probably jump out and say it wasn't that hot . . ."

I said more than I meant to say. I didn't mean to say anything, really. Somewhere in there, Lex finished his burger and was plowing through the last of his fries. Whitney looked like she was on the verge of tears. If the bar wasn't between us, I'd have probably been getting the air hugged out of my lungs. I didn't think anything I said was that sad.

Lex was surprisingly the first to speak. "You really loved her, huh." He shoved the last fry into his mouth and emptied his glass of water. "You seem like a real piece of work. The type women hate, and men only try to fuck, yea? I got a cousin like that. She relies on us, but you haven't been home in so long, you probably don't have that backup, yea? One of my boys got popped back in high school, so I know what it's like to lose your best friend. Ain't nothing I can say to make that shit better. But if you want to start to feel better, you gotta let your feelings out."

Lex stood up and put some money on the bar. He seemed to tower over me, like when an adult pats a child on the head. Or maybe like a giant tree in a forest that all the animals use as shelter from the rain and heat. "I just met you, but I feel like holding back like this ain't really you. You obviously feel some type of way about it. It's too hot for you to be bottling shit up. Somebody'll mess around and get hurt."

I smiled despite myself. He wasn't wrong.

"I'mma go wash up then head out."

As he walked towards the back, I realized I hadn't really looked at him before. Our first meeting was under such hot and miserable conditions that I let that color my impression of him. Lex had a good heart, and he was right. I wasn't acting like myself about this.

I didn't want to be back in this city. I didn't want to see my family again, especially not under these circumstances. And I damn sure wasn't trying to fuck with this heat. But none of that is an excuse. I don't make excuses. I make magic and get shit done.

"One more, Whitney." I went to the back to show Lex what my head was like when it was on straight. It turned out Lex was all of the man I thought he was.

When I returned to the bar, the place had filled out quite a bit. The lunch crowd was coming through. The ice in my martini had mostly melted. That just made it easier to finish quickly.

"Still here, Lex? Thought I missed you sneaking out. You have a rough time in there? You need to eat more vegetables. You're sweating something fierce."

"Nah, I ran into someone in the back and, yea . . ."

"Well, take care in this heat. Here, I got you some water to-go."

"Thanks. It was nice meeting you, LaShonda."

"Same here. It'd be nice for you to run into me again some time."

"Yea, yea." With that, Lex was on his way out of the bar, water in hand and sweat rolling down his everywhere.

It was almost time for me to get ready for the funeral. I had already decided I was going to face this head-on, so I needed to get a move on before I stopped feeling like it.

"Whitney, can you close the tab for me?"

"Sure thing, shugg." She pulled my card from somewhere under the counter and did some cashier things with it before handing it back to me with a smile.

I took her hand and held it tight. I was ready to do this, but honestly, I was still a little hesitant to do it alone. Lex was right earlier. My great-grandmother was basically my best friend growing up. We were so close, she was so much more than that, but if it had been anyone else that died, she'd certainly be the one I'd turn to to help me get over it. Without her around, I've been scared to think about what to do. I've always been able to rely on her to steer me in the right direction in life. Now, I'd have to trust she taught me enough to make it through without her. But that doesn't mean I need to force myself to do it alone. I could trust this girl; I thought so anyway. If nothing else, I was certain she liked me.

Since there were more customers in the bar, there were also more employees. Even if it was lunchtime, they shouldn't miss one bartender. (I knew this was a lie when I thought it, but I was going to steal Whitney away no matter what, so who cares.)

I called the person that looked like they were doing the least amount of work. "Hey, you the manager?"

She turned towards me without missing a beat. "Yea, what can I do for you? If it's about the AC, I know. We've got someone looking at it now."

"I'm stealing Whitney for the rest of the day." I held our hands up to show her. A spark of surprise flashed across both their faces. "She'll be back tomorrow, maybe."

Her manager wasn't buying it. "Do you know this person?"

Whitney was too slack-jawed to reply with a convincing response fast enough, so I intercepted.

"We've got a funeral to catch, and I've got some stress to relieve before that, so you can save this for tomorrow."

"You want to relieve some stress?" Whitney managed to ask.

I leaned over the bar and whispered into her ear. I could feel her temperature rising with every sweet nothing I spoke. When I was done, her face was so red I thought she might overheat at any moment.

"I, uhh, I . . . I'll try anything once, shugg."

Green light. I pulled her around the bar and sprinted for the door. What the manager had to say after that didn't matter to me. I took her back to my hotel room and relieved all of my stress and a good bit of hers. I kinda lost count after that.

After a shower and another change of clothes, we headed to the church for the funeral. Being the thicc queen that she was, none of my clothes fit Whitney properly, so we had to make a stop to buy her something funeral appropriate. Her bartender clothes wouldn't have cut it, even if they weren't soaked with sweat.

Once we arrived at the church, I realized that the concept of air conditioning didn't exist anywhere in the city. It was a bit nostalgic walking through those large wooden doors I used to go through every Sunday. I'm definitely not a religious person, but I had a lot of memories in this place. As I planned it, we were right on time. I wasn't on the schedule to speak or anything, so no reason to hang around any longer than necessary. I certainly didn't want to be harassed by my family before the funeral even started. Despite arriving right when things were supposed to start, that didn't save me from a confrontation I would have loved to avoid.

"LaShonda, you made it! But what are you wearing, child?"

My mom, the main reason I left this city, knows me better than I would like to admit. She was waiting in the main hall for me, ready to pounce as soon as I stepped through the doors.

"GG gave me this. 'For the specialest of occasions,' she said." I was wearing a slinky, silk black strapped one-piece and the pearl necklace she gave me for my twenty-first birthday. I've actually only worn them twice before this. "You know she'd be thrilled to see me in this."

My mom's face tightened like somebody farted. She knew I was right and hated not being able to say anything more about it.

"And this is?" she asked with a look to the woman on my side.

"This is Whitney, my girlfriend. If you give her any shit, we're leaving."

Whitney had been quietly watching the sparks fly between us this entire time. I don't think she expected to be brought into the conversation at all.

"Hello, ma'am. My name is Whitney. LaShonda is a very spirited and charismatic woman. Ready to take the world by storm. You must be very proud of her."

Unexpectedly high praise from the person I didn't even know a few hours ago. But she had the wrong read on my mom. We don't see eye to eye on anything.

My mom gave Whitney a thorough once over. She was wearing an ensemble decidedly less thottish than mine, but it was all we could manage since we were so pressed for time. She took a good long look into her eyes. Almost too long if you ask me. But, I was surprised at what she finally said to her.

"She's just like my grandmother, so of course I am. If she ever gives you any trouble, don't hesitate to call me. I can teach you all of her weak points."

I was left stunned for a few seconds. Those were words I never would have expected to hear come out of my mom's mouth, least of all when I was present to hear them.

"She isn't anything I can't handle, but you can tell me all of her weak points anyway." They shared a laugh.

I was frozen. It was too much to process at once. An unexpected compliment. Approval of my girlfriend. Them getting along and even cracking jokes, though at my expense, so that was easy to believe.

"Come on, child. We've saved you a seat." Whitney grabbed my hand and pulled me along behind my mom. We sat at the end of the third row of center pews. The first four rows spilled over with children, grandchildren, and great-grandchildren. Probably the one big difference between us is that I don't plan on having as many kids as she did. I'd hate to lose count after eight.

My great-grandmother knew a lot of people in her life and affected a lot of people's lives, for better or for worse. She was a good person, and this church filled to capacity proved that. Despite it surely being a fire hazard, especially in this fucking heat, people even stood all along the walls.

After things got started, the funeral proceeded nice and smooth. The choir sang her favorite hymns. Her oldest son and youngest grandchild spoke. A few local celebrities even had some personal stories about her to share. She really led an impactful life. Aside from the heat causing everyone to look like they just came out of a swimming pool, things flowed perfectly.

Until the pastor got up to speak one last time. "Our final speaker is a special one. This young lady was Grace's pride and joy ever since she was born. There isn't a person that knew Grace in her later years that didn't also know about her great-granddaughter LaShonda."

Everyone's eyes turned toward me. I looked over Whitney at mom. She didn't mention this shit at all.

She whispered across Whitney. "Your father forgot to tell you? Well, I don't know why you would think you wouldn't be speaking anyway. You were her favorite everything."

She was right. I should have known. I should have wanted to speak and asked to do it myself. I let my hatred of the thought of coming back here get in the way of someone really important to me. I was lucky to have the chance to correct that mistake.

Whitney gave me a gentle poke in the side, and I got to my feet. A lot of the crying stopped as I walked up to the casket. I took the mic from the pastor while ignoring the stares from everyone. My only focus at that moment was her.

It had been two years since the last time I saw her in person. She came to my graduation. Even though I didn't like the thought of coming back here, I always offered to for her birthday. But every time, she'd tell me, 'Live for the future, not the past.' This dress was a gift from her. She told me she had one just like it when she was my age. It's the reason most of us were even here today. The necklace was a gift from her father when she finally decided to get married. This woman has affected my life in more ways than I'll probably ever know. I don't know if I would be as confident in myself if not for her encouragement. I might not be able to say that I love both women and men with my head held high. I might not be able to openly enjoy sex as much as I do. And I definitely wouldn't be living my best life. There were so many times I relied on her words to give me strength. There are so many words I still haven't gotten to say to her. There are so many stories that I didn't have time to tell her about. Even though . . . literally every day of my life . . . literally every single day this woman was a part of my life . . . I . . . she helped raise me to be strong enough to look to the future. So I will.

Somewhere along the lines, I had started to talk out loud. I was on my knees beside the casket, holding my great-grandmother's clenched fist. The tears that I thought I didn't need to cry were spilling down the sides of my face. My mom was on one side of me. My dad, on the other. I don't know how long I knelt there crying, but I made sure she would know exactly how much she meant to me.

When I finally settled down, I realized there was something in her hand. It was a ring blacker than the 8th Light. Mom said she had been looking for it to give to me and wondered where it was. She was told to make sure I wore it. My younger great uncle said it was a ring she got from her grandmother. Didn't know anything else about it, but she always wore it until she got married.

I knew it was weird, but I liked to think she was holding onto it to give to me personally. There was a certain heat radiating from it, like the warmth of a hug from your favorite person.

When I put the ring on it burned hot. Almost like it was on fire, but it didn't burn until it did. It was on fire; I was on fire. I was fire. And it didn't hurt anymore. The pain of losing my great-grandmother slowly burned away as I realized my connection to her would always live on. I stared into my flaming hand

and was reminded of a memory from my childhood that I had long since forgotten. One night when the power had gone out, I started crying because I was scared of the dark. She made a flame in her hand and told me, "If the world ever becomes too dark, just become the flame that lights the way forward."

CHAPTER 5

Analog

Rae Harding

"Here we go. Cabin 6."

John worked the key into the lock, wiggling it for a split second before turning it to the left, sliding the bolt back. The door opened with a shrill creak.

"After you, madame."

Mary gave a tight smile at John's gesture. It was reminiscent of a game show model's hands as they emphasized the possible prizes a contestant might win. John always leaned towards flare and style when trying to sell Mary on how wonderful something was, especially when there was reason to believe she might find it awful.

And this cabin was awful.

When John suggested they get away for a long weekend, a secluded cabin in the woods of rural Tennessee sounded peaceful and romantic. Perhaps he booked an enchanting chalet in the Blue Ridge Mountains or an Airbnb along the Natchez Trace.

She was not expecting a defunct summer camp that had been renovated into an RV campground and a strip of blacktop flanked by a twenty-room motel masquerading as private cabins.

Mary inspected the living room and instinctively avoided physical contact with the furniture. The couch was brown and orange and goldenrod with a woven fabric and plaid design straight out of the seventies. It was flanked by two mid-century two-tiered cocktail tables with dark laminate tops and dainty, spindle legs, each donning crystal candy dishes. The coffee table was a rectangular maple Colonial Revival, pairs of drawers with metal pulls on each end and an open shelf in the middle. On top were a lace doily and a decorative glass bowl. Up against the knotty pine wood-panel wall sat a large armchair with an autumnal-colored synthetic velour in a repeating floral pattern surrounding a picturesque farm mill scene with a water wheel. On the bottom and sides were scrolling dark wood trim. A large floor model television framed in a dark wood casing sat in the corner near the front window. On top was a lace doily, and on top of *that* was a VCR and two remote controls. To the side was a tall, thin bookcase filled with VHS tapes—none of which were labeled.

"Oh my god, you rented my great-grandmother's house," said Mary.

John, who had just retrieved their suitcases from the car, took a look around the room. His eyes widened at the rust-colored shag rug, the Formica kitchen counters, the modified Windsor table chairs, and mustard-colored refrigerator.

"Okay," said John, each vowel drawn out for effect. "Not exactly what I imagined."

Mary gave him a pointed stare and folded her arms across her chest. This was John's signal that he was in trouble. And when John was in trouble, his only shield was his charming smile—a welcomed reminder of what attracted her to him at the beginning of their relationship. He went to Mary, sliding his hands up and down her upper arms, rubbing the tension, willing it to loosen with friction, and kissed her.

"It's fine. It's...vintage."

"It's ancient," said Mary, pouting, which made John smile even wider.

"It's three nights. We'll be spending more time outdoors anyway. There are several hiking trails. There's the lake. We could canoe! Or kayak! I hear there's even a zipline!" John's eyebrows raised into two half-circle arcs. "There's a market a few miles down the road. I know you love to find hand-crafted little gems to bring home. This...," John circled his head, "this is just a place to sleep. We won't even have our eyes open. Hardly."

"It's hideous."

"Agreed," laughed John. "It's hideous. But it gives us motivation to get out—be active. That's what we need. You. Me. The outdoors. An escape from the ups and downs of life. We'll make the most of it. I promise."

Mary wasn't convinced. She remained dubious about most declarations from John. His usual demands for perfection had melted away in the last six months, but she herself had not been able to relax, too conditioned by the last fifteen years. She continued her inspection of the cabin, wandering down the hall past the kitchen to find a bathroom on the right.

"John?" she called. "The tub is powder blue. And the toilet lid is covered in carpet."

John did not respond. Mary grimaced and turned back to the hall, making her way to the bedroom. Inside was a wooden dresser with an old digital clock radio and small vanity with a stool. Lamps rested on each small side table next to the queen bed, dressed in a floral pattern comforter and pillow shams. A quilt was neatly folded at the foot of the bed. It appeared to be handmade, and upon closer inspection, she saw cross-stitched birds and flowers in each square.

"Maryland. Pennsylvania. Georgia," Mary muttered. "It's each state's bird and flower."

While she did not appreciate its aesthetic properties, Mary could value the hard work involved in such an undertaking and wondered why anyone would leave it to rot in a cabin instead of passing it down to family members.

"Does someone live here?" she asked loudly.

"What did you say, honey?" called John.

"Does someone live here?" Mary repeated as she turned the brass knob of the closet door to discover what was inside: empty hangers and a shelf lined with beat-up boxes of board games that appeared to have been purchased in the sixties. "I mean, this place doesn't look like a hotel room."

"Well, it's not. It's a cabin."

Mary rolled her eyes. "All I'm saying is this place looks more like an old person's home than a vacation destination."

John entered the room from behind and threaded his arms under Mary's, hugging her waist. Mary resisted the urge to extricate herself. This encouraged John to give a quick squeeze. "Sorry you hate the cabin. Let's forget it. I'll go into the nearest town and find us some tents to set up on the campgrounds."

Mary smiled. "Oh. On second thought, this place isn't so bad."

John nuzzled her neck. "I thought you'd see it my way."

They sighed in unison.

John turned Mary around. "We'll have a great time. The point is relaxation. You deserve it. After everything we've been through lately. We need some time to tune into a new frequency. I promise. After this trip, you'll walk away a new person."

Mary lowered her head, but John gently lifted her chin with a bent index finger and kissed her lips. "It's getting late. Let's order a pizza. Maybe watch television."

"Well, I hope there's a phone because cell service is nil. Does this place even have cable?"

John frowned. "Didn't think about that. To be determined."

Mary frowned back. "There's no wi-fi either, is there?"

John made an abrupt escape, calling over his shoulder. "I plead the fifth."

"Don't blame me if you find yourself all alone in this cabin after tonight and no car in sight. It's the digital age, dear. I'm not a cavewoman."

Mary took one more glance around the room and exhaled. She marveled at how far John had come since leaving the behavioral health center six months prior. This weekend getaway had been entirely his doing. The year before, he couldn't even make it out of bed most days. He had been a stranger to her then and in many ways still was. She thought that feeling would have gone away by now, but instead of returning to the man she fell in love with and married, he came home a different person. On the surface, there was nothing to complain about. There were no concerns fully formed within her mind, but a constant nagging pricked her gut, especially when he was so agreeable. She could not reconcile the John she used to know with this John.

There was still tension, though. She made enough money for them to live comfortably, but John still had not found a job since being fired. His treatment had not been cheap. One big financial emergency could bankrupt them. In reality, they could not even afford this trip, but John had insisted, spinning it as a chance to prove how much he loved her, how she was his number one priority.

Perhaps, her expectations needed to be managed. She made up her mind to focus on gratitude. They had accomplished so much together. An outdated cabin was a far cry from the list of tribulations they dealt with in the last year. Not only did she have her husband back from the brink of depression, but he had become more loving, more patient, and more phlegmatic. Instead of hopelessness, their hardships had been met with adaptation. If John could endure and overcome a mental illness, surely she could endure three nights in a rustic cabin in the woods.

NIGHT 1

Mary woke to an instrumental version of the Star-Spangled Banner playing on the television while an American flag waved gently in the breeze.

There was not, in fact, any cable, and they had resigned themselves to the local television station broadcast after locating the antennae behind the wood casing. When the ten o'clock news started, they had paused their never-ending game of Monopoly to listen to the local weatherman's report warning residents on the possible storms coming through over the weekend.

"Well, there goes all the outdoor activities," said Mary.

"Maybe not," said John, always striving to be hopeful. "They may blow through quickly. Besides, it sounds like most of them will be at night."

John's optimism leaned on the side of delusional in Mary's opinion; she'd rather have John the Realist than the Idealist. She preferred to not have false hope and often debated whether the struggle to keep their marriage afloat was indeed a castle in the sky. She had already met with a divorce lawyer, but she owed it to John to try and salvage the broken pieces of their relationship, glue them together, and see if they hold water. She hoped this trip would reveal the more authentic John—the John she used to know—and there would be no reason to see a lawyer again. Storms would come, but if one of them refused to acknowledge them, what hope would they have in weathering them?

Soon after the weather forecast, with bellies full of pizza and exhaustion kicking in, Mary and John had fallen asleep on the plaid couch, her body in the fetal position, head in John's lap while his legs were propped on the coffee table.

Mary squinted at the television, a bright sun sparkling in the sky as the flag continued to wave. Beyond the dim light of the venti-hood above the kitchen stove, it was the only source of illumination in the cabin. She slowly lifted her head off John's lap and sat up, careful not to disturb him. His head was lolled back, mouth agape, snoring softly. She didn't envy the cramp he would have in his neck when he woke.

The song ended with a flourish, superimposed fireworks exploding in the sky above the flag for extra pizzazz. Mary imagined some high schooler interning part-time at the local television station, left to his own devices in a closet full of outdated technology to experiment with the most rudimentary of film special effects.

The picture flashed to a color bar test card screen, and a sine tone rang like a flat-lined heart monitor. Before Mary could reach for the remote control and turn the television off, the screen turned black, and a blue scrolling bar appeared in the center of the screen. White pixelated lettering trekked across to the left:

THIS CONCLUDES OUR BROADCAST DAY. STAY TUNED TO CHANNEL 66 FOR ALL YOUR LOCAL PROGRAMMING. IF YOU HEAR A KNOCK AT THE DOOR, DO NOT OPEN IT.

Mary's brows knitted. She rubbed her eyes, hoping to move the blur of sleep from her vision. But by the time her eyes focused, the words had scrolled away, and the screen had returned to the colorful bands. She turned the television off and gently rubbed John's leg.

"Hey," she whispered, hoping not to startle him. "Let's move to the bedroom."

John lifted his head, wincing slightly at the movement of his neck. "What is it?"

"We fell asleep," said Mary. "Let's go to bed."

John got up, still half asleep, and followed Mary compliantly down the hall.

NIGHT 2

The morning had been spent hiking a three-mile trail, and, after a lunch at the local farmer's market, the afternoon had been spent kayaking on the campground lake. It was as if they had the entire property to themselves—not a soul in sight. John had been right, though. No storms. Not one portent of what the weatherman had predicted. The sun was warm, but a cool breeze kept the temperature mild. Leaves were beginning to turn with splashes of red and yellow and orange, promising to overtake the green soon. Their reflection in the water gave the lake a magical appeal as gentle ripples radiated away from their kayak and to the shore.

Mary had never been a particularly 'outdoorsy-kinda-gal' as John liked to say, but she had thoroughly enjoyed her time with her husband. It hadn't been like the *old* John, but there were moments where she thought this *different* John might be okay too. Since returning home, John's disposition had improved on a daily basis, culminating with the idyllic attentive husband before her. Gone were the worries that plagued him daily with crippling anxiety and despair. The slightest bump in the road no longer sent him spiraling. This John made the most of the situation, able to salvage what they had going for them and carrying on with fortitude and hope, always aware of the bigger picture. Quite frankly, Mary began to believe she could learn a lot from his optimism.

They returned to the cabin from having dinner at Mom-and-Pop's Best BBQ exhausted. Mary's pink skin stung more and more as the sun set, revealing the slight sunburn they had acquired despite the copious reapplications of sunscreen. John unlocked the bolt, and the cabin greeted them with the loud screech of the door hinges. He moved aside for Mary to enter first. She made a beeline for the bedroom and flopped face-first onto the bed. John followed close behind, calling "Timber!" as he fell to the mattress.

"I love you," he finally said after several minutes of silence.

Mary turned her head to face him. "I love you too." She believed she meant it because she believed he meant it.

Knocking came from the front door.

"Who is that?"

Mary moaned. "I don't have X-ray vision."

John grinned and lifted himself off the bed. "Well, I got the short end of the stick with you, didn't I?"

Mary threw a pillow at John as he exited the room. She stared at the constellations found in the popcorn ceiling as his footsteps retreated down the hall and faded into the background. When she was young, her mind often tried to find patterns and images in random markings. She could find faces in the pits and crevices of tiles, animals in the rings and streaks of wood paneling, and ghostly figures in television static. Now she found Orion and Ursa, the moon, a comet...

She jumped as the radio blared and banished the quiet like a bomb.

Authorities ask residents to take shelter...

Mary was now sitting up in bed, putting as much distance as possible between herself and the radio, the headboard digging into her back. She stared at it, too frightened to make any sudden movements, as the radio popped and hissed with white noise and warped frequencies. But just as suddenly as it had kicked on, it once again became silent. With her heart hammering her ribcage, she launched herself out of the bed and darted to the radio to turn it off but couldn't find a switch. Deciding instead to unplug it, she once again failed—there was no cord.

The creaking of the front door echoed in the hallway. She recalled the strange incident from last night's television broadcast sign-off. She had been too tired to put much stock into it, but now all of her senses were heightened, ready to fight or fly. The scrolling bar predicted there would be a knock. There was, in fact, a knock. It had also instructed the viewer to not open the door.

John!

Mary darted down the hall. Her husband's back was to her, the last of the daylight outside making him a shadowy silhouette framed by the opened door. She could not see who he was talking to, but she could tell they were turning away.

"John!"

John turned to her, closing the door as he did.

"Who was that?" asked Mary.

John smiled. "One of our neighbors. Older gentlemen. Apparently, that storm is supposed to hit tonight. Should blow out of here by morning."

Mary took a breath, trying to calm her nerves. She felt a bit silly to be in such a panic. If it had not been for the radio, she wouldn't have given last night a second thought. She had to have imagined it in her drowsy stupor.

"What did he want?"

"To warn us about the storm."

"To warn us about the storm?" Mary echoed.

John chuckled. "Yes."

"How bad is it supposed to get?"

"Pretty bad, apparently."

Mary grabbed the remote control from the coffee table and turned on the television. It flashed, went dark, and then tuned into the local news channel. The weatherman's voice followed the closed caption on the screen.

This line of pressure is moving quickly, so we expect the storm to be out of the area by sunrise. There could be some power outages, so make sure you have a programmed weather radio with batteries to get any alerts issued throughout the night. We will interrupt our broadcast with any severe indoctrination warnings as we track the moon, so stay tuned to your local Channel 66 for all the latest.

"Did he just say…" Mary's eyes searched the closed caption quickly before it disappeared. …interrupt our broadcast with any severe weather warnings…She had misheard.

"You okay?" asked John.

Mary turned to him and gave a tight, but reassuring, smile. "Yes. Yes, I'm fine."

"Don't worry about the storm. We'll probably sleep through it. Don't we have a radio somewhere? I wonder if it has batteries."

"In the bedroom," she said. "It turned on a few minutes ago by itself. Scared me half to death."

"Hmm." John walked down the hall to the bedroom.

Mary stared absentmindedly out the window. The curtains were sheer, making the cabins across the blacktop path visible but hazy. The sun was down now, and the warm lights behind their own sheer curtains came from within.

"We lucked out!" said John from down the hall. "It's a weather radio. You must have heard the severe weather alert. There's batteries. Not sure how good they are, but it seems to be working just fine."

Mary closed her eyes for a moment of relief, hoping to shake her embarrassing freak-out from her mind. The radio had a perfectly reasonable explanation. She felt silly. Here they were, trying to relax. So why had she become so uptight?

She walked over to the window and pulled the curtains together. She glanced one more time at the line of cabins across the path, each identical with their windows to the right of the door.

And at each window of each of the ten cabins, behind a sheer curtain, stood a shadowy, statue-still figure.

"John!"

John appeared directly behind her. "What is it?" he asked in her ear.

Mary yelped in surprise, her body leaping violently. She had not heard him approach. John laughed and held her arms to steady her.

"You scared the crap out of me."

John continued to laugh. "I can tell."

Mary gave several playful swats at him. "Are you trying to give me a heart attack?"

"Sorry. Sorry. Why so jumpy?"

Mary shook her head. Trying to explain would just make her sound paranoid.

John and Mary played Uno that night. They had the television on but kept it muted. Other than the radar pop-up in the corner of the screen, there was no indication of severe weather. Not even the wind was blowing outside.

By the time John won his fifth hand, Mary decided Uno would have to end before she strangled him. "We should see what kind of movies they have."

"Honey," said John. "Those old things probably don't even work anymore."

You never know unless you try," Mary replied, pulling a VHS tape from the narrow bookcase. "None of them are labeled."

"Russian roulette," muttered John. "Just pop one in. It'll be a surprise."

Mary found the On switch to the VCR and inserted the tape. "Nothing's happening."

"Oh!" John grabbed the remote and pressed the input menu. The television screen went blue. Squiggly lines undulated across the center of the screen briefly before the picture went black. "There."

The production company's intro commenced with musical fanfare, and a blood moon traveled forward from the distance until the trademark filled the screen: *Harvest Entertainment Films*. It faded to black, and another title scrolled across the screen: *Enjoying Your Stay at Camp Cordova*. The picture changed to the lake at twilight, the reflection of the setting sun shimmering on the water's surface.

Mary turned to John with a shrug. "Guess we'll try another one."

"No, stop," said John as she went to press the eject button. "Maybe it will have a good tip or tell us about a hidden trail or something."

"Fine." Mary huffed as she plopped onto the couch, arms folded. "But if this is more than fifteen minutes, I'm outta here."

"Fair enough," said John, taking the seat beside her.

There was no voiceover, only canned music, so Mary and John had to read the text on the screen as the scenes changed from the lake, to the cabins, to the hiking trails. There was nothing revealed that wasn't already given in the information brochure they received when they checked in. It even showed the hidden waterfall they planned to find the next day.

Suddenly the tape hiccupped, and wavy lines danced across the picture.

"Told you these tapes are old," said John.

The picture changed to the exterior of a cabin. It was night-time, and a warm glow came from the front window.

OUR EXECUTIVE CABINS ARE COZY, PRIVATE, AND EQUIPPED WITH CENTRAL HEATING AND AIR. EACH CABIN HAS A FULL BATH AND KITCHEN.

"And no wi-fi," Mary grumbled.

The camera slowly moved forward, getting closer to the cabin. Even though the picture was dark, Mary could make out the cabin number: 6.

WE ASK OUR RESIDENTS TO STAY INDOORS AT NIGHT UNLESS TRAVELING BY VEHICLE TO DINE AT ONE OF OUR HALF DOZEN LOCAL RESTAURANTS.

A dark figure walked up to the door of the cabin, its right arm rising up.

IF YOU HEAR A KNOCK AT THE DOOR, DO NOT...

The screen resumed with fluttering lines, and the scene cut to a couple waving goodbye to the camera.

JOIN US AT CAMP CORDOVA FOR YOUR NEXT WEEKEND GETAWAY.

"Hmm," said John. "That was strange."

Mary thought it was more than strange. In fact, she found it frightening. Was she going crazy? Was she seeing and hearing messages on the television?

"Did you see that too?" she asked John.

"Um, I'm sitting right next to you."

"The creepy scene of the cabin? At night?"

John nodded. "Are you okay?"

"That was our cabin number."

"Was it?"

Mary ejected the tape from the VCR. "Last night, when we fell asleep. I woke up to the TV channel signing off, and I could have sworn it told us to not open the door if someone knocks on it."

"Okay. Weird."

"And now this tape," said Mary.

"It's an old tape. I'm sure it skipped a scene or two. It was just warning people about being out at night. It is the woods, after all. Coyotes may be out here."

"It didn't show a coyote, John. It showed a person about to knock on the cabin door."

"Guess I missed that."

"How could you miss it? I mean, it was dark, the film, I mean, and it wasn't clear—the person, but it plainly showed someone about to knock on *our* cabin door."

"You're a bit shaken, huh? I can tell from the way you're speaking."

"It didn't creep you out?"

"Honey, it's just an old, worn-out tape. There's nothing to be creeped out about." John turned the television off, stood, and stretched his arms. "Forget the tape. I'm beat. Let's hit the hay."

Mary tried to brush off the fear plaguing her. She reasoned that John didn't seem fazed in the slightest. Perhaps she too was tired, more than she thought, and it was causing her to make a mountain out of a molehill.

Reluctantly, she followed John down the hall. After getting ready for bed, they snuggled under the heavy quilt.

"Hmm," said John. "Looks like we're going to have a harvest moon."

"A what?"

"Look."

Mary leaned over to fix her gaze on whatever John was pointing at. Outside the window was a bright, gibbous moon, but instead of the ghostly white of most moons, Mary found a slight orange tinge.

"Why is it orange?" she asked.

"To match the furniture," John teased.

Mary gave a playful hit to his stomach. "I'm serious."

"To be honest, I'd have to look it up. Too bad there's no internet here."

"This is your doing," said Mary.

"We're having a great time. I'm happy to take all the credit." John smiled, kissed Mary, and rolled over. "Good night."

"Good night."

Mary watched John's chest rise and fall as he plunged into sleep. It wasn't long before her eyelids grew heavy staring at him bathed in rusty moonbeams, and she herself descended into the blackness of sleep.

NIGHT 3

If the storm had ever moved through the area, John and Mary slept straight through it. The weatherman that morning had not even mentioned last night's storm. Instead, this evening he was warning viewers about another storm that was expected to hit later that night.

John and Mary had spent the morning hiking to the hidden waterfall and the afternoon touring the local shops in the nearby town. Mary had picked up several items, including homemade fudge, a small pottery bowl she intended to put her jewelry in at night, a hand-knitted scarf, and a Christmas ornament hand-carved from wood. She carefully unwrapped each one and set them on the kitchen counter to admire.

"Don't know why anyone pays any attention to this guy," John said, nodding his head toward the weatherman on the television screen. "He kept saying how severe the weather was supposed to be yesterday, and we didn't even get a drop of rain."

"It's not an exact science."

"Still," said John. "I hate it when they freak everyone out for no reason."

"What do you feel like doing tonight?" asked Mary, hoping to move on from the weather or lack thereof.

"Haven't given it much thought," said John. "Wanna see about any more of those VHS tapes?"

"No," said Mary, remembering for the first time about the tape from last night.

"Well then," said John. "How about a stroll?"

"In the dark?" asked Mary.

"Why not?" said John. "Should be a proper harvest moon out there. We could head over to the lake. Bet it's pretty."

Mary smiled. "Okay."

"Okay?"

"Yes, okay. But didn't that tape ask guests to stay indoors at night?"

John wrinkled his nose. "That tape was a million years old. The brochure didn't say anything about staying in. In fact, when we checked in, the front desk lady mentioned how beautiful the lake looked at night and told me we shouldn't leave here without enjoying it one evening.

Mary gave a tight smile. How could she deny herself a stroll with her spouse to stare at the moon and stars by a lake? She had lived so long with a despondent husband that this was a welcomed turn of events. They headed out the cabin, a crisp breeze greeting them as their feet hit the blacktop path. The other cabins seemed empty and silent. Only the porch lights were on, illuminating their way to the lake.

John had it wrong. The harvest moon over the lake wasn't pretty; it was breathtaking. It seemed larger and brighter than a normal full moon and was blood red. Mary wondered how she could have lived all these years and never seen such a moon. They sat on the bench, watching the fireflies dance in the darkness, listening to the crickets chirping, and watching the bats flying overhead to catch their meal.

"This is nice," said John.

"It is," said Mary.

In the distance, an owl hooted.

John turned his body towards Mary, arm resting on the bench back. "I've been meaning to talk to you. Actually, that's not true. I've been waiting until now to talk to you."

"You have? About what?"

John exhaled. "You know how different I am now. Right?"

"Night and day," interjected Mary.

"Yes, well, the facility I went to...it was very much like this place."

"Oh?"

"It helped me so much. Obviously. Life-changing. I know this hasn't been the most romantic getaway we could have had, but I thought coming to this place might help you too."

The world grew silent. Nothing buzzed. Nothing chirped. Not even the lake made a sound.

"Help me with what?" said Mary.

"This past year hasn't been easy. How stressful it must have been for you. I want to take that all away. My gift to you."

Mary smiled. "I appreciate you recognizing how difficult it has been on me, John, but you don't need to worry. If you want to help me, continue helping yourself," she said. "This weekend has been nice, but tomorrow we will pack up, and head home and life returns."

"We don't have to go back."

Mary laughed. "You wish."

"No, I mean it."

"What are you talking about, John? I have a job. We have bills to pay. You need to continue therapy. We can't stay here."

John froze, eyes locked on hers.

"John?"

John did not respond. Other than a quick blink of his eyes, he remained stone still, expression vacant. It was as if he was no longer in his body.

"John, what is it? Speak to me."

John didn't move.

Mary glanced around, for a brief moment thinking John was about to spring a surprise on her. Far away, beyond the water, a red dot caught her attention. There were two, close together, coming from the woods. Flashlights? Laser beams? Who would be out in the woods at night? Behind John, another pair of lights appeared in the distance. Mary scanned across the lake. More pairs of lights appeared. She stood and turned in every direction. Not lights. Not lights at all.

Eyes.

A dozen or more red eyes lined the horizon.

"John." Mary's voice was a whisper, fright closing her throat. She grabbed John's hand. "We need to get back to the cabin. Now."

John did not say a word but followed her up the blacktop. They did not run, as John did not seem as panicked, but Mary found herself speed walking. At the cabin, her hand shook as she unlocked the door. She cursed the shrill moan of the hinges for announcing their arrival. Once inside, she locked it, being sure to add the chain for good measure. She hurried to the front window and glanced outside. Nothing.

In the back of the cabin, an alarm sounded. Mary raced to the bedroom.

The National Weather Service has issued a severe weather warning for your area.

She slammed her hand down on the dismiss button and ran to the living room to turn the television on to the local station. The weatherman was referring to a radar tracker with a large red blob directly overhead.

We urge you to seek shelter and stay indoors...

A tornado alarm sounded. Mary darted to the window and pulled back the sheers. No wind. No rain. No thunder. No lightning. Only the crimson harvest moon.

"I don't understand. It's like last night. There is no storm," said Mary, trying to quell the panic in her voice. "There is no storm."

"It's fine, Mary," said John. "We're safe. Those weathermen like to put everyone in an alarm to keep you tuned into the station."

Mary turned to John, who casually sat on the couch, slipped his shoes off, and set his feet on the coffee table. "Then why is the tornado alarm sounding? I'm going to find some candles."

"Better safe than sorry?" called John.

Mary opened the cabinets, searching for matches or lighters or flashlights or candles. After several attempts, she managed to locate a box of wooden matches and a flashlight she missed.

When she checked it, the bulb was a soft amber, indicating the batteries were low.

A high-pitched tone sounded on the television. The weatherman was replaced with the Emergency Alert System logo and a robotic voice.

This is the Emergency Alert System. All residents are asked to isolate themselves indoors. Keep all points of entry locked and secured. Do not answer the door—even to those identifying themselves as authorities. Please shelter in place until sunrise. Do not look at the moon.

Mary's body froze in terror. She couldn't think straight. "John?"

John's brow furrowed. "We'll be fine, Mary."

"John, this does not seem fine. Why does it not want us to stare at the moon? We were out there at the lake. What the hell is going on?"

A series of tones and beeps rang from the television. Mary thought it sounded like Morse Code. The screen turned red, and a white scroll bar appeared. Pixelated lettering traveled from right to left.

The EAS has rescinded the warning for all Cordova residents. We apologize for the false alarm. Please enjoy the moon.

"See?" asked John. "False alarm."

"Please enjoy the moon?" said Mary, her voice saturated with incredulity.

John shrugged.

"The sirens are still sounding," said Mary.

The lights went out, plunging them into darkness.

"Damnit." Mary held her hand out in front of her, feelers meant to keep her from running into the furniture on her journey to the kitchen counter for the flashlight.

"This could be romantic," said John, a disembodied voice in the void.

"Not even close."

Mary reached the counter and slowly moved her hand across until it hit the flashlight. She pushed the button at the bottom, and it clicked on. The light was dim, casting shadows across the wood-paneled walls of the cabin. John was still on the ugly plaid couch.

"How can you just sit there?" Mary said, exasperated.

John did not answer.

"John? Answer me."

"You like the new me, don't you?" he finally said, without moving. "The one without a care in the world?"

Mary took a hesitant step forward. "John."

"I'm not even the *old* old me," he said. "I'm a new man."

"Can we talk about this later, John? Maybe we should take shelter in a closet or the bathtub?"

The tornado siren was incessant, making it difficult for Mary to concentrate. She went to the front window. Outside, the harvest moon cast its ruddy shroud onto the campground. Along the blacktop were over a dozen neighboring campers, shadowy figures in the darkness, their backs to Mary and John's cabin, heads tilted up to the sky. Above, not a single cloud passed across the moon's face.

"John, everyone's outside."

"I told you there is nothing to worry about. There will never be another worry after tonight."

Mary turned to John. "What are you talking about? After tonight?" Mary's heart was pounding. Nothing was right. She couldn't make heads or tails of anything going on. John's behavior was normal, which under the circumstances was more than disconcerting. "How can you be so calm?"

There was a knock at the door. Mary pulled back the sheers and glanced outside. There was no one on the porch. Each person began to turn their heads slowly in unison to the left. Even from the window in the darkness, Mary could see their gaping jaws. Just as their heads could not turn any further, their bodies followed until each figure faced the cabin. In the next breath, their eyes lit up—the same red pairs of eyes she saw at the lake. Mary screamed, staggering backward, nearly toppling over the coffee table.

"John! Their eyes! Their eyes!"

There was another knock at the door. John slowly stood. "Answer it, Mary."

"Have you lost your mind?" she said. "I'm not answering that."

John started toward the door. "Then I will."

Mary moved in front of John. "The television. It warned us not to open the door."

"You saw for yourself, Mary. It was a false alarm."

"Those aren't people out there," said Mary. "Something is very wrong. The moon. I think it's the moon. We have to stay inside."

"They're here to help us, Mary. Through the storm."

"We don't need help, John." Mary's voice cracked with fear. Her mind was a ball swinging back and forth across a net, oscillating between the bigger danger: the people outside the cabin or the husband inside. "You're scaring me."

"I was scared too, Mary. But you'll see. It's time to open the door to a new life. You'll be a new person. You can't imagine it yet—how great it feels when the burden of control is lifted. On or off. On or off."

Another knock on the door sent Mary's head spinning. Not a knock. Banging.

"Go away!" she shrieked.

When Mary turned back to John, she found a pair of red, glowing eyes staring down at her. In horror, Mary sprinted to the bedroom and locked the door behind her. She tried to push the dresser, but it was too heavy. The sanguine glow of the moon reached into the room, sprawling on the bed quilt, bathing the state birds in blood. From the front of the cabin, Mary heard the front door creak open.

The brass doorknob rattled.

"Mary, dear?" said John from the other side. "The storm is here. I've let it in. Don't be afraid of destruction. After ruin comes rebirth."

Sobbing, Mary backed into the corner. In the window were two dark figures, eyes shining red, mouths agape.

"Leave me alone!"

The figures stood motionless. At the door, the tinny sound of a key hitting the inner lock alerted her to John's impending entrance into the room. The weather radio blared a single warning tone, and a programmed voice filled the room.

The National Weather Service has issued a severe storm warning for your area. All residents are asked to seek shelter immediately and to keep the moon out of sight. Do not believe anyone, including loved ones, who say the moon is harmless. Do not allow anyone into your home, as anyone outside has been indoctrinated. Symptoms may include...

The door opened. John poked his head inside, eyes aflame, smile from ear to ear.

"Honey, you've already been sown. It's why we're here. This is how we truly rebuild what we lost. Change is good. *This* change is good. There is nothing to fear. You're going to love this next part. It's time for the harvest."

DAY 1

Mary stepped out of the cabin, inhaling the fresh air. Last night's storm had come and gone with little to no damage. Even the power was restored quickly. She and John had awoken refreshed and ready to make the drive back home. She had felt a bit humiliated by her behavior, but John had dismissed it, assuring her he too had been that way before when it came to the storms of life. But now, they could see clearly. Fear is just static—snow on a television channel. Since the storm, Mary's brain was sharper. She could cut through the interference and keep her mind clear. Gone was the need to adapt to change or ride out every capricious alteration life bombarded her with. John was right. The change was good. There had only been two variables to choose between: on or off.

She had chosen off.

CHAPTER 6

Robert's Heart

Kathryn Skinner

Robert awoke from anesthesia one sense at a time on New Year's Day. First, he felt the pain of a semi-trailer resting on his chest. It hurt so bad he couldn't breathe. "Am I alive?" he thought. "What is happening to me? Why does my chest hurt so much?"

When he tried to inhale, he realized there was a machine breathing for him. " God, it hurts. God, it hurts so bad."

There was someone else in the room, not Jeannie, his wife, but a young woman, busily attaching tubes to him. He tried to raise his arm to get her attention. Nothing happened. He tried to speak. Couldn't. Something was in his throat. He panicked. His eyes opened wide. The girl put her hand on his arm.

"So, you're awake. Good. Nothing to be afraid of. Your transplant went very well. Try to relax now. I've got some pain medicine for you. Your wife wants to come in for a short visit, so we're going to get you cleaned up. Okay?"

That's the way Robert's new life started six months ago, though he would remember little of those first few hours after his heart transplant. What he would remember, and often thought about was the first time, and thousands and thousands of times since, when he realized a stranger's heart was pumping in his chest. It was a gift from a family he would never meet. He had a mental image of the young man who died in an accident so he might live. He imagined it was an auto accident, but no one told him that. He just imagined it.

At night, in bed, waiting for sleep to carry him away, and listening to Jeanie's soft snoring, he sometimes felt the presence of the young man, not physically, but somehow present. It was not something he could explain even to himself, and he was afraid to mention it to anyone else, even Jeannie. There were two nights when he thought he saw someone in the room. Between the bed and the closet, there was a tall figure standing with his back to Robert, as if walking toward the door. Robert wasn't scared; he wondered why he wasn't scared.

He remembered as a kid, sharing a room with his older brother. Ronnie would often tell him ghost stories at night and make moaning noises, so Robert had to cover his head with his pillow to shut him out, and he would hum to himself while he imagined he was riding his bicycle or going down the slide in the community swimming pool, two of his most favorite things to do. But this was different. This didn't seem like a spook but a friend. Jeannie's gentle snoring was soothing. It was normal. He loved the normalness of it. And he loved Jeannie. They had been high school sweethearts.

Robert was a simple man, just an inch or two shy of six feet tall and strong. He once lifted the rear end of a pickup truck on a dare. No one had ever suggested he should go to college, and he had been eager to get a job right out of high school, working as an auto mechanic for Mr. White, their next-door neighbor. When Mr. White died, Mrs. White asked him if he would like to buy the shop. "Sure," he'd said, and he was proud of how many customers depended on him for auto upkeep and repairs. He could bring almost any motor back to life. Now he had a new "motor," a rebuilt engine, a pump that once belonged to a younger man. He kind of liked thinking about it this way.

But with the new motor came some new ways of seeing the world around him. This puzzled him. Strange thoughts came out of nowhere.

On the first Sunday, he went to church with Jeannie, something he hadn't done in a long time; if you didn't count Christmas and Easter, he focused beyond the preacher at the podium, on the altar behind him. It was lush with flowers of every color, bright reds, yellows, and even blue. He leaned over to Jeannie. "Are those flowers real?" he whispered. She smiled, "Of course."

A few days later, while he was sitting on the porch rocker, he noticed that the birds were singing loudly, non-stop, so cheerful. Once he noticed them singing, he could hear nothing else. He walked into the kitchen to ask Jeannie if the birds were singing louder than usual. He stood at the door for a few minutes, watching the way Jeannie was using the kitchen space to make the pot roast for tonight's dinner. She moved two steps sideways from stove to sink and back again, twisting every now and then to open the refrigerator, never missing a beat. She was so well practiced at cooking for the three men in her life. How many sandwiches had she made over the years of raising two boys, and how many dishes had she washed? Hearing Robert sigh, she stopped and pointed to the window. Just outside was the window box he had attached to the house a couple of years ago. From it trailed purple verbena and red petunias. "Don't disturb her," she said. He looked again. A robin, sitting in a nest among the flowers. Robert whispered, "Maybe we should get a bird feeder."

Jeannie's Bunco Club came to their house one night because it was her turn to be the hostess, and from the TV room, Robert could hear them chatting, laughing, and teasing each other. He turned the volume down so he could eavesdrop. "It's always been important for Jeannie to have girlfriends," he thought. Then corrected himself, "At their age, they are women friends, I guess, but Jeannie still called them girls."

Jeannie was his girlfriend, still, after all these years. Still pretty. Still slim. Still the smiling, brown-eyed girl he fell in love with. What a rock she had been through all these medical problems he had had to deal with and the financial problems that had come with them. They may never see their way out of the money problems. She had even considered getting a job after all these years. She never complained.

Thump, thump. He could feel his heart beating; he could hear it beating against his eardrums. Robert turned his palms over and looked at the inside of his wrists. He could see his pulse. He put his right hand over the jagged scar that now defined his chest. Thump, thump. A strong thump, thump. Everything was working just fine. He wondered when he could go back to working on cars. That's what he wanted to do. He smiled and took a deep breath, and turned the TV volume back on.

His granddaughter Alexandria, nine years old, spent a weekend with them in the spring while his older son, David, and his wife, Jo, went to a friend's wedding out of state.

Robert loved being Alexandria's Grampa. She was the only little girl he had ever been around; he had only brothers in his family, and when David and Jo had their first child, as expected, Ricky was a boy. Robert remembered when Alexandria was born, David, dressed in a pajama-like scrub suit that doctors wear, walked into the waiting room where both families were anxiously waiting and announced, "Alexandria Marie Johnson, six pounds, six ounces, has arrived!" Robert remembered thinking, "Well, where on earth did they get that name?" Marie was his mother's name. That pleased him, but Alexandria sounded almost like a foreign language.

She will have a hard time learning to spell that name, he remembered saying to himself. But now, it seemed the perfect name for such a beautiful little girl. And she was beautiful. She looked like her mother, long, curly black hair, usually in a ponytail, and smiling hazel eyes, always twinkling, a happy child. Even now, she would climb into his lap when he was in his recliner and put her arms around his neck.

Alexandria had not wanted to miss any of her classes at the Children's Saturday Art School. It was something she looked forward to all week, so Saturday morning, Robert drove Alexandria to art school and promised to pick her up in front of the building at noon when classes were over. But when he returned, she wasn't there waiting, though all the other children seemed to be leaving the building. After waiting for a few minutes, he decided, "Maybe I need to go inside and find her." In one of the classrooms just inside the front door, he saw her. In fact, there were two others, all three of them leaning over the tables and painting.

Alexandria saw him and motioned to him to come closer and see what she had been working on. "Look, Grampa, we're learning to do watercolors today." The teacher, who had been at a sink at the back of the room, came forward to speak to Robert. "Alexandria is such a quick learner," she said. "Even though this is the first time the children have worked with watercolors, see how she has used such broad strokes to make that beautiful sky? A loaded brush here and diluted color there. You have quite a gifted granddaughter." Robert beamed. She went on, "Perhaps you, too, are an artist?"

"Oh no." Robert was quick to answer. "Never had any experience with art."

"Well, it's never too late. We have classes for adults, too. In fact, they are offering classes next fall to meet at the same time as the children's Saturday classes. Perhaps you and Alexandria could both come to class on Saturdays."

When Robert and Alexandria returned home, they found Jeannie in the kitchen cutting up a chicken. "I'm making your favorite for dinner, Alexandria, chicken and yellow rice. How was art class?"

"Great, Granma. We learned how to use watercolors, and the teacher told Grampa he should come to classes, too. I promise, she did."

Robert groaned, "Oh well, it wasn't exactly like that, but they are starting Saturday morning classes for adults in the fall."

Jeannie took a step back from the butcher block and wiped her hands on her apron. "You are going to art classes?"

"No, no. It was just something she threw out. They're probably looking for more paying students."

Jeannie smiled. "Maybe you would like it."

Robert hung the car keys on the hook by the kitchen door and circled the living room circling, pausing to study anything that was in a frame. He had never paid attention to Jeannie's decorations, though he had helped her hang some of the larger pictures. There was a black and white wedding photo of himself and Jeannie, and a framed piece of embroidery, brown with age, passed down from Jeannie's grandmother. Photos of his sons and their families that sat on top of the TV went unnoticed most of the time. And over the sofa, a large picture of a bouquet of flowers sitting on a dining room table. Robert walked closer. Was it a real painting? Probably not. It didn't look like real paint. He remembered how bright the blue was in Alexandria's painting. In fact, this one looked like a magazine ad that had faded.

Once, he and Jeannie had gone to an art gallery. One of Jeannie's Bunco girlfriends had a couple of paintings in it and invited them to a reception for the exhibit. But mostly, he just snacked on the dips and nuts while Jeannie made the rounds and talked with her friends. He had not examined the paintings as closely as he was now examining what Jeannie had chosen to hang on their walls.

Maybe it was because he had time on his hands. Dr. Wilson had told him to plan on taking at least six months to recuperate, go to rehab three or four times a week and come back to see him for the all-clear to go back to work part-time for a while, expect to take anti-rejection medicines for the rest of his life.

He was definitely getting bored. And it seemed his thoughts were running away with him. Especially thoughts about whose heart was beating inside his chest. He had been told the donor's family did not want their names known, and Dr. Wilson had made that clear. He hadn't given it much thought then. It hadn't seemed important.

At the auto shop, his son, Danny, had set up a computer program to track the billing and keep records of his customers' repairs. Danny had gone to junior college to study computers and ended up with a good-paying job working for a small company that sold new and used computers. He decided to ask Danny to show him how to use the internet so he could research the newspaper for stories that might tell him something about the source of his heart. From the way things went on the day he underwent surgery, he was pretty sure the donor was local or at least nearby. Maybe he could find out the answers to his questions. It seemed like he had the right to know. Then he would have a chance to say, "Thank you."

Danny said, "Sure, I can do that. It's about time you and Mom got with the 21st century, and after all, It would probably be a good thing to keep you occupied. You know... something to keep you busy." So, Danny brought home one of the refurbished desktop computers from work, hooked it up to the internet, and showed Dad how to use Google and Yahoo. It was Robert's new toy. He discovered something new every day. He learned how to send e-mails to Danny and to his older son, David. He learned how to listen to the radio on the computer, and he learned a lot about his surgery, including what all the pills he took were doing for him.

Robert found those who died the day of his transplant and those on the night before. Nothing seemed like a possibility. Of course, almost all the deaths were of old people, people in their sixties and seventies, like old man Shaeffer, 87, who had been part of his Dad's Friday night poker group. None could have been candidates for donating organs to a young man like Robert, who just turned 55 last June. Robert widened his search, and using a map, identified all the larger towns within 500 miles of Memphis, found their newspapers, and studied their obituaries. When he saw two of them suggested memorials be sent to the Heart Association, he perked up, but the dates of their death were not compatible with his date of surgery. He grinned with the realization that diseased hearts wouldn't be used anyway. No luck.

Robert scrolled back to websites that described heart transplantation again and researched the process of finding and matching donors and recipients. He felt the wave of gratefulness all over again for having been one of the lucky ones for which there had been a match. "Life is full of coincidences. That's for sure, and they worked in my favor. Somebody saved my life. Some stranger saved me."

He didn't understand all that he was reading on the computer. Most of the articles were published in medical journals, which in many cases seemed to be written in a foreign language using words that seemed only strings of meaningless syllables, but something leaped out to him in an article on what was believed to increase the success rate of transplants. The doctor who was reporting his findings wrote that it was not necessary to match males to males and females to females. It seemed *to make no significant difference in the success rate*. Robert pushed his chair away from the computer. "Whoa. How could that be?" he said out loud. Was it possible he had a woman's heart? He had been looking for obituaries of males. Of course. Of course, he had been looking for male donors.

He stood up and started toward the kitchen door. He had to tell Jeanie what he had discovered. She was in the backyard pulling weeds, trying to get the flower beds ready for spring planting. He paused at the top step. He wondered, "What difference it would make to Jeannie? What difference would it make to him?" He decided he would add this information to his list of questions to take to his next appointment with Dr. Wilson.

Robert didn't mention his suspicions to anyone. He asked himself, "Would he be embarrassed?" Or maybe she would worry about a female heart being sturdy enough and big enough for a strong and active man like him, a man who had been known to lift the rear end of a Ford pickup truck off the ground. He decided to keep this new information to himself. After all, it was just a possibility, not anything more than a possibility.

The next day at cardiac rehabilitation, in the Cardio Club, as his new buddies liked to call their group, they were excited about a 5K run/1 mile walk that had been organized for the first Saturday in April. Everybody planned to either enter the race or cheer the others on. They would have their own Cardio Club T-shirts. It would help raise money for the Memorial Hospital transplant program and raise awareness about the need for donors.

Robert enjoyed these new friends, male and female. They had so much in common, and he actually looked forward to Monday, Wednesday, and Friday mornings at 10 A.M. though he had never seen the importance of exercise before his heart problems changed his life. He assumed he got plenty of exercise climbing into engines and changing tires.

They all started out as a group that morning. Soon the younger, more serious runners became more competitive and moved toward the front of the group. Robert found himself walking at the same pace as a young woman who introduced herself as Ginny. Ginny seemed to need to explain why she was participating in the race today. Her sister had been an organ donor after she was struck and killed by an automobile while biking. Her sister was a Senior at the University of Memphis.

"She was studying Art History," Ginny said. "And here's the thing. Last year every member of her sorority had signed their willingness to be a donor on the back of their driver's licenses. One hundred percent of the sorority, but," she said, "My Mom was devastated. We all were. It was so hard for our family, especially at Christmas time. But because Terri was so certain organ donation was the right thing to do, I think that was the only thing that kept my Mom from giving up completely. We all were, the whole family. But I didn't think Mom was going to survive."

Robert was scared to ask the exact date her sister died. He was afraid, but he slowed his walking pace and said, "I am a survivor. I am one of the lucky ones who received a donated heart. Tell your Mom I thank her for the gift of life she made possible for someone."

Ginny stopped walking and grabbed Robert's sleeve. "I'm afraid to ask. I'm afraid to ask, but when was your surgery? Do you suppose...?" she yelled over the traffic. The walkers around them slowed but kept walking, seeing the two of them were only in conversation.

"Oh no. Surely not. But we were told it was someone nearby, a perfect match, they said. Do you suppose?"

Robert looked at her in disbelief.

"We're not supposed to know who the donor was. But what if it was your sister? What then?"

"Well, I would want to..." Ginny paused. "I don't know what I would want to do." She took a deep breath and slowly exhaled. "But my Mom - she would want to know. She has said many times, 'The corneas don't matter. Skin grafts don't matter. Kidneys, no matter, but Terri's heart is still alive and making life possible for someone. I would love to know that person.'"

"That's the way my Mom felt about it."

Ginny started to cry.

Robert had to lean in toward her to hear her whisper, "I'm so afraid to ask you. We gave them permission to pull the plug on Terri on December 31st."

Ginny choked, "When did you have your transplant surgery?"

Robert smiled.

CHAPTER 7

A New Face For Love

April Jones

I don't think anyone wakes up hoping to live forever. For most of us, the thought only tickles blank spaces in our subconscious. Most of us spend time dealing with the crap show life tends to be, only to spend our free time dreaming of stress-free places that don't exist.

I grew up on a healthy diet of anime and low self-esteem. It's not like I'm super shallow. I'm not. I'd settle for one of those average-looking faces. You know, the ones you pass by in the grocery store, as you peruse the cereal aisle, without a second thought. That's the kind of face I'd dream of while I slept, but when morning came, I'd wake up still looking like some monster from Power Rangers.

My teenage years quickly blended into an awkward adulthood where I toil my days locked away in a gray walled cubicle.

Mostly, my coworkers ignore me, and I find that more comfortable. I warm up my leftovers in the ancient microwave in the break room before scuttling back to the safety of my cubicle. I eat alone every day, far away from the chuckles of the community.

But humans are social creatures! That's what you're thinking, right? Sure, most of us need some kind of interpersonal relationship to keep us balanced. But if you spend your entire life being wounded by one person after another, you'll soon find having nothing to do with anyone else is better. And to be honest, how many "cool" thirty-year-olds do you know that are obsessed with anime? Right, so I'm not exactly batting away the cool kids. More like, we've reached an understanding. I stay in my corner, and they stay in theirs.

I eat my food, dump my soon-to-be Tupperware bomb back into my bag, and return to typing on some legal document no one will read anyway. I don't care. Either way, I get paid. It's not a meaningful job, but it allows me to eat takeout and renew my Crunchyroll subscription.

The phone on my desk rings, startling me from the hypnotic keyboard clicks. I reach over and wrap my hand around the thick plastic receiver.

"Lane and Lane Legal Services. How may I help you today?"

"Ari, can you come here a sec?" Mr. Flack, my boss, asks.

"Sure." I drop the receiver back onto the base and save my work before making my way through the labyrinth of cubicles to Flack's office. I knock lightly on the door and get the all-clear to enter.

"Thanks for coming, Ari. Why don't you have a seat."

I take one of the two leather chairs on the other side of his desk and try to figure out what to do with my hands. Put them in my lap? Fold my arms to hide them? It all feels awkward, so I settle with sliding them under my legs.

"There's no easy way to say this, so I'm going to get straight to the point."

I try to swallow, but the nervousness now coursing through my veins is constricting my throat, and I cough.

"The firm isn't doing as well as it was a few years ago, and we're at the point where we have to let some people go."

"You don't expect me to fire people, do you?" I blurt out, though I didn't mean to say it out loud in the first place. I don't know half of the workers here by name, even though I'm technically management. I can't imagine trying to fire someone when I don't even know their name.

"Ah... not exactly. More like, We're letting you go."

"What? Why me?" It's not like I'm Employee of the Month or anything, but I've never done anything wrong. I've never been called to this office for anything more than the typical yearly pay raise meetings. So why am I being fired? Why is my name on the chopping block?

"I'm really sorry. I know this is sudden, but we've put together a pretty sweet severance package for you."

"I've been here for ten years."

"Yeah. And it's been a great ten years. The market isn't what it used to be but, with your experience, you'll find a much better firm to work for. In the meantime, broaden your horizons a bit. Get out of town. Memphis is too hot anyway. Let your hair down. You know, Ari, all that stuff people say. Listen, I'm on your side here, but there's only so much I can do when it comes from the higher-ups. Sorry."

He promises to rave about me to any potential companies who call about me in the future, but it all sounds like bull to me. The type of empty words people say because they're afraid you'll cry in front of them because few things are more awkward than real emotions.

I nod as I stand and walk from the office, dazed. By the end of the day, my document isn't finished, and I don't care. Someone drops an empty box on my desk for me to put my things into, like I need it. A couple of Tupperware containers and a small cactus that's never bloomed; that's what the last ten years here amounts to.

I drive home. Without music. I'm too stunned to do anything more than signal when I have to. I pull into my driveway and shut off the car. I'm directionless. Lost. Where do I go from here?

Finally, I open the door and exit the car. I stop by the mailbox and half-heartedly pull the few pieces of mail out. When I get inside the house, I toss them onto the kitchen counter and sigh. I should start job hunting, but I don't have the heart to. It will be one rejection after another, like last time. My CV is good, but my face tends to turn people off pretty fast.

My phone buzzes, and I look down. My bank app says I've received money. I tap on the notification, and my mouth drops open. When Mr. Flack said it was a good severance package, he wasn't lying. I mull over his advice to get out of town for a bit.

If I was like everyone else, I would book a backpacking trip across Europe and post on social media about how life gives lemons and all that. But I'm not really the backpacking type, and I avoid social media as much as possible. There is one place I've always wanted to visit. It's a bit weird, but maybe that whole lemons thing isn't such a bad saying.

I smile as I stride to my room. I pull out a duffle and pack it with several changes of clothes. I take it to the bathroom and toss in some toiletries. I walk through the house to double-check everything is off, then I'm back in the car.

Eleven hours later, I cross the border into Michigan. I'm tired from driving all night, but I still feel jazzed. I've never done something this crazy before. Memphis has been my constant. It's my home. I grew up there, went to school there, and worked there. But something about the north has always seemed foreign to me in an interesting way. Another couple of hours, and I pull into a large parking lot. It's still early, but the sun is up, and just beyond, I can see the endless Lake Huron shimmering. I open the car door and peel myself from the seat. My body aches from sitting too long. For the first time, I ask myself why I came this far, but I don't really know why this is the place I've always dreamed of visiting. The water seems to nod at me like it knows why I'm here, and I smile.

I shut the car door and walk through a mushy field before my feet sink in the sand. I stretch my arms over my head and yawn. The coolness of the summer here shocks my body. I walk over to the water, kicking my shoes off before stepping in. The frigid water causes me to hiss, but I endure it. I pretend there's some greater metaphor about life in this experience and take off down the unpopulated beach, leaving my shoes behind.

Several minutes go by. Only the sounds of waves fill my ears. I don't feel more enlightened or anything, but I feel lighter. Flack and the law firm are some fifteen hours away, walking into the office for another day of meaningless work. Not that I'm having some kind of soul-altering experience, but at least I don't have to put up with them for another day.

I feel something wet hit my cheek and look up. The clouds have turned gray, and it begins to sprinkle. Then rain. Then pour. I look for cover but there's none.

Figures.

Even my attempt at letting go turns into a scene worthy of Hemingway. I sit down in the sand, and before I know it, tears stream down my face. The unfairness of being laid off. The uncertainty of the future. All of it wells up and comes to the surface. I ugly cry, and when I'm done, my head pounds. The rain has stopped, but I'm soaked and shivering even though the sun is back out.

I stand up and resume walking farther away from my car and problems.

Then I see it. A thing I've only ever seen in my anime shows. But instantly, I knew its name. How could I not?

Ningyo.

My mind becomes flooded with late-night Internet search results. This fish is the kind that changes fate. I have no idea why it's here of all places, but there it is. It should be somewhere in the waters off Japan, but it's somehow made its way to Michigan. To this beach.

Its golden scales shimmer in the sunlight as its gills fight to breathe on land. It isn't as big as I had expected it to be for a cursed fish. I had thought it would be at least as big as a person, but it's only a quarter of my size. Slowly, I make my way over to it. I'm worried it might disappear.

"I know those eyes," it wheezes as I come close. Its voice is neither male nor female. "I've worn them before...before I was this."

"Stuck on land?" I ask, kneeling down beside it. As if talking to a fish is normal. It's like I've suddenly become the protagonist in one of my shows, and the thought excites me.

"No." It says.

"Would you like me to put you back in there?" I gesture towards the water lapping up on the beach several feet away.

"We both know that's not how this will end. Will you at least listen to my story?"

A shiver runs through me. I don't know exactly how much this fish can see into my soul, and I'm not brave enough to ask. But I think we understand each other, so I nod.

"I once loved, but it was cursed. I was cursed. My love left me, and now I will pass that curse onto you, human."

"Why?"

"Because it is Fate's will you have found me here."

Maybe it's the sleep deprivation or the shock from being fired, but none of this registers as real to me. It feels more like I've wandered into a dream and none of the rules of real-life work here.

"Can I break this curse?"

"Perhaps. If your will is stronger than mine."

"What do you mean?"

"Can you live a life without love?"

It gasps for a moment before it stops moving at all. I know I should do something. Bury it maybe? But it did say I was cursed for finding it, and I know from anime that eating it will change my fate forever. A new life doesn't sound so bad. Can I live a life without love? Haven't I already? I grunt as I lift the fish and carry it back to my car.

I check into a hotel before carrying the fish and the supplies I bought at a local market into my room. Luckily, it's not tourist season, so there aren't many other people roaming the hallways as I make my way. I lower the fish into the bathtub and turn on the shower to rinse it off. Then I make my way into the main room to grab the newly purchased knife. When Flack told me to let my hair down, I highly doubt this is what he had in mind. The thought makes me smile.

Slowly, I saw my way through its neck. Its face looks more like a fish than old fables claim. Still, there's something human about its eyes that causes my stomach to churn. I drop its head into an open garbage sack sitting on the floor beside me. I slice along its belly and begin pulling out the guts. Something I've only ever seen on t.v. I'm not good at it. My hands slip often as I pull at the organs, and I gag.

I slice along its golden scales, pulling skin from the meat. I'm not sure how much I'm supposed to eat for the magic to take effect, so I work to get as much of the meat as I can. I pile it high on top of a paper plate sitting on my other side. When nothing remains but bones, I stand up and shake the stiffness from my legs. After I wash my hands, I take the paper plate back into the main room and sit down on the bed. I look at the heaping plate of raw fish.

According to the Internet, if I eat this, I'll become beautiful. I could also live forever. It's also possible that eating this fish could cause some kind of freak storm to rip up this coastal city in Michigan. I have no idea, but I'm willing to risk it all. Not because I want to be beautiful, and not because I want to live forever. I'm willing to eat this because I just want things to be different, even in my dreams.

I pick up a piece of fish and hold it between my index finger and thumb. I don't have much hope in this pink fish flesh doing more than giving me a bad case of food poisoning, but I also have nothing left to lose. I open my mouth and pop in the meat, and begin to chew slowly.

I'm surprised to find it doesn't taste like fish. At first, it doesn't taste like anything. But there's something about it that makes me want to eat more. I pick up another piece and eat it, and then another. Before I know it, I've eaten the entire plate full of fish, and I still want more. I make my way back into the bathroom, searching the bones for any more meat.

When I've licked the bones clean, I deposit the inedible parts into the trash bag with the head. I tie up the bag and throw it into the dumpster behind the hotel. By the time I make it back to my room, I'm exhausted. I change into pajamas and fall into bed.

I'm not sure how long I've slept when my eyes open again, but I feel nauseous. I bolt for the bathroom and drop to my knees in front of the toilet. I dry heave, but nothing comes out. As if the fish, and its curse, refuse to leave my body. My body tries its best to get the fish out, but nothing comes but spit and tears. Eventually, I curl into a ball on the cold bathroom floor and close my eyes.

When I wake up the second time, I feel new. Like I've just had the best sleep I've ever had. I feel like I could run a marathon right this second if someone asked me. I stand up and make my way to the sink. I turn it on and grab a handful of water to swish around in my mouth. I'm careful to avoid the mirror in case the fish was all a dream. I don't think I can handle knowing today will be the same as all my other days, so I chose to pretend today will be different. Then I walk into the main room and change my clothes. My phone says it's noon, which would explain my growling stomach. I grab my car keys and ask google for directions to the closest burger place.

The place is more crowded than I would have expected for a Thursday, but it looks decent enough. As I wait in line, I look over the menu and decide on a burger with jalapenos. I'm in the mood for something spicy.

"What can I get for you?" The cashier asks without even looking up from his register.

"A number eleven, please."

"One number eleven. What would you like to drink?" he asks.

"Lemonade."

He nods and reads off my total. I hand him my credit card. My stomach growls loudly.

"Must be hungry," a voice beside me says.

I turn. A man about my age stands beside me. He's tall, rugged-looking, with blue eyes. It's the first time in a long time I can remember someone talking to me first, and I'm at a loss as to what to say. So, I nod.

"Are you from around here?"

I shake my head. But more so because I can't fathom why he's still talking to me. Usually, it's me that speaks first, and I try to avoid those situations. I wonder if the fish wasn't all a dream. Maybe my fate has changed.

"Cool. Where are you from?"

"Tennessee," I say.

"Never been, but I've heard it's gorgeous down there."

"Yeah. It is." I know my response is lame, but my brain has gone blank from the shock of this conversation.

"How long you in town?"

"Not sure."

I've never been in this position before, but something about *stranger danger* haunts the back of my mind. I smile. Not because I've suddenly remembered something from grade school, but because of the utter ridiculousness of this situation. A thirty-year-old woman who's never been asked a single probing question by a man. I feel giddy. Eating that fish has changed something, and I want to find out just how far I can take this. I'm starting to feel reckless enough to ask him a question back.

"You've got a beautiful smile," he says.

I feel my smile fall as a shiver runs through me. I remember the fish's last words. "Can you live a life without love?"

Back in Memphis, I unlock the door to my house and walk inside. Finally, I feel like I can breathe again. I toss my duffle down on the floor and make my way to the couch. I spent the car ride telling myself it was all a fluke. The fish, the man at the burger place, all of it was nothing more than an anomaly. It won't happen here. In Memphis, I'm invisible.

A knock sounds at the door, and I pry myself off the couch to answer it. Through the peephole, I can see my neighbor Andrew. I undo the lock and open the door.

"Oh. Sorry. I was looking for Ari," he says.

"Andrew, it's me," I say. His eyes widen in disbelief.

"Yeah. Okay," he says awkwardly. "Uh, this came for you."

He hands me a package. I take it and nod my thanks before closing the door.

I toss the package on the counter and walk back into the living room to sit in the dark. I'm afraid of going to my room because I'll have to walk past a mirror, and I don't think I'm brave enough to see my new face again, even if it's beautiful now. I know now none of this is a dream if Andrew can't recognize me. We've lived beside one another for years.

I do this for several days. Stay in the living room, avoiding any reflective surface. But eventually, I run out of food. I shuffle sideways through my room until I reach my dresser. I pull out a clean shirt and pants. Once dressed, I shuffle back through and make my way to the car.

Inside the grocery store, I take my time wandering the aisles. I toss my favorite chips into the cart, along with some apples and spinach. Then, I make my way over to the Asian aisle to peruse the ramen. I turn the corner and run into another cart.

"Sorry," I say, but when I look up, I instantly want to cover my face and run. It's Andrew.

"No worries." He smiles. "Did you, uh, get a haircut or something? You look different."

"Something like that," I mumble.

"You look more alive," he says.

"Huh?"

"You know, before you looked sad. No offense or anything. But now, you look refreshed."

"Well, I did go on vacation," I say. *And I ate a magical fish that made me pretty.*

"Cool. Where did you go?"

Our grocery store conversation turns into coffee, and our coffee turns into dinner. Before I know it, We're dating. The warnings from the fish fade, and I enjoy all of the butterflies and stolen kisses. One night we're sitting on his couch watching some reality show, and he leans over. I turn to face him.

"It's crazy," he says.

"What is?"

"That you lived next door all those years, and we didn't get together until now."

Because I looked like a mutant dust bunny, I think. "Hmmm."

"I want to say something, but I don't know if this is the right place to say it."

"Go for it." I swallow, suddenly nervous that this dream will evaporate at any moment.

"I think I love you," he says.

I open my mouth to say something, but he leans in and kisses me instead.

Later that night, after I've made my way home, my calf starts itching. At first, I scratch at it, but the itch doesn't let up. I pull up my pant leg expecting to see a mosquito bite, but my calf has turned to golden scales. I scream and jump out of bed. I flip on every light and look at it again. But nothing changes. Where skin should be, there's a patch of shimmering scales.

I run to the bathroom and grab a set of tweezers. Once I'm in the bathtub, I sit down on the rim. I wedge the tweezers in between the overlapping scales and grab ahold of one. I yank at it, but it doesn't budge. I pull at it again, but it remains steadfastly part of my leg. The tweezers clang against the tub, and I begin to cry.

The fish's words ring in my ears again. It was right. I wasn't brave enough to give up on love, and now I'm cursed. I'm going to turn into a fish, and the only thing I can do is break it off with Andrew. But the thing is, I don't want to. I know it's stupid. I should go back to being alone all the time like I was before, but I can't. I'd rather turn into a fish than be invisible again.

I pull my pant leg back down and run for Andrew's house. I'm panting by the time I make it to his front door. I pound on it until he answers. The door opens, and he's rubbing his eyes.

"Hey," he says.

"I love you," I say.

"Oh. What time is it?" he asks.

I shrug.

"Want to come in?"

I nod and walk inside.

When I wake up in the morning, I'm in Andrew's bed. Every part of my body itches, but I don't lift the sheets to look. I know what I'll find if I do. The sun is pouring through the window, and I guess it to be mid-morning, meaning Andrew has left for work. I reach over and touch his pillow. I don't know how much time I have until there's nothing left of me, but I want to spend a few more moments buried in the sheets that smell just like him before I say goodbye.

I consider writing a goodbye note, but I don't. I don't bother to do more than grab my car keys and drive towards the river. The itching is unbearable, and it's getting harder to breathe. Finally, I see it, the mighty Mississippi River. I pull my car into a spot close to the river's edge and turn off the engine. I reach for the door. My hands are now covered in scales, my fingers more like fins. Awkwardly, I make my way to the water.

By the time I reach it, the world has grown bigger. Or maybe I've grown smaller. Or maybe I was always this. I can't remember.

The water smells, and it's too murky to see farther than a few inches in front of my face. As if by instinct, I find south and swim until I can taste salt. Slowly, mile after mile, the water turns clearer. The colors of the sea wave as I swim by. Greens, purples, pinks, and oranges. I've never seen colors this vibrant, and it would be beautiful if he was here.

The creatures of the sea don't know what to make of me either, so they avoid me. Days go by, and I lose track of how long I've been here. The quietness of the sea becomes maddening, and I start to look for a pair of eyes like mine.

CHAPTER 8

Wolf River Encounter

Susan Hopson

Standing in line at the shipping store, I shifted feet, thinking I could still beat the lunch crowd traffic, pick up my favorite carry out and make it back in time for a Zoom call. In front of me, the clerk and a young lady were talking. Focusing on their conversation, I tried not to think of the line forming at the restaurant.

"I'm sorry. What were you saying?" The young lady asked.

"Is there anything else you need?" asked the saleswoman.

"No, that'll be all for today," she said, inserting the credit card in the machine and waiting.

Suddenly, a jolt ran through my body--I tensed, and as I did, the young lady turned to look directly into my eyes, except I was wearing sunglasses. I found myself holding my breath, stunned by her light brown eyes and curvy, full lips. Just then, she looked away, putting her credit card back into a pocket of a crossbody bag. Her keys fell just as she finished putting the card away. We reached for them at the same time, our faces close.

"Hi. You dropped these?" My hand unfolded to reveal her keys.

"Yes, thank you." She said. As she took the keys from my hand, her fingers grazed my palm, causing another jolt to run through me. Our eyes met again. As she smiled, the tiniest dimple popped out to the side of her mouth. And what was that smell? Citrus, honeysuckle, and a touch of something?

Mesmerized, I shook my head. I could still smell her after she walked away. Wow. A long afternoon stretched in front of me, but climbing into my car, I wondered if I'd ever see her again. Grinning widely, I promised myself that if I did see her again, I'd be sure to ask her out! I just hoped she wasn't seeing someone or was married!

After dinner, sipping a beer outside on the deck and watching the sun falling into the arms of many tall trees, my thoughts returned to the woman at the shipping station. I wish I knew how to find her so that I could ask her out.

I wish you could too. The soft, gravelly voice filled my head.

I couldn't see him fully yet, but his shadow stood out in the woods behind the house, standing confidently, head held regally. I had grown accustomed to the appearances and the drop-in to my thoughts. No one would ever believe I had a familiar. An old word, but a very appropriate one. The wolf was both friend and protector.

"What's your interest in this?"

It's time you chose a mate.

"You didn't see her."

As a matter of fact, I did. I'm never far away. You should know that by now.

"You don't need to look over my shoulder. I'm a grown man."

True, but you have no mate.

"Maybe I don't want one. Maybe I like things the way they are."

She may be the one. I caught her scent.

"I don't need help finding a mate."

You need to find the right mate. Play is play. A mate is for life. That is if you find the right one.

"I'm not a wolf."

True. But I know you. The loneliness... I feel it too.

I sighed, finding no good answer to the wolf's last comment.

Running errands again the next day, I stole a quick look at the time. Great. I had enough time to get another ink cartridge before the client update this evening!

Hey. I found her. I picked up her scent. You're at Office Depot. She's at Home Depot. Why don't you "bump" into her?

"Don't you have other things to do?"

My family is fine. Where's yours?

"You are very annoying. I do want to see her. You're sure it's her?"

You have to ask?

"Ok, I'm headed that way. She was intriguing."

Definitely!

"Hi. Didn't we meet at FedEx?" I asked. Walking towards the young woman, I couldn't help but notice the shapely curves hugged by the red dress.

"Um...we didn't exactly meet, but I do remember you," she said. As she smiled, the tiny dimple flashed an appearance.

"I remember you, too." What to say next? Words escaped me. I looked down at the item in her hand. "What's that?" I asked.

"It's just a kit for replacing weatherproofing around the bottom of my doors. I'm not real handy, but this looks pretty straightforward."

"Ah. Good stuff. So, I'm Anthony. And you are?" I was certain I'd have no trouble remembering her name!

"I'm Taylor. Nice to meet you." She stuck out a hand quickly. Smiling, I took hold of it, savoring the sensation, noting the slimness of her hand and the long, tapered fingers.

"Since we've run into each other again, I don't suppose you have time for a quick lunch? Do you like Thai food? There's a good restaurant close by."

Hesitating, as if trying to decide if lunch was a good idea, she said, "Yes, I do like Thai food. I know the restaurant." She glanced at her watch. "I can meet you there."

"Great, see you there in ten!" He said.

I saw her enter the restaurant and glance around quickly, taking in the intimate setting. Our eyes met. Already seated, I stood and smiled. "Hello, again."

"Hello," she said and gifted me with another of her beautiful smiles. I pulled out the seat for her. Shaking my head, I tried not to notice how good she smelled! Fortunately, the waitress arrived.

"What would you like to drink?" asked the waitress.

"I'll have a sweet tea with lemon."

"I'll have the same," I said. As the waitress walked away, I asked, "What do you like to eat here? I like the spices; the flavors burst in your mouth. Not good if you don't like spicy food though."

"I like that it's not the everyday burger, and they have plenty of choices."

"Very true," I said.

After that, I noticed how easily the conversation flowed between us. After the drinks arrived, we placed our food orders.

Taylor said, "Hey, I notice you didn't buy anything at Home Depot. I hope I didn't interrupt what you were doing?"

"Not at all. I need a couple of tools, but what I need them for isn't something I have to do right away. A project. Maybe a new hobby. I'd already stopped at Office Depot for an ink cartridge. That was my main mission." I said.

"What kind of work do you do?" She asked.

As she tilted her head, curls fell around her face making me wonder how they'd feel if I reached out to touch one. Focus! "I'm a programmer. The work challenges me, and I'm always learning new things. Shrugging, I said, "I like the freedom of working from home too. I can fit in my workouts and run errands when I need to. What about you? What do you do?"

"I'm an ESL teacher."

"What's ESL?"

"English as a second language. I teach English to children online. They can be pretty entertaining at times." She looked like she was ready to laugh. The smile reached her eyes, igniting a fierce twinkle.

Wanting to hear more, I leaned forward and said, "That sounds interesting. So how old are the children you teach? And where do they live?"

"Most of them are in China. And as for their ages, usually, they're between five and twelve."

"And you like it?"

Nodding with emphasis, she said, "Yes, more than my old career as a recruiter. Recruiting was stressful. Long hours, and not a lot of happy customers. When there's an open job, you can never fill it fast enough."

Under the table, my knee made the slightest contact with her bare leg, setting off another ripple of tingling. Talk about chemistry. I wondered what a kiss would feel like. Heat pulsed through me. "So, you're not married, and you live nearby?" I said, forcing my mind to safer topics.

"You're pretty direct," she said, leaning back in the chair, smiling, and wiggling her index finger back and forth with reproach.

He caught another view of the elusive dimple. "Yes, but I'm also willing to share. I'm not married, and I live in a rental home nearby."

"I live in a condo about five minutes away, and yes, I own it. And to answer your question, I'm eight months out of a long-term relationship."

"Ahh. Lucky for me." I said. This day was getting better and better.

"Wow. Are you always this direct?"

Throwing my hands up as if to say, what do you expect? I said, "Hey, I'm a guy. I'd like to get to know you better." I smiled at her, putting my cards on the table and waiting for her response.

Humor, and something that looked like mischief, flitted across her face. Obviously, I'd caught her off guard.

She couldn't help but laugh. "Are the words 'go slow' part of your vocabulary?"

Leaning forward and nodding, I said, "I can go slow. How about we start with a walk? Do you know the entry to the trail a couple of blocks west of where we are now? We could meet there, walk, and talk? How does Saturday, ten o'clock sound?"

Studying my face, she finally said, "That sounds good. I'll bring the water!"

"Great! Here's my card. It has my work and personal number in case anything comes up."

Now that's progress!

I smiled, welcoming the contact with my friend. "You know, you're a terrible wingman, always in my ear!"

Come on, it's my job! We're kind of family, don't you think?

"Not exactly."

Ah, you break my heart.

I chuckled. "You, my friend, have strength and courage that far outweigh your size."

A torrent of memories flooded my mind, too fast to stop. The dark night I could never forget came back. Just a teen, I struggled to hold back the tears, my back pressed to the solid oak tree. My parents were gone in an instant, along with the life I'd had. My mother had been pregnant with what I'd hoped was a baby brother. A rainy night, a drunk driver, and my life was changed forever.

I hate to see you relive that night.

Rubbing the beginning of stubble on my chin, I said, "But you came that night."

I did.

Sighing, I said, "Worse night of my life, but I'm grateful to you for being there."

I couldn't leave you out there, unprotected and in pain. Losing parents, well, it's a pain I'm familiar with too.

"So, what happens after you....?" I finally asked the question. We bantered, but I dreaded the day he'd go.

Well, that depends on us. My life will end, and one of my children will stay with you."

"And will the link continue?"

Yes, it should.

Hovering over the lake was a shimmering blanket of fog. Soon, the heat would steal it away. Birds chattered, beginning their tasks of the day. The air was cool and fresh. The trees were in full bloom, the leaves providing an umbrella of shade over the trail.

"It's a great trail, don't you think?" I said.

Keeping pace with his long strides, Taylor said, "It is. I love the lake and the trees. I wonder what kinds of animals live in the woods?"

"I'm sure there are many kinds." Smothering a chuckle, I knew the wolf was monitoring our progress on the trail.

Glancing sideways at Taylor, I was impressed by her light, quick steps. It was obvious that she was in good shape. I also admired the leggings that stretched across her thighs. Was the temperature rising, or was it me?

Turning to Anthony, Taylor said, "You know, I keep thinking I see something out of the corner of my eye, but I never *see* it. It's so fast. I know it sounds crazy, but sometimes, I feel like there are eyes watching me. It's a little creepy!"

Chuckling, I said, "I understand. I've felt it too. Most wild animals are afraid of humans. They prefer not to be seen." I was sure the wolf was enjoying every moment of this conversation! "So, what do you like to do in your free time?" I asked.

"Well, I like to jog." Looking up at me, grinning sheepishly, she said, "I like trying out new recipes. But I'm not a great cook – at least not yet! What about you?"

"Let's see." Rubbing my hands together, I said, "I like sports, but I stay busy, so I don't always have time to watch them. I like to work out too. I don't cook much." Looking sideways at Taylor, I said, "You know, I might just be the perfect person to taste your new recipes! What do you think?"

"You're a gutsy one!" she said.

It's now or never. Just leap. "Speaking of food, will you go out to dinner and a movie with me?"

"Hmmm. That might be nice."

I noticed that the answer wasn't yes or no. What was she thinking?

"You know my relationship ended months ago, but what about you? Are you seeing anyone?" she asked, her eyes serious and locked on my face.

"I see you can be direct too!" I said.

Shrugging, with a mischievous smile on her face, she waited.

Maintaining the pace, while also keeping an eye on the surroundings, I said, "Let me answer your question. I was in a relationship before I moved here. It ended with the move. We weren't ready to commit to a future together. We parted on good terms. I date. But I haven't really found anyone that I could imagine a future with – until I met you." I put it out there. She knows I'm serious. And as I waited to see how she'd respond, I noticed how the curls around her face danced in the breeze, gently caressing the beautiful smoothness of her skin. Not only was she a gorgeous woman, but she was also smart, independent, and athletic. I found myself wanting to know more.

Taylor jogged forward a few steps, and turning to face me full-on, she stopped with her finger pointing at me. The expression on her face was playful. I wanted to kiss her right then.

"Hold on, Casanova! We've just met. How do you know where this is going?"

Undeterred by her feisty stop directly in front of me, I moved close to her face, my eyes dropping to her lips. "I don't know where this is going, but it feels different. And good!" Being around Taylor, my body heat automatically shot up without sending any messages to my brain!

Reading her face, I watched as Taylor's features changed from playful to serious. "I do want to see what we have in common - interests, values. I think it's important to get to know each other first; otherwise, what's the point? And no, I'm not looking for a "get busy" buddy! I'm at a point in my life where I'm looking for a real connection, someone who has goals, someone interested in growing together, dreams and all."

Still stopped in my tracks, I said, "A woman that knows what she wants! I like that! How about we each choose a date and see where this goes?"

"How would you feel about a date night cooking class?" she asked and watched as Anthony's hands flew up in front of him.

"I'll be honest. I don't know anything about cooking. If carryout didn't exist, I'd be a criminal, stealing food from all my favorite restaurants!"

"So, you really do need to join me for the date night cooking class!" She said.

I could see from her face that going to a cooking class meant something to her. And I was in this for the long term! My gaze settled once again on her lips. "If it means more time with you, and learning some cooking skills, consider me signed up! It's a date!"

A look of pure delight settled on her face. "Great. I'll text you about the class."

I like this woman. She knows what she wants. She's looking for a mate!

"I hear you. I like what I see, inside and out," I said, agreeing with the wolf's observations.

Taylor groaned, realizing the sun had dipped behind the trees. Now darkness and an eerie stillness accompanied her on the trail. The thick trees, now dressed in shadows, only served to intensify the quiet. She'd lost track of time and how far she was from the trail exit and her car. Picking up the pace, the rhythm of her feet hitting the trail was all she could hear now. She realized she hadn't seen a runner or walker in at least ten minutes. She'd been lost in thought replaying the conversation she'd had with Anthony on the trail.

Oh no. Seeing two men approach from the opposite direction, dread settled in the bottom of her stomach. As they neared, Taylor saw leering grins and eyes trained on her. Great. Reaching in her pocket, she realized she left the pepper spray at home. Placing keys between the fingers of her right hand, she knew she had to pass them. To turn and run in the opposite direction would be to show fear and to put more distance between herself and her car. Cutting a wide berth on the trail, she began to pass them.

"Hey, baby. You sure are beautiful." said one of the men.

She kept running, but now she could hear them jogging behind her.

"Wait up! We just want to talk."

Thoughts raced through her head, faster than her feet striking the trail. Taylor's eyes strained in the dimming light, seeing no other runners or walkers. Picking up speed, she realized that the wooded area coming into view was not visible to the road. Scanning for ways to escape, she hadn't noticed the men gaining on her.

One of the men grabbed her left arm. "Let go!" Yanking her arm free, she swung with the right hand, knuckles aimed upwards, and into his nose.

"You bitch," he yelled. "I'll get you for that!" Covering his nose, blood seeped through his fingers.

Positioning herself several steps back, she planned the next move. She couldn't outrun them. At least now, facing each other in a triangular position, she could see them both at the same time.

"You're a fine-looking woman. All alone too. I think we could have a little party together." said the partner of the injured man.

"I don't think so!" she snarled. While watching for their next move, Taylor continued to step backwards, trying to recall self-defense moves she learned years ago. Keys still linked through her fingers, and thinking fast, she knew that when she hit one, the other would likely grab her from behind. They approached, closer, closer. Her body tensed, preparing for the fight.

Grrrrrr. Grrrrr.

"What the hell was that?" said one of the men.

Pivoting towards the sound, the men turned their backs to her as an animal came up behind them, stepping out from the tall grass in front of the woods. Larger than a German Shepherd, dark in color with gray and black fur, the animal bared its teeth. Head and back lowered, it stood ready to attack.

Great. If two men weren't enough, now there was an animal! Taylor's eyes frantically scanned all directions, looking for ways to escape the men and the animal.

Training her eyes on all three threats, her chest rose and fell, her weight shifting from one foot to another, readying herself for the next move. A surge of energy mounted within her.

One of the men pulled out a knife. He started to wave it at the animal.

"Here, boy. I've got something for you. Want some?"

A deep guttural growl, accompanied by a menacing stare, came from the animal.

Run.

The command sounded in her head. What was that? That wasn't my voice! Propelled into action, she raced to the underpass, running as fast as she could, cutting right and straight up the exit trail.

"Come on! She's getting away." The guys ran behind her, still too close.

"Argh, Tommy! Help. He's got my leg!" One of the men yelled.

Taylor heard screaming, growling, and agonized cries. Then, nothing. She didn't look back.

Leaving the trail and entering the restaurant's parking lot, she was relieved to see cars. Falling forward from the waist, she breathed deep, ragged gasps of air. Quickly looking back over her shoulder, she checked to make sure she wasn't followed. What *was* that animal? Pulling out her cell phone, she dialed 911, hoping the police could catch the men on the trail!

I tracked your friend tonight on the trail. She ran into some trouble. I had to show myself.

"What?" Sitting straight up, my heart pounded in my chest, ready to spring into action.

She was jogging alone on the trail. A couple of guys wanted to have "a little fun" with her.

"Is she ok?" I asked, my body coiled tight, preparing for the wolf's response.

Yes, she made it to one of the exits. That lady can run! The guys weren't so lucky. But they'll live.

"What do you mean?" I asked.

I made sure they couldn't follow her.

Jumping up, "I should have been there to help her!"

You can't tell her you know about the incident.

"You think I don't know that?" I regretted the force of my words immediately, knowing my friend had only tried to help. "Thank you for being there, for watching out for her. I don't want to think about what might have happened if you hadn't been there."

I waited a while before calling Taylor, carefully choosing the words I'd say. "Taylor, hi. I thought I'd give you a call to see how the rest of your weekend has been going."

"I'm fine. But I did run into some trouble jogging on the trail this evening."

He could hear the tension in her voice. "What kind of trouble?" he asked.

"Two men tried to attack me."

"Are you ok?" Anthony's voice rose, despite already knowing Taylor hadn't been hurt.

"Yeah, I was pretty shaken up. I had to have a Jack Daniel's moment."

I remained quiet, listening to her recount the incident.

"I've never had a problem running on that trail. Usually, there are plenty of walkers and runners. Today was different. I ran too long and too late."

"Maybe we can run together sometimes, if you want to do it later in the day." I offered.

"Sure. I'm still upset by the whole incident. And the strangest thing happened. An animal that looked like a cross between a large German Shepherd and a Husky came out of the woods. I didn't like the sounds he, or it, made, or the teeth I saw! All

I could think about was how fast I needed to run! The animal provided just enough of a distraction that I was able to make it to the exit.

I smothered a laugh. "What happened then?"

"I called the police. They came, and I made a report. The policemen found the men on the trail and called an ambulance. They were alive and were carried off the trail. I hate to think what might have happened if the animal had caught me too! It was unreal. But there's something else."

"Something else? What do you mean?" I ask.

"I was facing the men after one had already grabbed me. I bust his nose with my keys. I saw the animal, and I was planning to run for it hoping they, or it, didn't catch me! And as I was thinking about what to do next, I heard a voice in my head telling me to run. But it wasn't *my* voice."

"What did it say?" I asked, stunned.

"One word: Run."

"Wow. That is strange. I'm just glad you got away."

"I know. I'm glad I made it to the exit. I've never been so happy to see cars in a lot. Anthony, I heard the guys screaming. And I could hear the animal growling and gnawing...the timing, when the animal showed up...it was so weird. I had just enough time to get away."

"I'm glad for that. I wish I'd been there for you. Do you need anything?" I asked, wishing I was there to hold her. She wouldn't need Jack Daniels.

"No, but thanks for listening."

As much as I wanted to comfort her, I didn't want to rush things. "I'm sorry about what happened. Get some rest. I'll call you tomorrow. I can't wait for our 'Date Night in Paris' class Thursday."

"I can't either. We'll see if you have *any* skills!" she laughed.

"What did you do to those men?" I asked.

I made sure they won't walk on that trail again for a looooong time. One took a bite below the belt.

Laughing to the point of choking, I remembered what Taylor said and asked, ""Did you tell her to run?"

I did.

"She heard you," I said.

She did?

"Yeah. How did that happen?"

Well, that's a new twist. I thought she'd think it was her own mind telling her to run. I've never heard of it happening outside of a link.

"Wow. She can hear you too. What are the odds? Lots of people *think* they know what their pets think. Maybe they do."

Trust me. They don't. If they did, there'd be fewer pets. People don't really want to know what "Fifi" really thinks about them! A union of the two of you would be interesting, especially given this new twist. I can communicate with her too. The possibilities! What will your children be able to do?

"Hey, let's not jump too far ahead!" I exclaimed. Images flashed in my mind. Taylor's face, close...the honeysuckle scent...cupping the back of her head, fingers lost in those curls. Moving against her soft, moist lips....

That's what I'm talking about!

"Get out of my head!"

Sorry. Your thoughts took off in the middle of our conversation! But I like where you're going!

"I admit I'm hooked. But she needs time to believe this is right too."

Oh, I think she will.

"Welcome, everyone! Tonight, we'll make a meal that's very typical for France."

As our chef for the evening spoke, I tried to focus. With Taylor standing just beside me, I imagined her body pressed to mine, cupping her face, being filled with her scent while kissing her. At his rate, I was going to need a personal fire extinguisher.

"Let me help you with your apron," I offer.

As she turned to face me, the spark in her eyes was playful. What was she thinking? I couldn't wait for the class to be over.

"Are you ready for this?" she said.

"Sure! I'm ready." Inside I was thinking, if you mean, am I ready to skip this whole lesson and make out in the car, yeah, I'm ready.

Despite feeling extremely distracted by my thoughts, conversation flowed easily between us. We competed in a friendly way, challenging each other to complete the tasks. Cooking together was really an exercise in intimacy. The closeness drove me crazy, but in a good way. I even learned a few things.

Sitting in the car in her driveway after class, I couldn't remember ever having that much fun with a woman. I wondered how she felt. "So, what did you think of the class?" I asked.

Throwing a hand up, she said, "It was a good class. I'm not sure I could make all the dishes again, but I'm going to try. How about you? What did you think?"

"If I'm being honest, I'm a grill-the-meat kind of guy. But the taste of the steak with the butter and herb sauce on top surprised me. It was better than I thought it would be." I said.

Nodding in agreement, she said, "It was good. And what did you think of the dessert?"

"I'm pretty sure I'll never make a cream puff again, but I could definitely eat one again," I said. I found myself thinking about putting some of that cream on her. Heat building within me, I moved closer. The friendly banter had dropped off, replaced by a heavy stillness.

It's getting steamy in there! Open a window. Get a room.

I ignore the wolf. Scents from her body mingled with mine, creating warm and intoxicating air in the car.

My head dipped, lightly teasing her lips with mine. Her eyes lifted to meet mine; her lips remained slightly parted.

"I liked the class, but I liked that even more," she said, slightly out of breath.

I leaned back, just far enough to look deep into her eyes. "I feel the same way."

Wrapping an arm around the back of her head, I pulled her closer, with an urgency that hadn't been present in the first kiss. She answered back, pressing closer to me, moaning as I deepened the kiss. This woman was driving me crazy.

Pulling back again, I said, "Taylor, there's something I want to talk to you about."

I could see the shift in her expression. A wariness crept across her face and seeing it caused me to hesitate before I continued.

"Remember when you told me you thought you heard the word 'run' in your head at the park?"

Tilting her head slightly, she said, "Yes, why? You don't believe me?"

"No, I do," I said quickly, not wanting her to get the wrong idea. Then, sighing deeply, I launched again, "That animal you saw, well, I've seen him too. The first time was years ago, when I learned my parents had been killed, and I hid in the woods for hours. He stayed with me. We became, well, linked. He can hear my thoughts, and I can hear his." Anthony waited as the silence stretched into the hollow spaces of the car and his heart.

She looked at Anthony, stunned. The heat they'd both felt, only minutes ago, had evaporated, replaced by a chill that filled the car. "I really didn't expect that from you." She said. "I feel like you're mocking me, Anthony. I did hear a voice out there."

"I'm not mocking you, Taylor. This is something I haven't shared with anyone. I don't want there to be secrets between us."

"I don't know what this is, Anthony, but I'm sorry. I don't do 'weird'. I think we need to end things here." she said, her hand reaching for the car door handle.

"Whoa. Taylor, I'm trying to be up front with you. I know how all this must sound to you, but I'm telling you the truth. He showed up to protect you. He's a wolf, and as unbelievable as it might sound, he's my friend."

She searched his face for a long moment, thinking perhaps this was all a bad joke.

"Thanks for everything, Anthony. You take care." Thrusting open the car door, she hurried out, not wanting him to follow her to the door. What had started as a promising evening, and relationship, was suddenly over.

Sighing, I watched her enter her house. I felt the chill and the silence seep through me. Looking one last time at the closed door, I pulled away. Taylor was special. Maybe the timing hadn't been right.

Man, I'm sorry that happened.

"So am I. Maybe I shouldn't have told her so soon!"

Give her some time. I know she's the one for you.

"It's over. It's not like I said something stupid that she can forgive! No, she thinks I'm mocking her, or worse, that I'm crazy!"

Give her time.

Normally able to fall asleep quickly, I couldn't tonight. I pushed back the covers and walked to the window, replaying the scene in the car, unable to get past the sense of loss.

The next morning, Taylor headed to the trail. Not wanting fear to keep her from her favorite running spot, she was prepared with pepper spray and keys. Spotting others on the trail, she began to relax and started her stretching routine.

Once again, she felt eyes watching her. Immediately she thought about what Anthony said, "He showed up to protect you."

Ignoring the feeling, she started to run, feeling the tension and disappointment fade away while inhaling the brisk smells of trees and damp leaves. Rounding a corner, there he, or it, was. Standing on the trail, close to the bushes, he stared directly at her.

Give him a chance.

"Are you talking to me?" she asked incredulously.

Yes. Give him a chance. He's a good man.

And with one last look at me, his mouth open in what looked like a wicked grin, he disappeared into the bushes, leaving Taylor staring with her mouth open.

Later, after a shower and taming impossible curls, Taylor flopped down on the soft leather couch and dialed Anthony's number.

"Hey, I'm sorry about the other night. I was wondering if you could come by tomorrow evening and talk about things? I'm going to make that Parisian meal, including the cream puffs!"

"OK! What should I bring?" I asked. A second chance? No way was I passing it up!

"Just yourself. 6:00. I've got everything we need." Well, not everything, she thought. "Just one problem."

"Problem?" I repeated.

"Yes, I think we might need to 'make-up' before dinner."

Images flew through my mind, including ones with cream. I realized I'd said nothing to her 'invitation.' I coughed, and clearing my throat, said, "I'll be there early."

"Hey, I brought some wine." I said, passing the bottle to her.

"Thanks, come on in. I thought we could sit outside for a few minutes while the dinner finishes cooking. Let me check on the food. There are wine glasses and a corkscrew over there on the counter.

"I like how you decorate." This woman was total class.

"Thanks, let's head out to the patio. We've got a little time before dinner."

She set her wine glass down on a side table, pulled a leg up onto the patio swing, and turned to me.

"Anthony, you have to know that what you said the other night is about the most bizarre thing I've ever heard!" She could see he was about to make a comment. Her hand raised. "Let me finish. After you left, all I could think about was how nice the evening was and how badly it ended."

"That makes two of us. I felt the same way. So, what made you change your mind?" Looking at her, I wondered what she'd say next.

"Well, I had trouble sleeping, so I went running on the trail."

"You went back to the trail?" I exclaimed, putting my glass down a little roughly, causing the wine to slosh over the sides.

Chuckling, she said, "Yes, everything was fine. I went in the morning. There were plenty of runners and walkers. And I saw your friend."

"You did?" I said, surprised, wondering why the wolf had said nothing. "What'd he say?"

"He said to give you a chance, that you're a good man."

Leaning towards me, she said, "Now, I think we left off right about here the other night." Locking her arms around my neck, she drew close. I could feel the tension begin to unwind from my body. Warmth flooded through me, and I pulled her even closer, treasuring the feel of her in my arms. Dinner no longer seemed a priority as our lips met and our bodies entwined with pleasure.

Owwwuuu.

Taylor pulled back first, hearing me chuckle, my fingers still laced in her curls.

If you have kids, name one after me.

We both laughed and picked up where we left off.

CHAPTER 9

Too Soon Forgotten

Rikki Boyce

"I wonder how often I wished upon a planet," Charlotte mused.

"Hmmm?" I nuzzled her hair, barely listening. Stretched on the hood of my daddy's Cadillac Seville, we were wrapped in each other's arms, shoulders pressed against the front windshield. Above us hung millions of stars on this moonless night. Below us, the Mississippi River whispered about its ceaseless journey to the Gulf of Mexico. Though the rhythms of the Bar-Kays still pulsed in our bloodstreams, we'd decided to leave our Senior Prom at The Peabody a touch early. Parking spots at Tom Lee Park to watch the "submarine races" would be at a premium tonight.

"You know that wishing poem 'Star light, star bright, the first star I see tonight?' When I was a kid, I bet I always wished upon a planet, thinking it was a star," she continued. "The first bright things we see in the night sky are usually planets, not stars."

"That explains why I never got my pony."

Charlotte giggled. I loved her giggle. I imagined champagne bubbles bursting into the notes of a piccolo. I kissed her midnight hair. She smelled of Herbal Essence shampoo. Not a whiff of hairspray. That's my Charlotte. "I'll never forget this night," I whispered.

"Me either."

Her white chiffon dress rustled as she snuggled closer, pressing her face against my pleated shirt. "Careful," I said. "Don't smear mascara on this rental, or I might not get my deposit back."

She play slapped me then abruptly sat bolt upright, staring hard into the river's darkness. "Tom! I saw something!"

"What?"

"I don't know what. But in the river." Her body tensed. She pointed. "There. Do you see it?"

"Probably a tree." I leaned forward, cupped my hands beside my eyes to block out the glare of streetlights behind us. Then I saw it. Dark, smooth, moving against the river's flow.

"I don't like it." Her voice had climbed an octave.

"Maybe it's an actual submarine?" I was doubtful. Watching submarine races was a euphemism for parking. Just like watching planes take off at the airport, though at least you could watch actual take-offs. If you wanted to.

Turns out we weren't the only ones actually watching the river tonight. Three other cars that had sat dark and motionless now lit up with engines growling. The sweep of their headlights as they turned to leave briefly highlighted the humped shape in the river, twice the length of my dad's Caddy. The lights and noise of the moving cars appeared to catch its attention because it turned towards the shore. And us.

Charlotte jumped off the hood, yanked the Caddy's door open, slid in, and locked it behind her. I followed her lead and gripped the ignition key but didn't turn it.

"Tom, I'm scared. We need to leave."

"Wait a minute. I want to know what this is."

"Russians," she hissed. The Cuban Missile Crisis was eight years earlier, and most people now focused on the war in Vietnam, but there was no way Vietnamese submarines would cruise up the Mississippi.

"Russians coming to Memphis?" To me, that didn't jive.

Charlotte's desperate clutch on my thigh tightened. "Please, let's go."

I started to turn the key when an extension rose from the top of the whatever-it-was. It emitted three flashes of blinding light, and the three cars that had started to leave vanished. Instantly. Without a trace.

I yanked my key away. "Maybe we shouldn't move." As one, we both slumped down on the bench seat, grateful for the Caddy's generous legroom. Charlotte slid further to crouch on the floorboards. Fear made me want to join her, but curiosity kept my eyes just above the level of the car's dash.

All the other parked cars made their moves, some keeping their headlights off in hopes of avoiding detection. It didn't help. More flashes of light and more cars disappeared. All of them. I heard Charlotte whimper and stroked her hair. "Don't worry, baby. It's going to be alright." Not that I believed a word I said.

The black hulk reached the stony bank of the park. The river was high, covering most of the reinforcing rocks, so when a faintly lit vertical slit appeared, the forms inside became visible. I squinted, trying to make out exactly what I saw.

Eerie green glows appeared in the opening, overlapped, separated, and moved slowly forward. As they came across the park—I couldn't exactly say they walked; it was more like gliding, floating—I could identify human shapes, but that was the only human thing about them.

They glowed like fireflies with a cold, green phosphorescence that obscured any details while making them seem translucent. And they were inching nearer. Too near.

Noiselessly I moved down beside Charlotte, folding my body over hers, so her white dress and my tux shirt didn't reflect any light—alien or otherwise.

Because I was positive, these were aliens. Not some Russian invasion force sporting weird new technology, not a delayed psychedelic reaction to the reefer we'd shared before prom. These were aliens. From another planet. Maybe another universe.

In Memphis. On a clear Saturday night in May, 1970. Aliens were sliding towards the city's downtown area where even now, our classmates poured out of The Peabody, heading to various after-parties or to spend a drunken night on the Sardis beach some fifty miles away. I said a quick prayer they would all reach their destinations. Safely.

The alien's green glow lit up the inside of our car as they oozed past. When it faded, I risked a look out the passenger side window. The wavering line of shiny green beings was crossing Riverside Drive, accompanied by the screech of brakes as motorists tried to avoid hitting them. One failed, knocking an alien to the asphalt. I expected to see that car obliterated, but nothing happened.

"What's going on?" A terrified Charlotte whispered from her place on the floorboards.

"The aliens are crossing Riverside. It's freaking drivers out. They're braking like mad, and one hit one of those green guys."

"What did they do?"

"Nothing. Weird. No reaction at all. Now they're headed up Union Avenue." I wondered why none of the other aliens seemed to care. And why they hadn't zapped that car like the ones earlier. Maybe no one was left on their spaceship, craft, whatever to fire the weapons? It was then I first noticed they left behind a slowly dissipating trail of iridescent green footprints on the ground. By my car, they were barely visible. On Riverside, they shone brightly.

Rising beside me, Charlotte cautiously looked around and gasped as she got her first glimpse of the retreating line of bright green forms. "What...what are they?"

"They for sure aren't Russians," I said.

"No kidding. What should we do?"

"I have no idea." I focused on the downed alien and the car that struck it. Two men got out of the car and approached the crumpled form by their front bumper. Only it wasn't an actual form anymore. It oozed over the pavement like a leaking water balloon. The guys carefully avoided touching the stuff, and after a lot of gesticulating, got back in their car and swerved around the growing pool of green.

I turned away from the scene and slid back to my side of the car to make room for Charlotte on the bench seat. I turned on the radio to see if I could find out more but got nothing but *Raindrops Keep Falling on My Head*. Twisting the dial got me Charley Pride singing *Kiss an Angel Good Morning* and Brook Benton complaining about a *Rainy Night in Georgia*. When I finally hit what I thought was news, it turned out to be some wise-ass DJ laughing about the pranks some students were playing downtown, dressing up in green, and scaring people. Disgusted, I turned it off.

"We need to get out of here," Charlotte said.

"Right." It was an automatic response but maybe getting out wasn't the thing to do. I stared at the craft floating on the Mississippi. Maybe we could accomplish more by taking over the ship and using it to destroy the aliens. Without that weapon, the aliens might be defenseless. They sure hadn't done anything when one of them got run over and destroyed. Literally, they'd done nothing. And if they were that easy to destroy individually, it might only be the spaceship we needed to worry about. And we might use it to save Memphis. And the world. Maybe.

"I think we need to get on that ship," I said.

"You're nuts."

I explained my idea to her. Charlotte stared at me, thinking, weighing options.

"You heard that, DJ. No one's taking this seriously." I looked deep into her green eyes. Charlotte was so beautiful. Beautiful as only she could be. Within seconds, I saw her eyes sparkle with determination and adventure lit up her face.

"Okay. I'm in. But I'm not going to die a virgin. Get our stuff out of the trunk."

While we'd been dating for two years, we hadn't had actual, real intercourse yet. Tonight was supposed to be the night. We'd planned to join the revelers at Sardis, have a few beers, then sneak off for a romantic first time. Just her mentioning sex was enough to get me excited.

"But not in your dad's car," she said.

That brought things down.

I went to the trunk and grabbed the beach blanket and clothes we'd brought for Sardis. Charlotte waited for me at the front of the car.

"I figure the grass will hide us a little bit if anyone's looking from the ship. Nothing will hide us from cars on the street but the Caddy."

That's my Charlotte. Always thinking. Almost always right. I spread out the blanket while she shimmied out of her prom dress and dropped down before removing her underwear. I stripped, knelt beside her, and managed to destroy one condom before finally getting a second one in place.

It was all over almost before it began. I could sense her disappointment, though she tried to hide it.

"Well, at least I won't die a virgin. I guess that's something." She reached for her clothes. "Still want to go on that suicide mission? Or join the others at Sardis and try this again?" she asked.

I looked at her then turned toward the ship where light still spilled from the opening as if inviting us in. "I think it needs to happen. We need to do something."

"Then let's get moving before I come to my senses." We scrambled into our shorts, t-shirts, and shoes and threw our formal wear on the Caddy's back seat. I locked the car's doors and pocketed the keys.

Charlotte snorted. "You really think we're coming back from that thing?"

I raised an eyebrow in mock bravado. "One must plan for every contingency."

Charlotte reached for my hand, and we slowly walked toward the river. And the ship. Its dark hulk soon filled our vision, the glow from the entrance lighting our way. As we inched closer Charlotte's grip tightened. "I'm scared," she whispered.

"Me, too."

One more step would put us in the light cast upon the park's grass. Without saying a word, we both moved to the left, so we remained in shadow while approaching the ship.

Beside the opening, I briefly placed a hand on the ship's surface. It was surprisingly cold, the extreme cold that burns to touch. I motioned for Charlotte to stay where she was while I peeked inside.

The ship's interior appeared to be a single space. And empty of aliens. I gave Charlotte a nod, and she joined me at the entrance. Together we stepped inside and tried to make sense of our surroundings.

The pale walls were curved with rib-like protrusions at regular intervals, like the inside of a cartoon whale. At the center of the ship was the device that zapped the other cars, mounted on top of a wide, dark-colored pillar riddled with holes. Cautiously we eased around the console but no alien crouched behind it posed to leap out.

We both let out a sigh of relief and moved closer to examine that central column that must be the ship's controls. It felt metallic, smooth, and cold to the touch. The holes were marked with Braille-style labels—raised bumps in different configurations. The holes were small, too small for a thumb to fit in but about right for a little finger.

Charlotte reached out and stuck her finger in a hole at random. Nothing happened. She looked at me and shrugged. I followed her lead. Again nothing happened. Stupidly bold, we continued to push our little fingers into one hole after another. The laser thing remained unmoved. The ship stayed silent and still.

We worked our way completely around the console, testing every hole we could reach with the same results.

"Well, this was a complete bust," I observed. So much for Charlotte and I saving Memphis. Much less the world.

"Maybe there's some sort of tool that fits these holes? Let's look around more."

Starting with the back wall, we each went in a different direction, carefully studying the walls, ceilings, and floor for other controls, tools, anything. We reached the front opening again. Nothing.

Except now, there was something at that opening. Phosphorescent green goo flowed across the entrance and into the chamber. We each leapt back and pressed our bodies tight against the ship's hull, taking advantage of the limited shelter the ribs offered. From our separate hiding places, we watched as the goo continued to come onto the ship, puddled just inside the entrance, then slowly transformed. However, it didn't change into a human shape like I'd seen before, but into something entirely different.

The alien that took shape looked a lot like an octopus, with six long, slender limbs topped by an oval, featureless body. Or maybe it was all a head. It still had a phosphorescent glow and translucence. As it moved toward the console, it left a trail of glowing round footprints on the floor that faded just like the ones I'd seen earlier.

Balanced on two of its limbs, it lifted the other four, with ends that transformed small enough to fit into the holes, and inserted them into different holes on the console. The ship's opening started to close. We both rushed towards it, hoping to escape, but the door was faster. We were trapped.

Clinging to each other, we faced the monster. "Keep away from us!" I yelled.

For a full minute, it stood in place, putting all six limbs on the floor.

Hoping it was as scared of us as we were of it, I pounded on the closed door and yelled again. "Let us out of here!"

Instead of using its limbs to do as I wanted and open the door, the alien walked towards us on five limbs while the sixth waved in front, like an elephant's trunk. We shrank against the door, and Charlotte whimpered as she hid her face in my chest. But the alien moved on and placed that searching limb on my forehead.

I tried to knock it away, but it stuck as if glued. The alien raised another limb, which snaked through Charlotte's hair. I could tell from her shriek that it had found her neck. The rest of the alien's body was out of my reach, so I was powerless.

For what seemed like an eternity, we all remained stationary. Then it dropped both limbs from our bodies, moved slightly away. And spoke.

"You've got a lot of dang gall coming on my ship."

It wasn't like my ears heard it. More like my brain did. And what I heard didn't sound angry. It almost sounded admiring. But what do I know about the nuances of alien speech?

Charlotte glanced toward the alien. Her expression told me she'd heard what I had. I could feel some of the tension leave her body, just like mine.

Maybe we wouldn't die. Yet.

As we watched, the alien transformed again, creating the semblance of a face—eyes, nose, mouth—in the top third of its body.

"I could change it all, but I've had a rough night and would rather not," it said.

I frowned in confusion, but then the penny dropped. "You're the one hit by that car!"

"Yes. Reassembling in an unfamiliar environment takes a lot out of a Dhahrai."

"Dha...hrai? You're a Dha...hrai?" I stammered. "Where are you from? Why are you here? What do you want?"

"I'm from here. Well, not exactly *here* here, but we've lived on your so-called earth for thousands of millennia. We've been here longer than you have."

"And stayed hidden all that time?" I scoffed.

"It's been pretty easy. You tend to ignore most of your planet. Especially the parts we prefer."

Charlotte stood straighter. "You live in the oceans, " she said.

"Yes. We arrived when your ancestors still swung in the trees. If we'd known what a mess your type would eventually make of things, you might not have had the chance to evolve into what you call Homo sapiens sapiens." It moved back towards the center console, though its face continued to "look" at us. "For a species that put the Latin word for "wise" twice in your self-designation, you're anything but."

Moving back to the console, it placed three of its appendages into select holes, and a holographic image of garbage appeared. Garbage floating on the ocean. "Look at this trash. We've been monitoring the increase—particularly in plastics—for some time. It's not too bad now, but the rate of increase has a perilous curve."

The image disappeared as he returned his appendages to the floor. "We are part of many teams sent to warn your authorities that if things don't change, we'll have to take action. We're a peaceful people but..."

"There wasn't anything particularly peaceful about vaporizing those cars with people in them!"

"Vaporized? Hardly. We transported them to that cobblestone area just up your river a bit because they were making a dreadful racket. The vehicles and the humans inside are perfectly alright, though maybe a bit shaken. But as I was saying, things must change, or there will be consequences. For you. Because this is our home, and we treasure it and will do whatever is necessary to protect it."

"Coming to Memphis late on a Saturday night doesn't seem like it would do you much good. You needed to go to the United Nations. Talk to everyone at once."

"We tried that."

Charlotte and I looked at each other in shock. "Impossible," I said. "It would have been all over the news. Aliens at the U.N.? It would be the biggest news ever."

The Dhahrai expanded to an aggressive height. "How dare you refer to Dhahrai as aliens! For countless generations, we have kept this planet safe. Since your kind lit its first fire, you have done nothing but destroy." He relaxed into his regular height. "But, yes, it should have been news. We do not know what happened, but our message did not reach the right ears then. We're hoping this rather unorthodox approach does better."

Charlotte shook her head. "I wouldn't count on it. Humans are great at ignoring things we don't want to hear, and you've got two biggies right here. First, we're not the smartest beings on the planet anymore. We're number two. Second, some buttinski creatures we've never heard of before want to tell us what to do."

"You're actually number three," the Dhahrai said. "Dolphins are number two. They bring us much news of your world. By the way, they aren't happy either."

"You speak dolphin?"

"We don't speak as such. But once we make physical contact with one creature, we can speak to them all.'

"So what was with that touching thing?"

"Being disassembled takes a lot out of a Dhahrai. I won't fully be myself until my others return and I can rejoin them. My language ability diminished to the point I had to touch you both to regain it." He stood stock-still for a moment. "I believe my others are approaching. Please step away from the door."

We did as instructed but prepared mentally for fight or flight. As soon as the door was halfway open, we started to dart through it only to face a sea of phosphorescent gel that slowly coalesced into a single entity that blocked our escape. We retreated behind the scant protection of a ship's rib and watched as this large blob of whatever oozed across the floor toward the console, where it merged with the Dhahrai standing there, though the rudimentary face remained. It then oozed around the console.

"We failed here." More appendages appeared, inserting themselves in various holes in rapid succession. "Reports from other teams show the same lack of results." The being flattened and spread to fill the entire ship, except the small area where we stood.

The single voice from earlier became a choir. "You were right in your assessment of your species. They refuse to acknowledge what their own eyes see and their own ears hear. Not only did they ignore our message, they refused to acknowledge us. Your kind dismissed us as illusions, costumes, pranks."

The entity withdrew enough to create a path between where we stood and the doorway. "Leave. But know that we will only stand so much. This planet can only stand so much. Since you won't solve the problems you created, we must find a way to eliminate the source of those problems. It would be with great sadness, but we will have to eliminate you."

I grabbed Charlotte's hand, and we ran from the ship and back to the safety of the Caddy. Once inside, we watched as the door closed, and the dark shape moved downriver until it could no longer be seen.

"That weed must have been pretty strong," I said.

"No kidding. I've never had a trip like that. Think you're sober enough to drive to Sardis?"

"Are you kidding?" I replied. "This is going to be the night. Our night. No drug-induced illusion is going to keep us from losing our virginity. And I guarantee things won't be like in that hallucination."

Charlotte nodded. "Don't worry about it. It's already forgotten."

CHAPTER 10

The Desk

Kathryn Skinner

It was a warm Sunday afternoon in late spring when her neighbors phoned and invited Susan to join them in a walking tour of homes in Central Gardens, the old part of town. Most of those houses had been built in the early 1900s. Susan knew that very well because she and her husband had owned one. She would love to go. She would enjoy revisiting her old neighborhood, and maybe she could share some of her personal history of Central Gardens.

She was enjoying doing just that, trying not to interject too much information about her old neighborhood or sound smug about her knowledge of the former owners. One of her daughters had been a babysitter for the residents of the first home they toured, she told them, and her third daughter had learned to somersault on a trampoline in the backyard of another.

The third house on their tour was a Spanish style home with a long circular driveway, a house she had always admired but had never been inside. It was owned by a well-known sculptor, a faculty member at the local College of Art. The three of them stepped into the coolness of a large foyer leading to a sunken living room on the right. That room was filled with the afternoon light from the floor-to-ceiling windows. She was thinking about how beautifully decorated it was. "But of course, it's the home of an artist" she murmured. Then she spied the table in the space between the two windows.

She started to cry but sniffed and swallowed the tears. "How odd," she whispered. "That *is* my desk." She turned to look at Glen and Rosemary, hoping they had not heard her. They were discussing the mahogany secretary on the back wall. They knew nothing of Susan's former home on Vincent Ave. They only knew her as the kind older lady in the house next door to theirs, someone to chat with when they were trimming their shrubs or planting begonias on summer afternoons. They may occasionally share a glass of wine on their patio or hers and catch up on the neighborhood gossip. They didn't notice her reaction. It was just another living room in another old house.

She pictured the desk in her downstairs hall where the back stairs led to the bedrooms above and the attic beyond. It was a simple table that straddled the return air vent for that cranky, undependable air conditioning system her husband had insisted on installing to replace the radiators and window units. *It was designed for commercial buildings,* he had said, and it would be the most efficient and economical way to heat and cool the house. It was neither efficient nor economical.

The desk was really just a simple table made of wood from an unknown species of tree. Not maple, not walnut, not oak. She had refinished it like every other table, chair, or chest she had spied in a second-hand furniture shop and brought home in her child-friendly station wagon.

Hers was a big house - four bedrooms to accommodate four children - and according to the date, scratched in the concrete supporting the furnace in the basement, built in 1907. Over the years, she had managed to fill every room and every empty corner with odd pieces from used furniture stores. Not heirlooms. Nothing fancy. Her friend, Marge, had suggested she call her home decorating style eclectic. This one was never a fine piece of furniture, but it had filled a space next to a wall of floor-to-ceiling bookshelves making a perfect spot for the family computer, the Apple II. She had to smile. "There's some history for you. I wonder what year the Apple II came out?" The desk had been at the center of the house, the heart of their home. Now it decorated someone else's living room.

She wanted to touch it. To rub her hand across the smooth surface as she had done many times during the sanding and refinishing process. She wanted to see if it still wobbled. Its legs were not designed to bear much weight. She had sometimes thought it might have been missing a lower steadying shelf or a dowel to support the tabletop, but there had been no evidence of screw holes or furniture makers' glue.

She started to step down into the sunken living room, then stopped when she realized her legs were pressing against a plastic yellow ribbon, like crime scene tape you might see on the nightly news. Of course. The guests were prohibited from walking through some parts of the houses on tour, and this one protected the owner's lovely, plush oriental rug from foot traffic.

She gritted her teeth, inhaled a long, deep breath, and thought, " I should never have sold that table. There were hundreds of things I should have never sold." She remembered the craziness of that Saturday yard sale. Her youngest daughter's boyfriend helped them to set it up. Whenever one of the family pointed to something, he would hoist it above his head and carry it down the stairs and place it for display wherever someone pointed, either in the open backyard or under the protection of the carport. A table, a chair, a print from the den wall, boxes of china, books, children's toys, clothing, a baby bed, Tammy's brass bed, even the quilt of red and blue bandanas she had made for that bed. There was the small pool table from the basement that one of the girls won in a raffle and the antique pumpkin pine washstand from the upstairs bathroom.

Her memory, like an old-fashioned slide show, rushed through projections too fast for the images to register - click, click, click - as if to hurry to the important photo at the end. She saw the precious things that had filled her home and her life for all the thirty-plus years she had raised four daughters at 1722 Vincent Ave. So many memories had to be left behind. She remembered the day her sister-in-law, Mona, brought a bottle of wine to share. It was a Reisling, Schwartze Katz. She liked it for the black cat on the label. In a reckless moment when the bottle was empty, Mona soaked the label, peeled it from the bottle, and slapped it on the wall of the small passageway from the pantry to the dining room, where it stayed, surrounded by all the labels from all the wine bottles from then on. If a label stuck to the wall, it stayed on the wall.

Now she was standing in a stranger's house, just four blocks from her former home, remembering.

Here, today, surrounded by fine antiques, was her desk. A deep blue plaid wing chair on the right and a peach corduroy loveseat on the left framed her desk. On it stood a small lamp with a beaded shade, a stack of oversized art books, and a black wrought iron sculpture. Together they made a simple still life, inviting a talented artist to admire it. It seemed perfect for its surroundings.

With Rosemary and Glen, she moved on through the other rooms - the bedrooms, a study, the kitchen, and finally the attached apartment for a mother-in-law perhaps. But she couldn't shake the shock of finding her desk in a stranger's house. As the afternoon wound down, she came to understand she should be proud that her orphaned desk had been chosen for such a prominent place in a beautiful home. She should be proud it was appreciated by someone else with eclectic taste.

CHAPTER 11

Rockin' Radish

Susan Hopson

Fingering the worn keychain in my hand, I flipped it over. Looking down, I sighed, thinking of Dad. What would he say right now? Even though he was gone, I still wanted him to be proud of me. He was always a huge supporter of my dream to open a restaurant. But it turns out that opening the restaurant wasn't the big challenge! Keeping it open is the real challenge.

I was proud to be the owner of *Rockin' Radish*, an up-and-coming, 1900-square foot restaurant off a main artery in the city. But I also didn't want my name and fame to be on the list of the 60% of restaurants that fail in the first year, or was it 80%?

Healthy, fresh, and reasonably priced options that you didn't have to prepare at home were the draw. Colorful sandwiches and wraps, trendy cool and hot drinks, and salads featuring none other than red radishes, were the main offerings. And yet, living in the south, the draw, or drawl, of southern fried anything could pull away even the healthiest eaters!

Turning the key in the lock and flipping the lights on, I set my iced coffee on the counter. Immediately the morning's scene in the coffee shop came to mind. Standing behind the two guys, I wish I hadn't heard the conversation!

"Hey, have you tried that new restaurant Rockin Radish? They've got some cool new wraps and salads. Man, the food is great."

"I don't know," his friend responded, twisting his mouth into a sour grimace. "I mean, who eats radishes these days? And when they get soggy, which they always do, they're worse than slimy mushrooms."

My eyes burned a laser-sharp hole in his back, at least in my imagination. At that exact moment, he turned, his eyes locking with mine with an intensity that froze all thoughts and actions. Eyes locked, and no words spoken, why did I have the feeling I had just lost a battle without even a chance to mount a strike back? Steel eyes one. Laser eyes zero. Not good.

What did he know anyway? You can't go into the restaurant business with thin skin. Not everyone will love your food! But radishes are so unappreciated! Rather than eating an orange and fighting all day to get orange pieces unstuck from between your teeth, you can just pop a few radishes in your mouth, and voila! You've got your vitamin C for the day and some crunch. What's not to like about that? The small superheroes even fight off free radicals in the body.

All sorts of thoughts flew through my caffeinated brain, but a quick look at my watch told me it was almost time to open.

Today's offerings were just about ready. I was humming one of my favorite songs as I flipped the light on my neon "Rockin' Radishes" sign, checked to make sure my hair was still pinned up, and unlocked the door.

Groaning inwardly, I said, "Hello, Jessica. What can I do for you?" I spoke in my most professional voice as I walked behind the counter.

With a slight smirk, Jessica said, "I'll have the Rockin' Radish Special. That is *if* you have it today. Looks like you're not ready for business. Are things so bad you can't afford help?"

Jessica worked for me until I discovered she'd stolen key recipes and opened a restaurant close by. Although more than a few months had passed since it happened, Jessica always seemed to think my restaurant was on the brink of closing. According to the restaurant app, she had her slow times too, but I didn't feel the need to visit her. Not even once. But a customer was still a customer as I grudgingly replied, "Sure, I'll have it ready in a few minutes." I rang her up and set about making the special.

"So, I heard that you were thinking about some sort of expansion?" Jessica said, eyes narrowed, looking like a cat focused on its next meal.

Shrugging, I said, "Well, you must have a friend over at the permits office. Yes, it's true. Just a small change." No way was I sharing more with her.

"What kind of a change?" Jessica boldly asked, deftly ignoring my comment about a friend in the permit's office.

The nosy cat was only missing a twitching tail. "I thought you already knew what I was about to do since you seem to have such great *intel*," I snipped.

"I have friends everywhere," she purred. "I always hear the scoop. But that's fine if you don't want to share. I know I'm just a *former* employee."

Steam built up inside me, and words spewed out before I could catch myself. "Just a former employee? Come on, Jessica. You tried to put me out of business so that you could start your own restaurant. And you stole some of my recipes."

"It was just a little healthy competition, that's all," she drawled, grinning widely, eyes crinkling with glee. She'd been hoping for a response, and she knew she'd hit a nerve.

"I'd say it was a little more than that! You called the Board of Health and recommended an inspection because you said the soup warmers weren't maintaining the 'required' temperature!" Now fuming, I couldn't stop myself. "I don't mind a little healthy competition, but that was pretty low," I spat.

Jessica, shrugging her shoulders and smiling broadly, said, "Well, I just wanted to get my business off to a decent start. Customers need options. Besides, no harm came of it. You passed the inspection." Bored with the topic, her eyes flicked around the shop, taking in everything.

"Whatever," I said and handed her the bag. Turning away, I hoped she'd take the signal that the conversation was over.

"You know, when I set my mind to win, there's very little that gets in my way." Smiling confidently, she pushed open the door, leaving me hot and cranky from the short interchange.

Jessica and I had been at odds for as long as I could remember, especially in high school. We'd both competed in track and field and for the lead role in the senior play. I was the better athlete. She was better at drama. No surprise.

Reflecting on the past several months, business had been good in the spring. Summer was great, so I'd been able to put money aside to spruce up the backroom. But I was worried about the cold months ahead. I needed a good plan to lure customers away from warm fireplaces and weekly reality tv. A new soup and sandwich combination? My head buzzed with ideas.

The backroom currently housed old equipment. Deciding to tear down the wall between the dining area and the backroom to create more eating space, or use the backroom for events, had been a tough decision, but I'd decided to go with renting the space for special events. Hoping to attract parents looking for the perfect spot for birthday parties, or even informal family gatherings, the potential was there! I just needed to get the word out and pick up a few parties or meetings. Hopefully, word of mouth would take it from there.

Already I'd come up with ideas for a few events. Arts and crafts activities would keep the kids busy. Moms could sit and take a break. Who couldn't use a glass of wine and some adult time? And if adults wanted to book the room for special events, even better.

The backroom didn't require a lot of renovation. My brother and his fire department buddies were coming tonight to move out the old equipment. After that, some minor patching of the walls, painting, and I could launch the new plan in time for the fall and winter seasons.

Hearing the bell over the door, I looked up to see my best friend, Savannah. "Hi, boss," she said. Savannah had the knack of bringing sunshine wherever she went. It was just part of her upbeat, creative personality. Nothing kept her down for long.

"What'd I miss so far?" she asked, slightly breathless as she pulled on the red and white apron with bright radishes splashing across the front.

"Jessica dropped in to get the scoop on the renovation," I said.

"Why is she always over here nosing around instead of focusing on her business? Were her claws in or out this visit?" asked Savannah.

"Mostly in. She said she'd heard that I was expanding the business. She point-blank asked what I was going to do with the restaurant. Like I'd tell her."

"Did you tell her it was none of her business?" snapped Savannah. Had she been working when Jessica came in, I'm sure Savannah would have taken Jessica on. Savannah's loyalty was to me and to the restaurant. I couldn't ask for a better friend.

Shaking my head, I said, "No, but I did tell her I was surprised she didn't already know what I was doing since she's obviously getting information from someone in the permits office."

"We need to find out who her source is," Savannah said, eyebrows drawn in a grim line.

The rest of the afternoon passed in a blur. Between customers, I jotted down more ideas about themed events and new soups. Savannah, excited about the upcoming changes, had started sketching a mural to dress up the backroom wall. Peeking over her shoulder, I could see a castle, woods, and the outline of a princess. "Is that Rapunzel?" I asked.

"Yes! What do you think?" Savannah turned to me, face beaming.

"I love it!" How did she come up with such creative ideas so fast? Savannah's mural would be a perfect backdrop for the kids' events, and we could cover it for adult events.

I didn't worry about Jessica and her mother running a restaurant in the same neighborhood. Jessica was right about one thing. Our neighborhood didn't have many restaurant options. I just needed to create a unique twist. More focus on my plan, and a speedy 'no demo' reno, could make all the difference for the upcoming months.

Looking at my watch, I realized it was almost time for my brother, Jordan, and his friends to show up. Right on time, they arrived at 7:00 pm. I unlocked the door to let them in. Savannah and I were still cleaning and prepping food for the next day.

"Red, what do you want us to do first? And what do you have to snack on?" My big brother never failed to amaze me. He was always hungry.

Laughing, I said, "You know I've got food. Is this everyone that's coming?"

Jordan smacked his friend Reed on the shoulder, causing Reed to grin and push him back. "Just these two knuckleheads. This is Adam." Jordan tossed his head in Adam's direction. "I think we can handle it. I promised them food, so I hope you've got me covered!"

"No problem! Thanks for coming. Reed, you already know Savannah. Adam, I'm Red, and this is Savannah, my best friend." Making eye contact with Adam, I tried to sound normal, even as I felt the telltale heat creep up my face. Adam's gaze locked on me, just as it had this morning, never shifting to Savannah when I mentioned her name.

The look I got from most men, the "feed me" look, was not what I was reading from Adam. A flicker of surprise, curiosity, all passed over his face as he continued to look at me intently. I had to stop myself from blurting, "Oh great. What are you doing here? And by the way, not all radishes are slimy." Suddenly self-conscious, I pushed several stray hairs behind my ear and said, "Well, there's the backroom. I've put orange tape on everything that needs to go." Hoping they'd all move to the backroom, I needed a moment to process that the man from this morning, with the gorgeous but intense eyes, and *rude* opinions, was standing right in front of me.

Surveying the backroom, with hands on his hips, Jordan said, "This shouldn't take long. I'll bring the truck around to the back. Good thing we brought the ramp."

As Jordan left, Reed and Savannah started discussing one of the new reality TV shows. Their conversation reminded me how out of touch I was with popular tv, let alone current events. I rarely had time for TV.

Adam approached quietly, opting not to take part in the conversation with Savannah and Reed. I guess working in a restaurant hadn't killed my sense of smell. Adam's fresh masculine scent tickled my nose, and I craved more of it. His eyes were brown but much lighter than mine. His hair was almost black. The shadow of a beard spread across the lower part of his face, adding texture that made me wonder how it would feel to touch it. Wow. Where did that come from? He towered over me by a good foot and several inches.

"So, Red, we meet again. Now I know why you were glaring at me this morning. Must have been my comments about radishes."

Looking around, taking it all in, he said, "You've got a really nice place here. How did you come up with the idea for a radish restaurant?" Adam asked.

I wish I'd thought to put on lip gloss and check my hair. I had ridiculously crazy hair that often seemed to have its own personality! Thick, long, and brown, today I'd braided it. Pulling it around and gently pulling on the thick braid as I thought about how to answer his question, I said, "Well, I suppose you've guessed already," as I threw my arms around to highlight the restaurant interior. "I like red. Hence, the nickname. And according to my father, my mother craved radishes when she was pregnant with me. And out I popped, totally smitten with radishes!"

He chuckled, and at that moment, I felt a spark between us. Judging by the look on his face, I think he felt it too.

"That's a cool story." Looking around, Adam continued, "I like the design of the restaurant. It's...," Adam searched for the right word, "unique. I bet you do good business."

"I'm committed to serving fresh, not slimy, food." Ah, score one. The satisfaction of seeing his face change from relaxed to a grimace told me I had hit the target. He laughed and said, "Ouch. You got me. Any chance I can get a do-over? I'm willing to approach the food with an open mind. I'm just grateful to not have to find food tonight."

Laughing, I said, "No one wants slimy anything unless it's oysters." And we both laughed.

Returning to the topic of business, I said, "I've had a few good months. I haven't been open a year yet. But research says the colder months can be slow, so I'm hoping that renting the backroom will give me a competitive edge and carry me through the slower months."

"What kind of events are you thinking about?" he asked, tilting his head.

I could tell he was genuinely interested. "Kids birthday parties, maybe a few themed events, crafts for the kids, wine and hor d'oeuvres for adults. I'm open to the idea of adult events too." Other than Savannah, not even Jordan knew what I'd been thinking. I was still working it through in my head. It was easy talking to Adam.

"If I can ever help in any way, let me know." Adam offered. "I'll work for food. I'm not big on cooking."

As he said that, a smile appeared, taking away all the seriousness on his face. I suddenly realized I'd been staring at his lips, unusually pink for a man! Embarrassed, I looked away and pulled on my braid, even as I felt the heat creep up my neck.

"Next up on the list of tasks is patching and painting. Savannah can't paint the mural on the wall until that's done. I don't suppose?" I looked at him with the question floating in the air between us.

"Yeah, sure, I can patch and paint. I could come a couple of days after work next week. Monday sound good, about 7:30? That would give you some time to close up the shop, and we could work for a couple of hours."

"I'm not going to pass up that deal. We can eat a quick meal, then start working."

Neither of us knew what to say next. Fortunately, Jordan broke the silence. "Hey, people, let's do this!" And with that, the backroom began to swirl with movement. I couldn't believe how big the room was once the equipment was removed. I might have to buy a table or two more than what I'd planned.

The next day, Savannah couldn't wait to ask me about Adam. She'd noticed us talking and how no matter where I was, his eyes kept track of me. "So, what's the deal with you and Adam?" she said.

"Nothing. He asked about the renovation and offered to help any way he could," I said, not meeting her eyes, pulling out dishes to prepare a salad.

Spinning around from cleaning the counter and smiling mischievously, she said, "He is hot! Are you going to take him up on his offer?"

Still avoiding eye contact, cheeks flushed, I said, "Well, he did offer to come by Monday evening to patch the walls and paint. I told him I'd feed him as payment for his help."

Hands firmly planted on her hips, Savannah said, "Red, you do realize he's interested, right?"

The simple question brought on a wave of thoughts like, 'When *had* I last shaved? "Yeah, ok. Whatever," I said, wanting desperately to change the subject! "And what's going on between you and Reed?"

Laughing, Savannah said, "Reed's a sweetie. We're just like brother and sister. He's easy to talk to, no more than that!" said Savannah.

"Right," I mumbled, "Heard that before."

The rest of the weekend flew by. I'd gotten a manicure and pedicure just to relax. At least that's what I told myself. And I bought paint. As Monday afternoon pressed on, I was quiet, nervous about being alone with Adam.

Savannah, one to notice subtle changes, asked, "Why so quiet?"

"I'm just a little nervous about tonight," I admitted.

Savannah had the gift of feeling at ease in most situations. "Look, just turn on some music. Then if there's a gap in the conversation, you go with the music or toss some paint on him. Have fun. It's not a date. Ask him some questions about himself. And don't forget to text me later to let me know how the evening went. Hey, switching topics, do you mind if I leave a few minutes early today? I need to study tonight. Big exam tomorrow."

Looking around the restaurant, only a few tables were occupied. "It's already slowing down. Why don't you go? I can handle it here."

"You sure? Thanks, that'd be great. Don't forget to text me later!" she said.

Waving my hand, I said, "Go on, I've got this."

Savannah pulled off her apron and ran her hands through her hair as she freed it from the hair net. "And Red?"

"Yeah?" I paused, having no idea what she was about to say next.

"Before Adam gets here, do something with your hair, and change your top, ok? A little makeup wouldn't hurt!" With that, she sailed out the door with a cheerful grin.

Sighing, I continued to work. Soon enough, it was time to lock up. I'd already put the keys into the lock, not expecting more customers. Hearing the bell over the door, I looked up. I'd already packed away most of the food, minus what Adam and I would have for supper tonight.

"Jessica, what a surprise." Looking at my watch, I said, "What brings you in so late?"

Her eyes flicked from side to side. Her shoes clicked in rhythm as she approached the counter. It was easy to imagine what Jessica would look like with a real set of whiskers. Her lips twitched frequently, invisible whiskers responding to her thoughts.

"I'll have a wrap and a radish side salad – to go. I can see business is slow again. We still have customers coming in. Do you really think your restaurant will last another year? And where's Savannah?"

Throwing her meal together as quickly as I could, I looked straight into the pale green eyes. "I think we'll be just fine. How about you?" Despite the force of response, I was more than a little worried. Moving from behind the counter, I opened the door and gestured for her to exit.

Jessica snatched the bag and, with a parting glance, said, "We'll see about that."

I wondered what she meant as I locked the door, flung the keys on the counter, and hoisted my purse up beside them. Time to finish up. I started with the tables. Checking things off as I cleaned, my mind ran free, picturing Adam, wondering what we might have in common. Did he like sports or movies?

Changing quickly, I pulled on a clean, bright pink T-shirt and jeans. Pulling my hair out of the hair net, I shook it loose. Even hair needed to be set free at times. I was fortunate to have a good crop of hair, which stretched to my lower back. Friends complained about thin hair. Not me. I brushed it firmly, braided it into a ponytail, and freed some tendrils to frame my face. Adding just a light amount of makeup and gloss, I surveyed the results, turning my head side to side. I mean, we were painting, right, not going on a date! What was the big deal?

Looking at the clock over the counter, I realized that Adam would be here in less than an hour. I headed to the freezer room, just off to the side of the counter in a recessed alcove. It was a small room, enough to house two large trays, where we stacked salads and wraps. Surveying the room, I was satisfied that we had enough food prepared to start the day tomorrow. But sometimes customers surprised you. Maybe I'd prepare one more .... I heard the door click and close behind me. I swung around.

Panic seized me. "Hey! Who's there? Unlock the door. Can you hear me?" Wow. Robbers. I guess yelling to them for help wasn't a great idea! My purse and phone were on the counter outside. Great. I'd never thought about something like this happening. Running in and out was one thing, but to sit in the freezer room for hours was another thing altogether! I realized Adam wouldn't be able to get in. He'd knock on the door and maybe text, but he'd probably think I'd forgotten and gone home. And Savannah wouldn't expect a text from me for hours. Shivering, I dreaded the cold night ahead in the freezer.

I could only remember a little about hypothermia. I was shivering; I knew that was a good sign. Trying to keep my mind off the situation I was in, I paced until I grew tired. Anything to stave off the cold. Starting to feel a little groggy, I sang my favorite song. And then another. How long had I been inside? Looking at my watch, a half-hour, maybe an hour. I loosened the braid, the fanned hair adding a little warmth to my shoulders and the back of my neck. But sleep, cool and comforting, crept to my side and overtook me.

Jolted awake by what I thought was a strange sound, I stood and walked to the back of the room. I yelled for help, desperate to get out. Was someone there?

Suddenly, a voice! "Red, is that you? It's Adam."

"Yes, it's me! Can you get me out? It's freezing in here!"

"Hang on! I'm calling for help."

"Ok..." Too tired to walk, I sat cross-legged on the bottom of one of the trays, imagining a big toasty fire in a fireplace.

Time trickled by. The door snapped open, and Adam ran in and rushed over to me. Pulling me to my feet, he took me into his arms, holding me for several seconds. Then, he walked me into the main area of the restaurant. I could see at least two fire-fighters. Folding a blanket around me, Adam pressed me into a chair and ran to the hot water dispenser. He filled a mug and rushed back to me. Pulling me up, he held me to his warm chest and folded the blanket around the two of us.

He smelled so....so...why wouldn't my brain work? I wanted to hold on to him and go back to sleep. Beginning to shiver violently, I heard one of the firefighters say, "Adam, let her sit. We need to check her vitals."

Adam stepped away, and one of the two firefighters came forward. After assuring themselves that I was ok, Adam put the hot water to my lips. He folded the blanket around us again, thoughtfully leaving enough space this time for me to hold the mug and to sip.

Not taking his eyes off me for one second, Adam said, "I've called your brother. And he's called Savannah. They're on the way. Red, do you have any idea who might have done this? The police will be here any minute.

I wasn't fully alert. Icy tendrils still gripped my brain. "What do you mean? It wasn't robbers?"

Adam looked at me oddly. "Red, the money is still in the cash drawer. Your wallet and purse are here. That's how I knew you were inside. I saw your purse and keys through the door. I don't think this was a robbery.

"You mean someone *wanted* to hurt me? But why?"

Adam grabbed the mug as I stumbled. His other arm circled my waist quickly, holding me up. "Yes, it looks that way. The police will want to know more, like if you've had a disgruntled customer or a threat of any kind."

Jessica's face floated before me, along with her comment about winning. Surely, she wouldn't stoop to something like this. Maybe I was wrong.

The police came, followed closely by Jordan and Savannah. I told them what I knew, which wasn't much. I mentioned the visits from Jessica. I shared with the police that I didn't believe that she'd do something like this. We'd competed for years, but this would be taking things to a whole new level. The police did consider her a suspect and planned to meet with her immediately. They dusted for prints on the freezer, but given that it was a restaurant, prints were everywhere. Jordan talked to the police as well and cased the restaurant, searching for clues in every corner.

Adam and I rescheduled for Wednesday night, giving me a chance to rest and recover. Savannah was beside herself with worry. I assured her that I'd install a new lock, enabling us to get out of the freezer room from inside. Hopefully, we wouldn't need it, and nothing like this wouldn't happen again.

Wednesday night came, and after discussing the incident, Adam and I set about patching the walls. We worked well together. Like a good tennis match, our conversation bounced back and forth across various topics. As we worked, we discovered that we both liked basketball games and the Fast and Furious movie series. As Adam stretched to reach a corner with the paintbrush, a section of his bare back came into view. A fit back. I covered a smile with my paintbrush. But my eyes took in the view with appreciation. The memory of being in his arms after the freezer incident still made me warm. With those memories, I might make it through the winter with no coat!

A few days after Adam and I patched and painted the walls, Savannah started on the backroom mural. I'd already worked out the details of at least six themed events. We would have a night reveal, inviting our customers to come in, tour the backroom, and learn about upcoming events. I was busy planning the menu of bite size-snacks, wine, and beverages. The days were flying by with preparations. The freezer incident was never far from my mind, and a part of me wondered if the person was out there, lurking, waiting to strike again. But with the reveal coming, I didn't have time to dwell on it.

Savannah, ever the friend, was like a dog with a bone. She kept muttering, "I know it was Jessica. She reminds me of that crazy cat from the Alice in Wonderland movies, always popping up and causing trouble." But I still had trouble believing it was Jessica. Call it a gut thing, but something didn't feel right. Oddly, the message from last week's fortune cookie came to mind. It said, "Sometimes distrust is the best defense against betrayal." Ok, I'm not Confucius. What the heck did it mean? Shaking it off, I continued to prepare for tomorrow's special.

Dating Adam was on my mind. A lot. With our busy schedules, I was satisfied with him dropping by in the evenings when he could, offering a helping hand, and keeping me company. In return, I fed him. A great arrangement. I hadn't seen Jessica. With the police having questioned her, she kept her distance.

Reveal night came. Savannah, Jordan, and Adam arrived early to help. The mural would be unveiled as part of the ceremony. Savannah and I made extra hors d'oeuvres, unsure how many guests would come. We dressed in our new T-shirts for the event. We had appetizers with radish garnishes, radish dip, wraps with radishes – and new soups. Combined with an assortment of drinks and wine, we were ready.

The door swung open at seven, and the first guests appeared. After that, it was a blur of activity. Jordan left early for his shift at work. Stationed at the door, Savannah greeted everyone and handed out the Rockin' Radish events flyer. Everyone was eating and chatting happily. I saw cameras flashing. I could only hope for positive feedback on social media.

"What are you doing here?" hissed Savannah, causing my head to spin towards the front door.

Jessica, smiling widely, stepped lightly through the door as she said, "I wouldn't have missed this for the world."

Moving quickly, I planted myself directly in front of Jessica. "Look, this is a special night for me. If you're here to cause trouble, just go."

Pausing for a few seconds, lips twitching and considering her words, she said, "Red, how could you ever think I'd do something to hurt you? We may not be friends, but what's a world without a little friendly competition?" And with that, she sidled away, heading straight for the wrap tray.

Savannah was beside herself. "I'm not letting her out of my sight. She's nothing but trouble. I don't trust her."

A short while later, Savannah and I posed for a photo. So far, everything was perfect. We had great traffic, lots of customers, and the food was delicious. It wasn't exactly my fifteen minutes of fame, but positive publicity was exactly what the restaurant needed!

Until I heard the scream.

Customers rushed out the door, not waiting to find out what was happening. Adam was clutching his face. Savannah was yelling, and Reed was trying to calm her down. I couldn't figure out what was going on!

Jessica, appearing out of nowhere, said, "Red, I've called 911. Apparently, Adam and Savannah had an argument."

"What? That can't be!" The night was quickly turning into a disaster. All the guests had flooded out the doors; the fire department had arrived, and many of the customers were being treated for pepper spray exposure.

Rushing over to Savannah and Reed, I looked from one to the other, "What happened?"

Savannah hesitated, looking at Reed. Reed spoke up. "Adam accused Savannah of sabotaging the restaurant. She felt threatened when he got in her face. I pushed him back. She wanted to stop a fight between he and I, so she sprayed Adam. You know the rest."

"Savannah, why did he accuse you?" Looking around the lot outside, I could see Adam sitting on the end of a fire truck, talking to one of the guys treating him. I planned to talk to him next.

"Red, don't believe anything Adam says. He's lying. I would never do anything to hurt you or the restaurant!"

"What are you talking about?" I asked, trying to piece together what had happened. Savannah was babbling, and after listening a few minutes more, I went in search of Adam.

Approaching Adam, I wasn't sure where to start. "Adam, how are you? Are you okay?"

"I think I've got new respect for pepper spray. My eyes don't feel great, but I'll survive. One of the guys is giving me a ride home. I'm so sorry about ruining your night. But Red, we need to talk about what I heard. Can I call you tomorrow?"

"Sure. I don't think I'll be sleeping much tonight." And I meant that. Something just wasn't right.

I had plenty of time to think, cleaning up after what had started out as a promising night. Surprisingly, Jessica offered to stay and help. I was really beginning to wonder who I could trust. Remembering the mysterious fortune cookie message, I declined the offer.

While cleaning, Adam's words came back to me. He'd overheard something. That *something* had caused the fight between him and Savannah.

Suddenly I knew what I had to do. After being locked in the freezer, the police captain had recommended I install hidden security cameras – and tell no one. He assured me that I needed to consider the possibility that the person who'd locked me in the freezer was someone I knew. I was glad I'd followed his advice.

Dropping everything, I flipped on my tablet and began to playback the evening. I had the ability to zoom in on different areas. I quickly found Adam. Despite the evening's disastrous end, my mouth curled into a smile, following Adam through the camera's eyes.

"There!" I exclaimed out loud. I could see Adam standing near Savannah and Reed, who were talking in low tones. Adam was surveying the room, but I could tell when he began to listen to what they were saying. And suddenly, Adam burst into their conversation and confronted Savannah. I couldn't believe what I heard next.

"How could you lock your best friend in that freezer? Are you crazy? She could have died!"

Everything from that point played out quickly. Reed and Savannah tried denying what Adam had heard. Reed pushed Adam in the chest. Adam advanced on Reed, and Savannah pulled out the spray and let Adam have it.

I felt sick. Why did Savannah do it? I dialed the police station. It was late, but I was promised a return call from the captain. I couldn't have been more relieved that the next day was Sunday. I needed to recover from the night's events.

I texted Jordan to meet me at my apartment. Once there, I played it all back for him as well.

Savannah was arrested on Sunday. Reed was arrested as well. Jordan and I were still reeling from the events. Adam called, and I shared the updates. We arranged to meet Monday evening at a restaurant. The least I could do was to thank him personally and feed him.

As I entered the restaurant, Adam stood up and hugged me. "At least we know now who locked you in the freezer. But I'm sorry you lost a friend."

As we both pulled back, I looked into his eyes, soft with concern. My eyes teared up as I said, "She wasn't a friend. I just thought she was. I'm still upset. I asked the police why she did it. They said she was jealous and felt I should have made her my business partner. I never knew she had those feelings. And Reed was one of Jordan's closest friends."

"I guess you never know. I wasn't sure you'd believe me when I called. You haven't known me very long. I'm glad you had those cameras installed!" Adam said.

"Nothing like a confession caught on tape. I'm lucky you were there. And you know, you don't look so bad in red!" I grinned at him wickedly.

"Seriously, I will be so glad when these burns are gone!" Adam said.

Leaning into Adam, I kissed his eyes. "Does that help?" I asked, in a low voice thick with promise.

As he leaned closer, his lips claimed mine. "It's a start. Now how about our date?" he said.

CHAPTER 12

Window Pain

Daniel Reece

The Munfords were arguing again. They prefer to argue in their bedroom. From there, I can't hear them yelling, and their blinds are typically drawn, so you might not think they were arguing. But I can see Cheryl pacing back and forth in front of the shades with the bedside lamp behind her, casting a perfect and upset silhouette on the window. Every few moments, she'll gesticulate suddenly with her hands. She likes to talk with her hands; mostly she just yells with them. I think it's nice that the Munfords usually wait to argue until after the kids go to bed.

It's the weekend, and Sammy, Grace, and Penny are inside the house watching television in the living room. So the Munfords go to the backyard to do their arguing. Cheryl paces back and forth in front of the infrequently used trampoline. Raymond sits on the back steps taking the pointed admonitions quietly. They aren't yelling-arguing. They are arguing in civilized tones. There is lots to argue about from their points of view. From my point of view next door, they only argue about one thing. She thinks he drinks too much, and he thinks she thinks about his drinking too much. They're both right, and they're both wrong. They are the kind of couple who won't divorce until Penny turns eighteen, but that's a long twelve years to go.

I step away from the window and return to my study. I set the binoculars down next to my computer as I take a seat at my desk. My philosophy teacher mother loved to hurl pearls of wisdom at me every chance she could. When I'd complain about going to the store, she'd say, "*Esse est percipi*." Then she'd wait patiently until I replied, "To be is to be perceived. George Berkley." Mom would clap a strange sort of golf clap before making me get in the car. When I told her I didn't want to go to the movies with her, she'd bring out the big guns. "*Stone walls do not a prison make/Nor iron bars a cage*." Then she'd wait patiently while I begrudgingly gritted through my teeth and say, "To Althea, From Prison. Lovelace." She'd smile her professor smile, and I'd make my way to the high mileage Chevy Cavalier so we could go watch some artsy, French with subtitled monstrosity.

The last thing my mother ever said to me was her own pearl of wisdom. "Don't let this prison become your tomb." Then her heart that had always been breaking, broke one last time and she was gone. Mom was worried that I'd succumb to my agoraphobia and never leave the house. I put on a brave face and a week later went to her funeral at Memorial Park.

That was five years ago, and I haven't stepped foot out of my house since.

The modern world is built for prisons, especially the ones we make for ourselves. Those are inescapable. I didn't drop out of college. I was able to avoid people by taking all my courses online and graduated in two years. I got a job writing software which fulfilled my only two requirements for employment: 1) work from home 2) do not interact with humans. Amazon delivers my goods, Kroger delivers my groceries, and Netflix delivers my entertainment. I live in a contained universe, a self-maintained aquarium.

I finish my work for the day and walk to the east side of my house. I look through the blinds into Leonard's house. Leonard is in his mid-60s and lives alone. He reminds me a bit of Louis Gossett Jr. with his bald head and greying beard. Leonard is a relic of this block, having lived here even longer than mom and myself. I think Leonard was a bit sweet on my mom though, to my knowledge, they never did anything more intimate than sit on his porch. That's intimate enough, I think. He frequently invited her over for sweet tea and sugar cookies. Leonard loved to bake, especially any variety of pie with the season's flavor. Peach cobbler in the summer, pear streusel in the winter. He would bring his confections over about once a week. After Mom passed, he would leave a tin of cookies on my doorstep every week. That dwindled down to once a month. These days he delivers them just every now and then. Strangely, and admittedly, rudely on my part, but I've never actually met Leonard face to face. I have sampled hundreds of his creations, and we've lived next door to each other for every one of my twenty-four Memphis years.

I watch Leonard every day, just as I watch the rest of my neighbors every day. He is my rock, an ever dutiful creature of habit. Gets up at six and reads the paper on the porch. Goes for a walk, and then he eats lunch in the kitchen. After lunch, he takes an afternoon nap. I watch him sleep in his La-Z-Boy recliner, his chest rising and falling with each breath. After dinner, he falls asleep in front of the blue electric glow of his television.

Behind my house is a rental property. The families never stay for more than a year, sometimes for only a few months. In the summertime, the line of willow oaks block my view, and my backdoor neighbors might as well be in Barcelona. In the summer, my outside world closes in, and the bubble of observation is limited. In the fall, I can invite myself to peek into the backyard to watch young kids throwing footballs around, teenagers sneak outside to take timid puffs off cheap cigarettes or watch barbeques abound with burnt hamburgers and red Solo cups brimming with lukewarm beer. In the winter, I gaze through windows and backdoors to see multi-colored tree lights twinkling and chimneys pumping out streams of smoke. I wonder about the warmth around the fireplaces within. Leonard and the Munfords are my family. The backyard people are my distant relatives who only visit around the holidays.

The windows in my study look out across Vinton Avenue to the black hole of my universe. It used to be old Lady Weissenger's place. She was a miserable woman who hated the outside world as much as me. Her shades were always drawn, and the curtains were so thick I couldn't tell if the lights were on or off. She posted a big sign next to her door proclaiming "No Solicitors," then let her yard grow over into such a dilapidated state which made everyone in the neighborhood rejoice that they didn't have the *worst* yard on the block. It's no wonder her body wasn't discovered for nearly five days after she passed.

The mailman noticed she hadn't picked up her post in a week and called the fire department to check on her well-being. Two burly firemen broke down her door, and later two less burly technicians wheeled her out on a gurney zipped inside a white bag. My mail is delivered with a somewhat contemptuous push by the mailman through the slot in my heavy oak front door. If I should suffer an aneurysm and fall unconscious to the floor, it will be several months before I am discovered. If possible, I shall attempt to die on the first floor to make it more convenient for the body collectors.

The Weissenger house sat empty for almost two years. A *For Sale* sign appeared in the front yard six months ago and beaconed buyers, but alas, there have been no takers. I wouldn't put it past the old lady to rattle chains in the basement whenever any prospective buyer should come around.

One day, the *For Sale* sign just disappeared. I was a bit disappointed that I didn't get to see a realtor proudly place a bold *SOLD* sign atop the *For Sale*. Still, it's a wonder I even noticed the missing sign at all. These days it's become too much of a chore to look outside. A week after the sign's departure, the sound of a truck backing up brought me to my closed blinds to spy upon my new neighbor for the first time.

It was steadily raining the day she moved into the old Weissenger house. She ought to have waited for a sunnier day. The large moving van backed into the driveway, barely missing the mailbox but squarely running through a flower bed. My eye caught her standing on the sidewalk in the rain as she supervised the three movers unloading the truck. She wore a yellow raincoat, with red galoshes while a clear umbrella rested on her shoulder as she surveyed their folly.

I spied on her from my office on the second story. I hadn't been spending as much time watching Leonard or the Munfords the past few weeks. Every time I looked out the window, I felt like a penny being dropped into a well with a hollow echo on the inside. I lost interest in the world beyond these walls. You could say I am captive to my own indifference or a hostage being held by himself.

The last human to come to my house was the guy who delivers my groceries, a wonderful young man named Chip. I tip Chip five bucks. I think he likes me because of my generous nature. I have never met Chip. I leave his tip wedged into the backdoor. He leaves my groceries just on the inside of the en-closed back porch. We have a good thing going, Chip and I. We are not unlike sharks and pilot fish.

Before the lady of the yellow raincoat and red galoshes entered my life, I hadn't turned on the television in four months. I keep paying for Netflix because the shows were my last meaningful connection to the outside. I felt tethered to all those people who liked watching Sherlock endlessly. But I cut that tether quickly, and all other ties I severed slowly. I have no friends or family. My employers only acknowledge my existence by electronically de-positing money into my account every other week. I'm not sure what I expected to accomplish with my self-imposed solitude. I've not dedicated myself to learning the arts nor to a meditative search for inner peace. I am not writing a novel. I am not search-ing for anything.

If my mother was right and to be is to be perceived, then is invisibility annihilation? I've often wondered if the rose that blooms under the bush is still beautiful. Or is existence merely a matter of perception? I'm out of sight of the world. I wonder if I stay hidden long enough, might I cease to be? Every day I feel a little less there. I feel that I have faded a little more. With any luck, someday I may fade completely until even I have forgotten about my being. Suicide by evaporation.

At least, that was how things were going. I was on the verge of being able to wink myself entirely out of existence. Then she entered my life with the incessant beeping of a haphazardly backing up moving van. The steady thrum caught my attention on the rainy day and snapped me back to reality. My curiosity drew me in further.

I was lying on my bed staring at the ceiling and working myself into a deep trance when the unremitting beeps needled me like water torture. I sat up with a dazed look like a science fiction astronaut awaking from prolonged stasis. I stumbled to my office, which was totally dark, and pulled up my blinds a bit. I was assaulted by gray light. Even though the light wasn't particularly bright, it stung my atrophic eyes.

The first thing I saw was the van backing over the azaleas. I shook my head and grinned. Then I saw her on the sidewalk. One hand on her hip, she turned and smiled and threw her head back with a monstrous laugh as the rain drizzled over her face like chocolate syrup over a white sheet cake.

We were probably the same age, even though I looked ten years older than I should. She was cute. Or maybe she was beautiful. She probably was beautiful, but with my poor sense of the aesthetic, I'd never know it. She had pale skin and her long red hair tied into a messy ponytail. Her wet red hair flung about as she tossed her head back and let the rain fall into her open mouth as she watched the movers.

I liked her. It wasn't her hair, her smile, or even the slowly revealing fullness beyond her white shirt in the rain. I think it was the galoshes. I couldn't recall if I'd ever seen an adult wearing galoshes. She seemed playful. I watched as the mover opened up the moving van, which was packed full. The movers began unloading a collection of boxes marked with the rooms they were destined for in black marker. I was impressed by their ability to move everything in such a quick and efficient manner. My yellow-coated neighbor grabbed a box labeled *Fragile* and carried it into the house. She seemed so unlike a thing to be encased in bubble wrap or sheets of old newspaper. She was the opposite of porcelain.

I sat at the window, unable to tear myself away. This was a movie of my very own, which caught my attention for the entire day and well into the evening. The moving van had long since gone, and she was alone in the old lady's house, which I should come to think of as the new lady's house. I couldn't take my eyes off of her every movement. Under her raincoat, she was wearing a pair of blue denim overalls. She turned on every light in the house and worked methodically, going from room to room unpacking her boxes. It was past midnight when she finally got to her bedroom. I was beginning to nod off myself. Her bedroom was on the second story directly across from my room. It had two large windows. If our houses had eyes, they would have been looking longingly into one another's soul. She had yet to unpack the blinds or curtains, so I could see clearly into her well-lit room.

She put her bed together and dropped the box springs and mattress onto the rails. She brought over a box marked "Bedroom" and unpacked her bedspread and sheets. They were sky blue. I watched her make her bed up. She had unbuckled her overalls, letting them fall to the floor, and just as quickly took off her shirt. My eyes widened, and my heartbeat quickened. She stood there in her white cotton bra and pink panties. I looked away for a moment, blushing with embarrassment. I put my hands over my face and smiled. I looked back and peeked through my fingers. She turned her back to me and took off her bra, then slipped a green silk nightgown over her head. It tumbled softly over her body like water cascading down a mountainside. She crawled into her bed and turned out the light. My mouth turned slyly for a minute, then I dragged myself to bed.

That was how it started. I was on the brink of vanishing, and the stranger across the street resuscitated me into existence. She became my only connection to the outside world. Actually, she was my outside world. I've always thought that my voyeurism was a sort of perversion. Now I'm sure that it is. I have learned that it's not entirely sexual, though. Unlike Leonard and the Munfords, my new neighbor seemed to treat her private and mundane moments with equal reverence with respect to her blinds and curtains. She never closed them.

I found that I enjoy watching her wash the dishes as much as I enjoy watching her shower or dress in the morning. It was probably the guilty pleasure I got from invading her privacy. I say guilty, but it's hard to feel guilty about watching a beautiful woman with a tendency to keep the drapes open, more like human nature. Well, human *man* nature at any rate.

We fell into a routine. Each day, I sit at my office desk casting furtive glances across the way. When she's not home, I work, and when she is there, I watch. My binoculars sit shamefully on the edge of my desk and taunt me. Old Lady Weissenger never opened her blinds or drew back her curtains. I learned every room of her house that I could see through her windows. I could see her kitchen, living room, bathroom, bedroom, and a corner room upstairs that I think she used as a studio. I first thought that perhaps she was some sort of exhibitionist. But, after watching her for a few weeks, I discarded that idea. I think she was just the opposite of me in that she soaked up the outside world that I chose to filter. I was the shoal keeping back the ocean, and she was the tide thrashing against me. I think she loved the light I cowered from.

I began to fill in the missing gaps of her personality with her habits. She rarely watched TV and liked to read. She must be artistic because she played her music too loud and liked to sing along with the lyrics. She liked her coffee with sugar, so she must be excitable. She was forgetful. She had to keep a spare key in the planter next to the side door. She locked herself out of her house at least twice in the month that we'd become acquainted.

She couldn't cook anything more complex than Ramen Noodles and had food delivered four to five times a week. She really liked Chinese food. I suppose she had a generous nature like me since the delivery boys always left smiling. Then again, maybe it wasn't her tips more so than her smile. She smiled all the time. Maybe her smile was infectious because I often found myself grinning for no reason while I was watching her. Through my invader lenses, I learned every curve of her smile.

I didn't know her name. I could have done an online record search and probably learned it, but my obsession was creepy enough already. Besides, my construct of her was surely better than the reality. Of all the quirks she had, there was one which I liked above all others. She had a least one Monet print in every room of her house. She had a particular affinity for water lilies. I am more of a Van Gogh myself. There was a guy who understood the value of oblivion. At any rate, I began calling her Claudia, which seemed as good a name as any.

The other eccentricity Claudia had, other than her paintings and open windows, was her affection for the company of men. About two weeks after she moved in, they would begin dropping by like suitors to Penelope's side. With no Odysseus in sight, they had the run of the house. Every couple of days, it was a different man and never seemed to be the same man twice. As a distant admirer, I would be quite the hypocrite to judge Claudia based upon the frequency of her love interests. Sometimes they would visit for a few days, sometimes just a few hours. Every so often, they would spend the night then be sent scurrying away in the morning.

I was not privy to these intermediate interludes. The light in her bedroom would go out, and the room would go dark. Watching the darkness, I would wonder what it would be like to be with her. Would she be playful or forceful? Would she be docile or seductive? None of my business, I know. In the morning, I would see her standing on her porch in her blue bathrobe waving goodbye to the current Mr. Moment.

I think Claudia was searching for something. The perfect man, perhaps? She might as well be searching for a yeti or a phoenix. By having so many boyfriends and sending them away to wherever it is used men go when they are tossed aside, perhaps she was hoping to find true love. What a foolish endeavor. For what it's worth, I was rooting for you, Claudia. Even though I can't decide what elusive quality she was on a quest to find. I knew it must have been something like honesty or integrity. It was probably something moral which would, of course, immediately disqualify me from vying for her affections. She could never see me. *What is essential is invisible to the eye*, said the Fox to the Little Prince.

We continued in this manner for several months. Me the Watcher and her my tether to reality. Then one day a tall man driving a red sports car came to her house. Claudia left with him in his car. I supposed he took her on a date. They returned around ten that evening. They retired to her bedroom around eleven. He went to the window and closed the blinds; a moment later, the light went out. I felt a twitch of jealousy and reluctantly went to bed. The next morning, I got up expecting to see his car pulling from the driveway and Claudia adorned in the Farewell Bathrobe bidding him adieu. Instead, his car was parked in the driveway and stayed there all weekend. Since then, I have seen Claudia less and less. Her new beau has come into her life and taken her out of mine. My tether was being severed.

I became a war correspondent to a private battle going on between Claudia and her new man. She keeps opening her blinds, and he keeps closing them. Sometimes I can see into her world, and other times I'm kept out. He stays at her place most nights. I find myself dreading to open my blinds and look out my window lest I find his red car parked in front of her house. It sits there like a crossroad demon taunting me with a slithery grin. My heart can't take much more of this. Again I am becoming cut off from the world though not by choice this time. It is so much worse to fade away against one's will. My tether is now my noose.

Claudia doesn't seem the same either. She seems to smile less often. At first, I thought I was just seeing what I wanted to. She was smiling as much as she was before the new guy entered our life. But I had seen her smile more than anyone else. The corners of her lips were sagging a little. Her sparkling eyes were a little less sparkly. I couldn't nail it down in concrete terms. Her smile was powered by her warmth, and now there was a coolness behind her mask. Part of me wanted to yell and scream my undying devotion to her. The rest of me advised me to sit down and shut up. I sat down. I shut up. I shut down.

One day I looked up from my work and saw Claudia standing in front of her bathroom mirror in her bathrobe. I tried to look away and focus on my work, but it was pointless. She was staring motionless into the mirror. I picked up the binoculars. It's probably none of my business, I told myself. I set the binoculars back down. I sighed, cursed my indecisiveness, and snatched the binoculars again. Something told me that I had to look. I brought the lenses to my eye and looked in on her. I sighed a heavy breath. She had a black eye and was crying softly as she applied heavy foundation to her face. I shook my head, set down the binoculars, and drew my black curtains closed.

A few days passed before I could bring myself to look out my window again. I wasn't quite sure how I should feel. Should

I pity her? Should I say something to her? Why would she keep him around? Obviously, I couldn't tell her that I had been spying on her since she moved in. I'm certain the local constabulary wouldn't look too kindly on my watchful gaze. Perhaps it would be better if she did call the police. She could have me and her boyfriend arrested for indecency. But our crimes were not equal. I might be an aberration, but at least I have the courtesy to be ashamed of it.

I didn't know what to do, so I did the one thing that was obviously wrong. I watched and did nothing. This went on for the next two months. I was certain it would go on for years. I knew how it would be. Things would be fine, then they would be bad, then there would be an apology and an empty promise, then things would be fine again. I had known men and women like the two of them. My grandparents immediately came to mind. They were married almost forty years. The day my grandfather croaked would have been the happiest day of my grandmother's life if she hadn't already died three years before him. I saw a lot of my grandfather in Red Sports Car. I knew they could carry on this relationship like lover gladiators until the inevitable end. *Morituri te salutant.* Those who are about to die salute you. Does that make me Caesar?

It was late at night when I woke up. I yawned and furrowed my brow in confusion. There was a red light flashing softly on my bedroom walls. I sat up in bed and shook my head. I thought perhaps that I was still asleep. I walked in a daze to my office and raised the blinds. There was an ambulance in front of Claudia's house. Sports Car was talking to a paramedic as Claudia was wheeled out on a stretcher. She was wearing a neck brace, and her arm was immobilized in a soft splint. The EMTs loaded her into the ambulance. I placed my forehead against the cold window. My breath began fogging the glass. The ambulance left, and he went back inside the house. I lowered the blinds.

I called the hospital in the morning and told the nurse that I was a concerned neighbor. I know honesty isn't my strongest suit, but I couldn't think of a passable lie. After some small talk, I got the nurse to look up Claudia by her address (her name is Julie, but I'll continue with Claudia all the same). The nurse told me that she had been admitted for a broken arm and a moderate concussion. She had apparently had a bad fall in her house said the nurse, but we both tacitly agreed that there was a more likely scenario evidenced by the older bruises painted all over her body. She would be in the hospital for a few more days. I thanked the nurse and hung up.

I raised my blinds and saw the red sports car. It was mid-afternoon. Around two, a blue car pulled into Claudia's drive-way. A long-haired blonde in a short skirt got out and met Sports Car at the front door. They kissed and went back into the house. All the blinds and drapes were down. She emerged later that evening, got into her car, and drove away. I stared at the closed blinds until midnight.

I stood up and walked downstairs. I went into the kitchen and took a pair of white plastic gloves from beneath the sink. The gloves fit on my hands snugly. I looked through my kitchen junk drawer and grabbed a small flashlight. I put on my jacket and slipped the flashlight into my pocket.

I stopped at my front door. I couldn't remember the last time I had used this door. I clenched my left hand in a fist to quell my beating heart. I placed my hand on the knob and opened my door, which had been closed for so long. The door stuck a bit, and I had to muscle it open. I stepped outside and took a deep breath feeling the chilly night as the crisp air burned good in my lungs. The outside atmosphere was filled with sweet particles, unlike the filtered air of my sanctum prison. Munford's house was quiet as they were all tucked in and sleeping at this witching hour. Leonard's television light slowly flickered as he slumbered in his recliner. I moved briskly across the street to the side of Claudia's house and took the key from the flower pot outside her side door. I snuck around to the side of the house, unlocked the kitchen door, and slipped inside.

I should have felt odd to be in this house. Instead, I felt completely at home. I knew every inch of her kitchen. I knew the sugar container was in a green canister next to the flour, and the never-used good plates were over the sink. From her pantry, I took out a large plastic freezer bag.

I crept to her refrigerator and opened the freezer. Methodically and quietly, I placed several ice cubes into the plastic bag, then closed the fridge door, moved to the living room, and over to the stairs. The stairs were uncarpeted and polished wood. I wasn't sure if they would creak as I crept up them, but they were as silent as mouse slippers. My heart thumped as a marching band clanged inside my chest with each step I took. Each breath I drew in was a betrayal which to my ears sounded like cold wind rushing through a cave. My head was light, and I could almost hear the blood pumping through my head. I breathed deliberately and tried to calm the brass section of my innards as I made my way to the top of the stairs.

I reached the top and stood still, hearing nothing at first. Then I detected the subtle sounds of snoring emanating from Claudia's bedroom. I wondered what my mom would say to me at this moment. I think she'd say, '*I have spread my dreams under your feet,*' then patiently wait for me to say Yeats.

I opened the bag and closed my latex fingers around the cubes, then strategically set the ice cubes on the second and third steps from the top of the stairs. After I was satisfied, I crept back down the steps with a slightly heightened sense of urgency.

I returned to the kitchen and pushed the now-empty plastic bag into my jacket pocket. I opened the side door and walked outside, pulling the door in but not closing it completely shut.

The night street was still, quiet, and empty. I waited for a beat then rang the doorbell next to the side door. I listened closely but did not hear anything. I rang the doorbell again. Would nothing wake this Cyclops? I was about to ring the doorbell a third time when I saw a bit of luminance spill into the living room from upstairs.

I could see the bottom of the stairs through the kitchen. Then I heard a grumbling sound followed by bated silence. I put my ear to the door jam and listened. A moment later, there was a loud yell and crash. The living room was shrouded in the darkness, but I could make out the form of the crumpled body at the foot of the stairs. He was wearing Claudia's Farwell bathrobe, and he wasn't moving. I waited for a minute. I waited for another minute.

I opened the door and moved through the kitchen, making no effort at stealth this time. I entered the living room and saw Red Sports Car was motionless. He was misshapen and lying in a tangled mass which reminded me of *Woman Descending a Staircase*. His right leg was twisted into an impossible angle at the knee. His right arm had a protrusion of bone poking through it and was bleeding slightly. Unfortunately, he was still breathing. I shone the flashlight on the mangled monster. He couldn't see my face with the light in his, not that he would recognize me. His eyes were wide open, and blood was trickling from his mouth. His broken neck was purple, and he was choking. Sports Car looked at me with tear-filled eyes and croaked, "Help...me." I looked at him with neither impish smile nor damning scowl and said, "*Sic semper tyrannis.*" I switched off the flashlight, turned, and left. I locked the backdoor and replaced the key in the planter.

I was looking out my window two days later when Claudia came home. I didn't want to watch, but it was my burden to see the end of our passionless play. The ambulance came, then the police, then the coroner, and finally a tow truck arrived, and the last remnant of Mr. Sports Car was hauled away. I didn't feel vindicated or that I had performed some great deed. Later that day, Claudia went through her house and opened up all of her blinds. I felt gleeful at first, then guilty, and then just a general feeling of comfort. I turned away from the window.

My victory was short-lived. Claudia apparently couldn't get the ghost out of her house. Two weeks after the *accident*, the "For Sale" sign went back up in her yard. She wasn't there when the moving van arrived. I never saw her again.

I never got around to oblivion. I started doing my own grocery shopping and going out to the movies from time to time. I started a garden in my backyard. I was working outside when

Cheryl Munford saw me working and asked me if I had just moved in. Later she invited me over for a barbeque. I brought potato salad which the kids really seemed to enjoy. I even baked a cake for Leonard. We sat on his porch and sipped lemonade while we watched the street quietly and talked a bit about mom. I swept the dust from my life and began to see my existence in tones less sepia.

One sunny day while I was working at my desk, I heard a beeping sound and looked out of my window through raised blinds. There was a moving van outside running over the mailbox in front of my neighbor's house. A brunette wearing yoga pants jumped out of the van and sighed at her handiwork.

I immediately went downstairs and out my door. I strolled across the street up to her without hesitation.

"Could you use a hand?" I asked.

She smiled warmly and said, "That would be nice, but you don't have to."

"It would be my privilege," I said as she opened the back of her van. Inside I saw a large telescope and asked, "Amateur astronomer?"

She blushed a bit and said, "From time to time."

Without thinking, I said, "*Ad astra per aspera.*"

She smiled and replied, "To the stars through hardship."

I picked up a box and carried followed her inside. Later on that evening, I helped her hang her bedroom drapes. A while later, I watched her draw them shut from the inside before she turned out the light.

CHAPTER 13

The First Day of Practice

Justin Siebert

The parking lot of the Glenview Community Center in Orange Mound is lined with campaign signs as my mom rolls my wheelchair to the passenger door of our battered Toyota Avalon.

"This all sounds stupid," I say, grabbing my legs and swinging them outside the car door.

"Don't call things *stupid*. Besides, Trey, you love basketball," Mom says.

"I used to. When I could still play."

My mom purses her lips and raises an eyebrow. I'm busy pulling myself into the chair, so I don't see her do those things, but I know the disapproving face she's making.

"Trey, you're only as disabled as you let yourself be," she says for the millionth time since I got shot back in June. Like, what's that even mean? She's got these catchphrases for everything. It's her way of avoiding the truth that I can't do anything I used to.

This isn't the first time she's tried getting me back on the court. At rehab last month, she told the physical therapist I used to play ball and insisted I would again. So they made me try shooting baskets at the hospital's gym. The previous year, I had the sickest crossover on the JV team. Now, sitting down, I could barely get the ball up to the net. When they started lowering the basket for me, I couldn't take it. I just left.

The therapist followed us out to the car to tell us about the Memphis Rollin' Grizzlies, this whole team of guys who play basketball in wheelchairs. She gave us the coach's number. When we got home, Mom dialed the number and shoved the phone into my hands because I sure as hell wasn't going to choose to make the call myself. Seeing a group of grown men in wheelchairs pretend to play basketball like I'd just done sounded depressing.

But here we are.

I hear basketballs dribbling to my left as we enter the community center. Through double doors, guys in chairs streak past faster than I expected. We sit in the doorway and watch them shoot free throws for a bit. Empty wheelchairs similar to mine line the far wall. The chairs they're playing in look way different, with slanted wheels and this bar that extends around the front of their feet. Practice started thirty minutes ago, but on the phone Al, the coach, said to get here whenever. He'd kept saying I just needed to get in to see a practice.

"Alright, fellas, back on the line!" Across the gym, a small white man in a wheelchair calls out instructions, blows a whistle. The ten players push hard down the length of the court. At the end, they turn faster than I've ever been able to in my chair. One dude even goes up on one wheel around the turn. The coach waves us over.

Coach Al asks about my injury, and I let my mom answer all his questions while I watch the guys pushing down-and-backs up and down the court. I'm staring at the hoop when I hear Al explain that most of the rules are the same as "able-bodied" basketball, which is what they call regular basketball.

"How high is the basket?"

"Ten feet. Everything about the court is the same."

"You have to dribble?"

"Yep. You can't do more than two pushes without dribbling."

I nod, wondering how they're supposed to push and dribble at the same time, let alone things like crossovers or three-pointers. I think back to our final post-season game last year. That three-pointer I barely missed against Melrose would have put us within one basket with under a minute left. Half of us were in tears after losing that game, and I vowed I wouldn't miss the shot next time.

"I guess y'all don't really do three-pointers in wheelchair basketball," I say, realizing I'll never get that second chance.

Coach raises an eyebrow, then calls out to one of the guys. "Hey, O! Shoot a three." Al tosses a ball to this tall dude with no legs. He's wearing a durag and a glove on one hand. He pulls up and drains a shot from a few feet *behind* the three-point line. Someone tosses the ball back to him, and he does it again.

I close my mouth, which was just hanging open. I try to picture myself making a shot like that, but I can't shake the image of me struggling to get the ball up to the basket in that hospital.

Coach checks his watch, then blows his whistle. "Alright, gentlemen, get some water!"

Everyone's breathing heavily as they get water and start shooting around. A couple guys come over and introduce themselves: a redhead man in his thirties who towers over us. A lanky light-skinned black guy with muscled arms who looks like he could play for the able-bodied Grizzlies team if not for his skinny legs.

They ask me questions, and I tell them about my gunshot injury, how I was in the wrong spot at the wrong time, running with some guys I shouldn't have been running with. I leave out the depression that came after I woke up and realized I wasn't dead but that my life was over. I don't mention all the tears I cried about things I'd never do. Play basketball. Drive a car. Have a girlfriend, maybe a family someday. Talking to them is different, though. Their faces say they feel sad for me, but not sorry for me like everyone else has up to this point.

This isn't what I thought it was, and I finally admit to myself how much I want to be a part of it. But my mind flashes back to rehab...

"You alright, Trey?" Mom asks.

I nod slowly and mumble, "I don't know if I can do all this."

Al puts a hand on my shoulder and his voice changes to that of a father giving advice. "Don't cut yourself short. These guys were all in your same position at one point."

"This takes time, you feel me?" says Archie, the lanky, light-skinned guy. "We gonna get you out here hoopin' though."

Al calls out to the guy who was draining threes. "Big O! Come here for a minute."

"What's up, fam?" O says, shaking my hand.

Al points to me and tells Big O how long I've been in a chair.

"Man, you're real fresh," O says. "This junt don't get easy, but it gets easier, you feel me?"

I nod and listen to Big O tell about his accident, how he coped with everything and still is coping, how he was intimidated to get out on the court at first, too. I watch him go back out on the court and post someone up on the block, and I wonder how he was ever scared.

"What do you think? You gonna come back Wednesday?" Al asks as the players scrimmage. "We'll get you in a ball chair; see how that feels."

I look to my mom, who I can tell is holding back an *I told you so* smirk. "Maybe. I'll think about it," I say. I'm sure Mom is rolling her eyes because she can tell how much I want to be part of this.

Once practice is over, everyone convenes out in the parking lot. While most of the players debate about what defensive set they should run against some of the teams they'll face in an upcoming tournament in Alabama, the guy who was hitting reverse layups before comes over to me.

"It was Trey, right?" he asks.

"Yeah. And your name was…"

"Justin," he says, giving me a fist bump. "Four months ago, huh? That's tough. You're still relearning how to live life. I bet you have a lot of questions."

I shrug.

Another guy leans over to us. "He's wondering the same thing we all wondered after we got injured, and the answer is yes, you can still have sex."

"Manners, A.G.!" Justin says, nodding toward my mom.

I'm avoiding eye contact with her and dying of embarrassment inside, so I change the subject.

"Well, like, how do you drive a car?" I ask.

Justin takes me and Mom over to his car, and he shows me how the hand controls work, how he gets his chair inside. He shows me a picture of his wife and his two-year-old daughter sitting in his lap. He tells me about playing basketball in college, becoming a science teacher, about how disability is never an excuse for not doing something in life.

Then he says something that makes me cringe.

"You know, I've seen a lot of disabled people never try things because they're afraid of failure. Don't make yourself more disabled than you actually are."

My mom is beaming. "Now that's some great advice! Sounds like something I'd say."

I glare at her, then roll my eyes. "Mom's got a new catchphrase now. I'm going to be hearing that twice a day."

Justin laughs. "Well, I think there's a lot of truth to it. Anyway, I need to go. We going to see you Wednesday?"

I look to my Mom, who indicates it's my decision, then back to Justin.

"Yeah. Yeah, I'll be here."

CHAPTER 14

Cast Aside

Rikki Boyce

Already battered by another frustrating day at the office, Janet sagged on her crutches when she saw the handwritten "Out of Order" sign taped to the elevator. Her office at Maxwell and Associates Advertising was on the second floor but going down even one flight of stairs in her current broken-bone state presented her with a major obstacle. In the vain hope a coworker played yet another prank, she pressed the call button anyway and thrilled to hear the ancient elevator creak to life.

"Not funny, Bobby," she hissed as she reached to tear the sign off the door as it opened. Arm outstretched, she froze. A man lay crumpled on the floor inside, face ashen, a pool of blood congealed beneath him, the handle of a knife protruded from his chest, the iron stench of blood drifted out. She stared in horror as she realized it was her boss. "Dan! Mr. Maxwell!" she screamed.

In a panic, she fished her phone out of her carry-all. Struggling to control it, the crutches, and her bag at the same time, she fumbled and watched in shock as her phone slipped away and clattered down the adjacent stairs.

As the last to leave the office, she'd set the office door to automatically lock behind her. As she didn't keep an office key, her only options to get help were the stairs or the single elevator.

Not the elevator, she shuddered and moved towards the stairs. Lowering her crutches to the first step, she swung her leg with its heavy cast forward and almost toppled headfirst down the flight.

Heart pounding at her near miss, she decided bumping down on her rear might be safer, though far less dignified. She lowered her rump and thump-thump-thumped her way down the worn wooden steps until she was low enough that her crutches would help leverage her upright. She shuffled to the street door, pushed it open with her shoulder, and screamed into the dark street, "Help! Murder! Police! 911! Help!"

Her panicked call sounded ridiculous to her own ears. *But it's the frigging truth*, she thought as she scanned the crowds for someone helpful.

Historic Beale Street, home of the blues, thronged with after-work revelers even on this frosty winter evening. Lined with old buildings and popular bars, the pedestrian-only street was busy with many people, and lots of them pulled out their phones. A few even placed emergency calls before documenting the scene with videos and pictures. Janet sagged against the doorframe and waited for help to arrive.

Hours later flashing police lights illuminated the glass-fronted ground floor entrance area where she sat, offering rubberneckers a good view of one bedraggled redhead in a short winter coat, with a snazzy lace-up boot on one leg and a white cast encasing the other. It had taken an hour before someone bothered to bring her a chair from the bar next door. All that time, uniformed police and the homicide team swarmed up and down the stairs, securing the scene and occasionally stopping to pepper her with questions.

Slumped on the rickety chair, she glared at the crowd. *Probably think I'm the murderer. Or at least a suspect.*

Her eyes widened as she realized she might *be* a suspect.

As if on cue, a police officer approached. "We need you to come to headquarters to take your statement."

She indicated her cast. "I can't drive."

He nodded. "We'll give you a lift."

The police drove her to the station, but after hours of intense questioning where she told her story innumerable times, she opted for a Lyft driver to take her home. *No need to excite the neighbors with a police escort,* she thought.

She struggled out of the back seat of the sedan and stumbled through her apartment door, emotionally and physically drained. But when she crawled into bed, sleep refused to come. Her mind buzzed. *Dan Maxwell was dead. Murdered. Stabbed to death. Who could possibly want to kill him?* But as she considered it, it occurred to her that more than one person might have a motive.

When Janet finally summoned the energy to return to the office the next afternoon, crime scene tape still marked the elevator, so she reversed her rear end thump-thump-thump up the stairs. When she reached the top, she couldn't manage to stand up, so she crawled to the office door, dragging her crutches along. Once there, she used the door handle to help pull herself upright before entering.

The office coffee station buzzed with the hushed gossip of her coworkers. She hadn't expected to see them. After all, their boss had died. His employees had neither devotion to him nor to hard work, so why show up? Instead, they stood clumped together in their Memphis-cool office: part of a repurposed cotton warehouse with scarred wood floors and original brick walls festooned with assorted neon signs. Practically every ad agency in downtown Memphis had the same vintage, faux-hip look. Just like every ad agency in town had the same mix of tattooed, pierced, and artfully dressed would-be hipsters.

"Hey, Gimp, why'd you do the boss in?" Bobby heehawed at his own joke, inciting embarrassed titters from the others. Janet sensed their underlying shame at laughing with Dan's body barely cooled.

She didn't have the stamina to put up with Bobby's lack of sensitivity and course humor. "There's nothing the least bit funny about this, Bobby. Dan was murdered. Murdered!"

Undeterred, he continued, "Yeah. I guess we're all out of jobs? That's not good. But I wasn't kidding about you. I heard that huge fight you two had yesterday afternoon."

She startled. "A fight about a client rejecting one of my radio scripts? Hardly a killing matter."

"Well, I told the cops about it when they interviewed everyone here this morning. It was a command performance for all of us. That's why everyone's here. So where were you?"

"I was at the station getting questioned until 1 a.m. this morning."

Bobby whistled. "That's not good."

"Remember, I found the body." Tears glazed Janet's eyes as she limped towards her cubicle. Waking her computer, her rewrite of the rejected script filled the screen. She'd accused Dan of not making any real effort to sell it. Heatedly and loudly. It was ridiculous, but the timing could be enough to make her a suspect.

She idly scratched under her cast with a pencil while opening a new document. She stared for a moment at the blinking cursor, then typed "Potential Murderers" and started a list:

Emily Maxwell. Dan's long-suffering wife might have had it with his constant philandering and shady business deals. Janet wouldn't blame her. Dignified, smart, and with an enviable figure, she deserved better. Far better.

Eric Stilwell. Dan's now-former partner had wanted to cash in his ownership shares and retire. But Dan's cooked books made it look like the agency's debts outweighed its resources, making Eric's shares worthless. Instead, Eric had to take a job at a rival agency and promptly started poaching Maxwell and Associates' most profitable clients. Janet shook her head. He'd already gotten his well-deserved revenge. But could he want more? Janet's trusted confident for years, she couldn't picture him as a killer.

Cindi Boliver. This raven-haired beauty was the latest of Dan's mistresses and a sales representative for a newspaper conglomerate. Dan's women were always advertising or media reps of some kind. This made it easier to claim he was conducting legitimate business when spotted with a beautiful, vivacious young woman and reduce rumors of extramarital activities. Some.

Bobby Christophe? His contempt of Dan was obvious and mutual. She didn't understand why he still worked for him. Laziness. Which meant he was probably also too lazy to murder anyone. But she couldn't stand him, so his name remained.

She stared at Cindi's name, remembering a rather drunken night at Silky O'Sullivan's bar a week or so earlier when that tramp slid onto a barstool next to her. Cindi cooed on about what a great boss Janet had in Dan. When she could stand no more, Janet turned on her with full venom. "You're just the latest of his floozies, you know. I bet he told you he was leaving his wife. He tells that to all his girls. He told me that. He won't leave. He never will."

Cindi had narrowed her eyes. "Jealous bitch," she'd spat and flounced away.

Was Cindi capable of murder? She was certainly a cut-throat sales rep, tough as nails making deals and readily slicing and dicing her competitors. But slicing and dicing Dan? Janet couldn't be sure.

Why did I tell her about Dan and me? Their short affair happened over a decade ago. They'd moved on enough that she felt comfortable coming back to work for him recently. Still, it was a slip she shouldn't have made. But recent events made it appear her revelations about Dan's many mistresses and lies actually helped Cindi see the light.

Yesterday during lunch, Janet spotted Cindi among the crowds of tourists on Beale and quickly averted her eyes. To her surprise, the rep ran up and grabbed her in a bear hug, whispering, "Thank you for saving me." Then she raced off before Janet could respond. Flabbergasted, she'd watched Cindi's retreat, a wry smile on her lips. It was a completely unexpected reaction, but she felt good about it.

"Janet!"

Jarred from her thoughts upon hearing her name, she deleted the document.

"Yeah?"

"Someone's here to see you."

"I'll be right there." She grabbed her crutches and worked her way to the reception area, where two police officers waited.

"Yes?"

The taller one spoke. "We need the coat you were wearing yesterday."

"Sure. It's in my cubby." She indicated her crutches. "Would you mind getting it for me? It's black. In the second cubicle on the left."

The officer nodded and left, returning in less than a minute with her coat in an evidence bag.

"What's this about?" she asked.

"We got an anonymous tip."

"About?"

"We need to check it out. Then we'll see."

Only then did his partner speak. "Meantime, don't leave town. Don't even think about it."

They really say that? She wondered. Numbed, Janet watched their retreat. She *was* a suspect. She was still standing there when Emily Maxwell came in. For a brand new widow, she didn't seem too devastated. Her blonde hair was perfectly coifed, her eyes showed not a touch of red. She flashed Janet a quick wan smile before bellowing, "All right, everyone! Come to the front desk right now."

The few employees in their cubicles piled out, all offering vague messages of condolence when they saw Emily. She responded with appropriate thanks and waited until everyone assembled before stating her piece. "I know we're all shocked and saddened by my husband's untimely death…"

Janet was impressed by how steady and strong Emily's voice sounded. The woman showed control and confidence. Almost as if she'd known.

"…and there's a lot to process. But I want you to know one thing: Maxwell and Associates will live on. I'll take over for Dan. That means, at least for the foreseeable future, your jobs are secure. So take care of our clients. Do good work. Fill in your timesheets. I'll see you soon. And often." After a nod and sad smile, she made a sharp turn and left—back straight, head high.

Bobby was the first to react, "Well, that's good news. I'll quit updating my resume." The others had similar responses but didn't seem anxious to return to work. Janet, however, hobbled her way after Emily as fast as possible. She called out to stop her from going down the stairs.

"Emily! Do you have a minute?" She swung closer and continued, "Do you know anything about the investigation?"

Emily looked vexed by the question, "Is that something to ask a grieving widow? Jeez, Janet. But the answer to your impertinent question is 'no,' though they spent long enough questioning me last night."

"Me, too."

"*Cherche les femme*, I guess. And in this case, there are plenty of *femmes* to *cherche*." Seeing Janet's startled look, Emily half laughed. "Don't think I'm so blind I didn't know about Dan's affairs. I even knew about you. Now, so do the police. About all of them. But I don't think you need to worry. You never had an ounce of killer instinct. Too much the doormat."

Janet frowned at the description but said, "I'm not sure the police agree with that. They took my coat. The one I had on when I found Dan. Said they had an anonymous tip."

"That's strange." Emily frowned. "The tip wasn't me. I don't hold grudges. Plus, there's been plenty more women since you. Worse ones. Like this last one." She grimaced and headed down the stairs. At the bottom, she paused to look up at Janet. "I don't have an alibi for last night. You're not the only one on the suspect list."

Janet watched her leave, momentarily lost in thought, then returned to the office. In her absence, Bobby had broken out a bottle of scotch, and the atmosphere felt more festive than sorrowful. He thrust the bottle towards her and whooped, "We get to keep our jobs!"

She took one look at the happy group, swung her crutches around to leave the office, and mentally prepared herself for another bottom-driven descent. Stepping onto Beale Street, she shivered. Shadows were long, and the many neon signs were bright, but the after-work crowd still had an hour or so of paper shuffling to get through before wending their way to the street's various bars. She, however, felt no need to wait and swung her way down to Silky's as quick as possible to get out of the winter cold. The Beale Street Flippers looked warm enough as they warmed up for their daring runs of flips and handsprings, all performed for spare change from the tourists. Beale Street was like that; an active, fluid community. Musicians played on the streets as well as in the clubs. Why not? On Beale Street, drinks were allowed inside and out.

Steel beams supported the aged, three-story facade of a building long-since demolished. Behind that imposing edifice stood a simple one-floor bar with an adjacent open courtyard, deserted in winter except for the mascot—a beer-guzzling goat. Many of the buildings on the tourist section of Beale Street were like that— aged facades with new structures behind them, but only Silky's had the audacity to keep the beams that signaled the underlying faux nature of the place.

Silky's was a regular hangout for the advertising crowd, making it a substantially prosperous business even when tourism was slack. It reeked of stale beer, unbridled ambition, and desperation. Even this early, she recognized several creative types from other downtown agencies. Offering them waves or nods of acknowledgment, she headed for the corner of the bar against the wall. Perched on that stool with her back to the wall, she could survey the entire room and its customers. It was her favorite spot, even if now she had to prop her cast on a chair to keep it from weighing her down. As she nursed a Manhattan and scratched beneath her cast with a straw, she thought about Dan's murder when Cindi waltzed in and spotted her.

As she hustled toward Janet, the girl said—none too quietly, "I heard you're the main suspect." Heads swiveled in Janet's direction.

"What?!" Janet exclaimed.

"The police think you killed Dan."

Discombobulated by Cindi's claim and the attention her statements drew, Janet sputtered, "That's ridiculous! Where did you hear such nonsense? I've got no motive."

"I know what I know."

"Yeah, sure." Janet gave a dismissive wave though the worry lines that appeared on her face spoke otherwise.

Cindi plopped on the adjacent bar stool and ordered a beer. "I heard all about your coat."

Janet's eyes narrowed. "How exactly?"

Cindi shrugged. "Just around." She took a hefty pull at her beer before glancing at Janet's cast.

"Hey, he signed your cast before you offed him. Think I'll sign it too." As she spoke, Cindi whipped a pen out of her purse to write before Janet could protest. In loopy letters, she wrote: Hope you get away with it. Love, Cindi.

"Jeez, girl! What...?"

But Cindi laughed over her shoulder as she headed towards the door, beer bottle in one hand while the fingers of her other waggled a farewell. Just before she exited, she turned with a small frown and called across the bar, "Do you have a cat?"

"A cat? Lord, no."

"Good." Cindi flashed a fake smile and sashayed away. Janet glared after her. *A cat? What was that about?* She then turned her attention to her new cast inscription. Something about it teased at the edge of her memory, but the more she tried to retrieve the thought, the further away it slid.

Cindi today was a 180-degree turn from Cindi yesterday. Of course, this time yesterday, Dan still lived, which could explain a lot. Still...

Grabbing her phone, she texted Eric Stillwell, Dan's former partner: Meet me at Silky's? Need to talk. Within seconds she received a positive reply, signaled the bartender to make two more Manhattans and moved to a more comfortable—and private—booth.

Then her phone rang. It was police headquarters. She answered and heard a man say: "Do you have any pets, ma'am?" She told them she didn't, and the call ended. *What is up with people wanting to know about pets?* she wondered.

Eric's appearance minutes later coincided with their drink delivery. "You must have flown," Janet said.

"I heard that cocktail shaker a-going and started running," he laughed, then turned somber. "I heard about Dan. I'm sorry. Sort of."

They toasted Dan and each other and took first sips (for him, anyway) with serious faces. Eric said, "Dan was an SOB to me—just like he was to you all those years ago—and I hated him for it. Come to think of it, he was an SOB to everyone, and I for one, am not too sorry to see him go."

Janet started at that revelation. *Could Eric be the one?*

He continued, "But tell me what's going on with you. Why'd you call?"

"I think I'm murder suspect number one."

"What?! Outrageous. You don't have an ounce of killer in you. Everyone knows that. You're the most pliable, easiest-going person I've ever met."

"I believe the word you're looking for is 'doormat.'" She sighed. "But I'm a doormat who threw a huge screaming fit at Dan the day he died."

"Really? Why?"

"Another piece of rejected copy. A radio script. I think this broken ankle has broken me in other ways, too."

"It's a lot to deal with." Eric glanced at her cast, then did a double-take as he read aloud: "*'Hope you get away with it. Love Cindi.'* Really?"

"She did that right here mere minutes ago. Claimed I was the prime suspect. Knew about my coat."

"Your coat?"

"The police took my coat into evidence."

"Why?"

"I'm not sure. They said they got an anonymous tip. That's all they shared."

"Strange."

"Then Cindi asked me if I had a cat."

Eric arched his eyebrows in surprise. "Maybe you better tell me everything from the beginning."

Janet started her tale with the elevator, but he stopped her.

"Start earlier. A lot earlier. From the beginning of the day."

She frowned as she described her day: Took a Lyft to work. Worked on a brochure for an agricultural client. Went to lunch at Dyers alone. Ran into Cindi on the street afterward.

Eric held up a hand. "Cindi was on Beale Street?"

"Yeah. She said she was glad I told her about Dan. Gave me a big hug. It surprised me."

"Wait. What did you tell Cindi about Dan?"

"It was a few evenings ago. Here, as a matter of fact. I was a bit potted, and she went on about how great Dan was, and I lost it. Told her she was one in a long line of floozies. That he always lied about leaving Emily. And I knew because it happened to me."

"Whoa! Not the best admission. How'd she react?"

"Called me a jealous bitch and stomped out."

"That sounds like our Cindi. That big hug does not." He paused to finish his drink and signaled for another round. "Something's off. Cindi is not the kind of girl who takes kindly to learning she's been used and duped."

"True enough."

"Go on."

"I went back to the office, had the shouting match with Dan about my rejected script, then spent the rest of the afternoon in a sulk while I rewrote it." She looked up at Eric. "I felt ashamed of my outburst. Knew everyone heard it. So I made sure I was the last to leave. Dan left about 15 minutes before I did. He didn't say goodbye, but I heard him shout, 'Be sure to lock up.' Which let me know I was alone. I waited until I figured he had left the building then left the office, locking it behind me."

"And then?"

"This part is tough, Eric." Her eyes started to shine. "I know he was a hound, but it's still hard." She took a shuddery breath and continued. "I went to the elevator, but there was a sign on it saying it was broken. Bobby's been playing jokes on me ever since I busted this ankle, so I hoped it might be him. It was handwritten. Didn't look official." She frowned; something important flitted at the edge of her consciousness. "So I pushed the down button anyway and heard the elevator coming up. I was about to pull the sign down when the door opened, and there was Dan." She started to cry.

Eric patted her hand in sympathy. "Skip that bit. Tell me what you did next."

She told him about the phone incident, bumping down the stairs, screaming for help, waiting for the police to arrive, and giving her statement. "That's about it." She downed her drink and stared into its emptiness.

"You want another?"

She shook her head. Then nodded. Eric signaled for two more, then turned back to her. "Was there a sign on the elevator at the bottom?"

"Now that I think about it, no."

"So Dan was headed down to the first floor, and you know he used the elevator because that's where you found him. The sign was on the second floor, and you were on the second. Whoever put the sign up..."

"It was probably Bobby."

"But then Dan would have torn it off. You said he was the last to leave besides you, and he used the elevator."

Janet looked shocked. "You think Dan put it up?"

He shook his head. "That man didn't understand practical jokes, much less pull them. Someone put that sign up for you to see, but it wasn't Dan."

Janet furrowed her brow in thought. "Eric, I hate to ask you this, but what were you doing yesterday around 5:30?"

Eric sighed. "I was with Emily."

Janet started. "But Emily said she didn't have an alibi?"

"Yeah. She would." He grimaced. "The manner in which I was with her could make us both suspects."

"Eric! Good lord!" Her eyes swept the bar as she came to grips with this new information. *Emily and Eric? Yowza!* "How long has this been going on?"

"It started not that long after I left the agency."

"So you were poaching clients and the wife."

He frowned. "Don't be like that, Janet. It doesn't suit you."

Abashed, she looked down at her drink. She'd long harbored hopes their friendship could turn into something more, but with Emily being free, not to mention being Emily, there was no chance of that.

To cover her disappointment, she let her gaze sweep the growing crowd, ending with a contemplative look at her cast. Her eyes then widened with sudden understanding.

"I've got to go, Eric. Now." She gathered her belongings and leaned on her crutches. Staring at him, she said, "I think I figured it out. I think I know who did it. But I need to check something first."

Without another word, Janet left the bar in a fast, crutch-driven bounce. Eric called after her but she didn't stop.

Janet worked her way down Beale then turned onto Main Street. She panted from her efforts. *Crutches are my cardio*, she thought. With much huffing and puffing, she traversed the seven blocks that separated Beale from the building where Cindi worked. The old structure once housed an upscale department store. That had morphed into a hive of small offices for media empires of varying sizes which all needed to maintain some local presence—like one person. Cindi worked on the top floor, the sole representative of American Media.

Grateful to find a working elevator, Janet impatiently waited for it to reach the fourth floor. She then wandered a maze of depressing hallways until she spotted the American Media logo and pushed open the door.

Cindi, on the phone, looked up with a client-worthy smile until she realized who it was. "I've got to go," she said and hung up. "Why are you here?"

"You left that note on the elevator."

"What?"

"You left the note on the elevator. Why?"

"What note? Why do you think I left some note?"

"This." Janet pointed to Cindi's loopy inscription on her cast. "You've got pretty distinctive handwriting."

Cindi eased out of her office chair and came around her disk to better confront Janet. One hand fidgeted with things on her desk, the other swept back her long hair. Both betrayed her nervousness. "What are you implying?"

"That you murdered Dan. I know it. But why did you leave the note? It makes no sense."

Cindi didn't even try to deny Janet's accusation. "I knew you were still upstairs. Dan said so. Said you'd hear us fight, but you didn't. After I gave him what he deserved, I put up the sign so you would use the stairs. Clumsy as you are, I expected you to fall. And die. But you had to push that button, didn't you? If you hadn't, no one would have found Dan until today. That was my plan."

Cindi picked up a brass pyramid paperweight, put it down, picked up a pencil. "Good thing I had a backup plan."

"But that very day, you thanked me for helping you. So why try to kill me?"

"You think you helped? With that drunken confession? I only hugged you to plant some cat hairs on your coat. Dan had a white cat. Its fur was always on his clothes, including those he kept at my house. I used some."

"To frame me."

Cindi grinned. "That was my backup plan. You thought that hug was sincere? Idiot." She toyed with the items in her pencil cup then picked up the paperweight again.

"It's a shame you came here. Now I have to defend myself against a killer. I would have preferred you went to jail... since you didn't have the decency to fall down those stairs and die."

Cindi stepped forward, aiming the point of the paperweight at Janet's face. Janet quickly swung one of her crutches, hit Cindi's arm, and sent the paperweight crashing into a file cabinet. Off balance, she then crumpled to the floor.

Cindi glanced at her arm. "Thanks for the bruise. Evidence of self-defense." She retrieved the paperweight while Janet struggled to get up. Looming over her victim, Cindi screamed bloody murder as she brought the paperweight down with all her might. Janet tried to dodge the blow, but it still punctured the side of her head.

Bleeding and dizzy, Janet reached for a crutch to defend herself while Cindi wound up to strike another blow.

At that moment, the door burst open, and the room filled with police officers.

Dropping the pyramid, Cindi cried, "Thank God you're here. She tried to kill me."

"I think you've got that backwards." Eric Stillwell stepped into the room.

It took a few minutes to determine who was the victim and who was the criminal, but they quickly sorted things out. One officer cuffed Cindi while reciting her rights and frog-marched her out of the room. Two others helped a shaking Janet onto a chair while a fourth called an EMT.

Janet stared at Eric. "How?"

"It didn't take a rocket scientist to figure out Cindi's cute message caused your reaction Though it did take me longer than it should. But going after her? Alone? In your condition? I called in the cavalry then came after you myself. "

Janet touched her bleeding head. "Thank God."

EMTs bustled in to treat Janet's wound, which looked worse than it was. Getting an all-clear from them, one of the officers turned to Janet and Eric. "We really need you two to come to headquarters to make statements."

They both nodded. Eric helped Janet reclaim her crutches, and they followed the police out.

After making their statements, Janet and Eric went back to Silky O'Sullivan's, selecting an oversized booth so Janet could stretch her leg out.

"Manhattan?" Eric asked.

She shook her head. "Not with these pain meds. Diet Coke, cheeseburger, fries. I'm starved."

Eric ordered for both of them. "So turns out Cindi is a bit psycho."

"If killing a married man for lying to you is psycho, absolutely. An officer told me she believed matching cat hair DNA from my coat and Dan's clothes would get me convicted. She read about something like that online but thought the results came in a lot faster."

"Like on TV."

"Yeah." Their food arrived, and Janet adjusted her position on the bench. "I do wonder why she wasn't picked up on a surveillance camera. They're everywhere on Beale."

"It all happened last night. They might not have had time to check the tapes. Plus, there's that door between the first-floor entry to your building and Wet Willie's. It's never locked. Cindi could go there, have a drink, come through to commit murder, then go back and enjoy all the excitement in complete safety."

"While enjoying a cocktail, no less." She paused and frowned. "Think I'll ask Emily to add a camera to that vestibule."

"I'll back you up."

Janet gave him a considering look. "Do you think you'll come back to Maxwell and Associates? Now that he's gone?"

He shook his head. "Love and business don't mix too well. I'd rather keep the love at this point in time."

"But you'll have to at least quit poaching clients."

"And that was such fun."

With a moue of irritation, Janet grabbed her dinner knife and slid it under her cast. "This itching is killing me. I'll be so glad to get this cast off."

"How much longer?"

"Next Tuesday. But a police officer has to be with me. They'll need it for evidence."

They looked at each other then burst into laughter.

CHAPTER 15

Radio Demon

April Jones

I'd like to tell you that I had nothing to do with the end of the world. But that would technically be a lie, and I don't have anyone left to lie to.

Like all other stories that begin this way, it started on a Monday morning. I was running late for work, so I awkwardly jogged to the car with a half-eaten piece of toast in my mouth. I sped down I-40 towards the ever dreaded Malfunction Junction. As I crested 75 mph, I swallowed the last bite of my dry toast and switched on the radio. I thumped the steering wheel as I waited for it to automatically connect to the familiar playlist on my phone. Soon the sounds of old pop music filled the car.

The cars slowed, signaling that I was approaching the bit of interstate perpetually clogged with commuters. The music stopped, replaced by my husband's ringtone.

"Hey, babe. Can you grab some milk on your way home today?" he asked.

"Sure," I said.

We hang up, and the music resumes. It's weird. I'm the one who always buys milk even though he's the only one who drinks it. The things we do for love.

Traffic slows to a crawl, and I sigh. The music stops again. I look down from the sea of tail lights, but I can't find any issues with the radio. It says it's playing a song, but nothing is coming out of the speakers. I reach down to adjust the volume, and the metal knob sends a sharp electrical shock up my arm. I pull my arm back, hissing.

I look up to find the cars still crawling through the chaos that is the morning commute before reaching back down for the radio knob again. The radio screen now shows an error message, and I make a mental note to have my husband check it out later.

"Why?" a pleasant voice asks.

"Because he's handy with things like..." I say before I realize I've just heard a voice. I look around the car, but no one is there. Where did the voice come from? I look down at the radio again.

"I'm not in there anymore," the voice says. It's a man's voice, higher pitched, but it doesn't sound like anyone I know.

Surely this is some practical joke from my husband. He loves things like this. Tossing cold water on me while I'm showering or scaring me as I walk up the stairs. Granted, this is more elaborate than his usual pranks, but it's definitely not outside of his capabilities. It's been a while since his last prank, and I conclude I'm due for one.

The voice sighs. "Humans are always like this. You have such difficulty accepting things as they really are."

Had the shock messed up my brain? Maybe I should signal and change directions towards the hospital.

"It won't do you any good," said the voice. "They won't be able to hear me."

Talking back to the voice in my head seemed like a bad idea. Perhaps it was simply stress. My boss wasn't exactly nurturing. He was a hoverer, the type that is never satisfied even when there are no imperfections in the work itself. Maybe I needed a vacation?

"You're not stressed," he says as if bored. "You're possessed."

I'll admit I don't know much about possessions, but I was pretty sure they involved bodies floating in the air and spinning heads. Creepy voices, screaming, and vomit. Nothing like this pleasant voice in my mind. And as far as I could tell, I wasn't levitating yet.

I signaled to change lanes. The hospital was sounding better every second.

"I'm a radio demon," he said. "I grant wishes."

"I'm pretty sure that's not how this works," I said. If I was going to be possessed, I might as well see where talking to this voice was going to get me. Maybe I'd be able to rule out seeing a doctor altogether. Which would be great considering our crappy insurance plan.

"That's how radio demons work," he replied. "What do you desire most?"

"What if I say to not be possessed? Will you go away?"

"Nope."

"So are we going to be a duo forever? Or is this like an Aladdin-and-Genie kind of relationship, and you'll disappear back into the radio after I make three wishes?"

"You're awfully concerned about the rules here. Don't you want anything?"

I take the off-ramp and slow my car. At the red light, I wait to turn left. "Sure, but you are a demon which means that telling you my wishes is going to make this situation go sideways."

"I'm not tricky like the genies you read about in those old human myths. I'm more sophisticated than that."

"Then why are you granting wishes for humans instead of, oh I don't know, vacationing in the Bahamas?"

"Let's just say I'm trying for a promotion. I have to put some good energy back into the universe before I can be forgiv...er...I mean promoted."

"What did you do?"

"This is not about me," he says. "This is about you. What do you want?"

"Why did you choose me of all people?"

The voice sighs. "You've got some good Karma built up. Good job for being a nice human."

I chew on his compliment for a moment. I mean, I try to be nice to people, but I still roll my eyes when my boss isn't looking and let my dog poop in the neighbor's yard. Sometimes I tell little white lies, mostly to avoid hurting people's feelings, but it's not like I'm some kind of saint. I haven't done anything downright bad, but nothing in my recent memory points to anything suggesting this kind of reward if that's what this is.

"For now, let's go to work," I said. "I'll think about what I want later."

"Sure," the voice agrees. "You're the boss here."

"Do you have a name?" I ask.

"Twitch. And yours?"

"You possessed me, and you don't even know my name?"

"I'm not God. Plus, it's less intrusive for you if I ask first, even if I know your name is Anna. I'm but a humble radio demon."

"You keep saying that as if I should know what that means. Where I come from, there aren't any radio demons."

"Aren't you going to go? The light is green. If it's easier for you, let's say I'm from Kansas. Nothing even remotely exciting ever happens there."

I follow the stream of traffic until it's time to pull into the office parking lot. I jog from the car into the building and try to slide into my cubicle undetected. I'm only three minutes late, but if Steve notices, he'll act as if I stroll into work whenever I feel like it.

The day passes quickly. The voice remains quiet, and I begin to wonder if he was ever there at all. I clock out and head for the door, but Steve calls out to me right as I reach the door.

"Anna, can you come here for a second?"

I sigh quietly and turn around, faking a smile. "Sure."

I'm not sure who chose the paint colors for his office, but the dull brown doesn't do much to cheer up the place. The only personal effects to be found in this standard-issue office are a small replica of Big Ben and a picture of Steve when he still had hair.

"Have a seat," he says.

I take a seat, setting my purse on the floor beside me. Steve sits down in his chair, and his lips curl into a predatory smile.

"I noticed that you were late again, Anna."

I don't like the way he says my name. I don't know if it's the pitch or tone, but it makes me irrationally grossed out. "Sorry about that. I will be on time from now on."

"That's what you say every time, and yet here we are." He rests his arms on the desk in front of him. "Which is why you're now on probation. If you're late again, I'm afraid it's the chopping block for you."

I nod my head. Trying to argue is pointless. I retrieve my purse and stand.

"Want me to take care of him for you?" Twitch asked.

Looks like I didn't imagine him after all. I shake my head.

"Do you have something you'd like to say?" Steve asked.

I shake my head again and exit the office. I spend the day working in my cubicle and trying to avoid seeing Steve again, so he doesn't invent another reason to reprimand me. During the drive home, I don't even have the energy to complain about the traffic as I pass through Malfunction Junction.

"I could get rid of all these cars for you," Twitch suggested, but I ignore him. He seems to take the hint and remains quiet.

I pull into the driveway, switch off the car, and shuffle my way inside the house. The only thing I want is a long, hot bath. Today has sucked, and I want to wash it away.

Once the water is ready, I lower myself into the hot water and try to forget I have to see Steve again tomorrow.

"I could fix this for you. If you want," Twitch says.

"No thanks," I mumble.

I lower myself into the tub until I'm fully submerged. Under the water, I can hear the clinks and clanks of the pipes running through our house. I pretend they are sympathizing with me. When my lungs burn, I slowly crest the water to find my husband.

"Did you get the milk?" he asks, though he's not looking at me. He's staring at his phone, scrolling up with his thumb.

"Sorry, I totally spaced it."

He sighs, never looking up from the screen, and walks out of the bathroom. It looks like his Monday didn't go any better than mine.

"I wish we had milk," I mumble as I stand and step onto the bath mat, leaving soppy footprints.

"Done," Twitch says.

"Huh?"

"You wanted milk. Now you have milk," he says.

I wrap a towel around myself and pad to the kitchen. My husband is sitting at the table drinking a glass of milk.

He sets the glass down. "I thought you said you forgot."

"Guess I forgot I bought it," I say. His phone buzzes, and he picks it up.

I turn and walk back into our bedroom, shutting the door so my husband can't hear. "How did you do that?"

"I told you I grant wishes," Twitch said. "You wished for milk, and poof, there it is. Cool, huh?"

Suddenly, the possibilities of having a wish-granting demon flood my mind. "Can you get rid of my work probation?"

"Just say the words," Twitch says.

I smile.

Weeks pass, and Twitch grants all of my wishes. True to his word, there were no tricks. If I wished for milk, then I got milk. Which was great considering the sudden milk shortage in Memphis made it nearly impossible to find it stocked anywhere. If I wanted the clock to stay still for a couple of minutes so I wasn't late for work, that's exactly what happened. If I wanted the bananas' spots to disappear, I was left with perfect golden bananas. Also great considering the only bananas I could find in the store nowadays were ridden with brown spots and black scuffs. I knew I was getting greedy, but Twitch seemed happy to grant whatever wish I came up with.

"Why do you only ever wish for small things?" Twitch asked.

I rinsed the last dish and turned the water off. "I guess I don't have any big wishes."

"I'm not complaining necessarily. I mean, I'm racking up points because you keep making wishes, but if you make a couple of big wishes, then I can finally be promoted."

I try to imagine my days without Twitch and instantly grow sad. I would have to go back to dealing with all of the daily annoyances I've avoided for the last few weeks. But, I can understand his ambitions. It can't be fun for him to replenish empty milk jugs and return library books so I don't accrue late fines.

"What did you have in mind?" I ask.

"I get major points for improving cities," he says.

I think through the streets of Memphis, the places that could use the most improvement. I don't want to do one of the sweeping I'm-trying-to-be-a-good-guy-but-I'm-really-insane kind of things. I want to do something small but effective.

"We should improve Malfunction Junction," I say.

"Not quite as grand as I was hoping, but it's still a good place to start."

The next day I drive to Malfunction Junction and pull the car off to the side of the road. I turn my hazard lights on and turn off the engine. Cars zip by, rocking my car slightly as they do.

"Why do you want to be promoted?" I ask.

"I messed up a wish," he says in a tone begging me not to ask him what happened.

"What did you do?"

Twitch sighs. "You still asked."

"What does a radio demon get promoted to anyways?"

Cars continued to buzz past us as I wait for Twitch to respond. A comfortable silence sits in between us. I realize there isn't much I know about my constant companion or the world he comes from.

"I wasn't always a radio demon, but I chose the wrong human last time. And now I have some repenting to do, which is why they sent me to a nicer human like you."

I nod. "What's first?"

"All you have to do is say the magic words."

"I wish that Malfunction Junction was fixed, so it's not so dangerous."

Time pauses as the overpasses and underpasses unwind and reform to create a perfectly sensible interstate exchange. Something that would have easily taken the state years to complete, but for Twitch, it was only a moment's worth of work. As the last overpasses fuses in place and time resumes, a large black blob with yellow eyes floats out and smiles at us. Then it turns and flies off into the trees.

"What is that?" I ask, pointing.

"Oops," Twitch says.

"Oops? What do you mean 'oops'?"

"I should have checked to see what was living in here before I granted your wish. Of course, a Blightkeeper would be here."

"What is a Blightkeeper?"

"Have there been many deaths here?"

"Of course, there are dozens of accidents here daily."

"A Blightkeeper's favorite meal, fear."

"So what does this all mean?"

"It means that I'm not going to be promoted anytime soon."

"Do we need to go catch it?"

"Nah. It will find a new feeding ground. I just did a good deed for nothing." Twitch sighs.

But I'm not so sure. It seems like a bad idea to free something called a Blightkeeper. Still, I turn the key and rejoin traffic. If it was that bad, surely Twitch would tell me, right?

Several weeks pass. The milk shortage continues, and banana prices skyrocket. Twitch and I go around fixing smaller things like broken park swings and burned-out street lamps. We even tried to work Twitch's magic on my indifferent husband, but it seems that Twitch is only good on things and not people. He still replaces the milk that only my husband drinks, but I can tell he's itching to try something bigger again.

Another Tuesday finds me at work when Steve comes running out of his office screaming for us to turn on the news. Someone pulls it up on their computer, and we all gather round. A lady with perfectly styled hair and angry looking eyebrows talks at us in an emotionless voice.

"Fallout from the nuclear bomb launched moments ago is expected to extinguish the better part of our beloved country. The final words from the President are resolute, 'We will continue to fight for America well after the bombs land. Those who attack us do so at their own peril. May God be with us all.'"

My fellow workers look at each other in disbelief, and the office erupts in panic. Within minutes the entire office empties, and I am left alone looking out the window beside my desk before the reality of the situation dawns on me. We're going to die unless someone can save us. I jump up, grab my purse, and sprint to the car.

"Twitch, can we fix this?" I ask though I'm afraid of what his answer will be. I turn the key in my ignition and bring the engine to life. What should I do first? Call my husband? Drive? Cry? I'm not sure. I suddenly wish I would have read more about how to survive a nuclear fallout.

"I've been waiting for this moment my entire life!"

He sounds excited and not as if the entire country is about the die. Still, if he can save us, I will forgive his callousness in this moment. I close my eyes to make my most fervent wish yet.

My phone buzzes. I open my eyes and look down at a message from my husband.

"Anna, I think I'm going to die."

I immediately text back, "I can fix this."

"What?" He responds. He still doesn't know about Twitch, and I'm not sure there's a good way to tell your spouse you've been possessed, so I have no intentions of telling him now or ever.

"I wish that the bomb would disappear. I wish we would be safe again." I say.

I pull up the browser on my phone. I type 'news station' into the search bar and click the first website on the list that appears. The same stoic anchor from before is reporting.

"Military efforts were able to subdue the bombs heading for the western and eastern coasts. By way of the United States joint military operations, the bomb has appeared to change directions. America is safe, though the same cannot be said for those who originally launched the bomb. The President has already signed a declaration of war..."

I click the X in the upper right corner and try to remember how to breathe normally.

"I'm definitely getting promoted this time," Twitch says.

"Twitch, I wish the bomb would *disappear* and not change directions."

"I've been meaning to tell you, but that's not really how this works."

"What?"

"There's a price for magic?" Twitch offers weakly.

All the fairy tales I've ever read rush to mind. "You mean the milk shortage?"

"All me. Well, really it's all your husband, though we both know there's no way he can drink that much milk."

"And the bananas?"

"Yep."

"Twitch, what am I supposed to wish then? I wish the bomb would stop."

"Then we'll be dead. You sure you want that?"

My phone buzzes in my hand again. I look down.

"Anna, I want a divorce. I met someone else and, since we didn't die, I'm going to spend my life with her."

"WHAT?" I type, but he doesn't respond. Five years of marriage, and he breaks up with me over a text.

I set the phone calmly on my dash. I don't know if it was the weeks of wishes granted, or some kind of late-onset rebellion on my part, or the shock from learning my husband wanted a divorce, but something inside me snapped.

"Twitch?" I say.

"Oh no. Don't do it."

"Can you bring that bomb back?"

"There goes my promotion."

Why Malfunction Junction?

In 2011 the American Transportation Research Institute ranked two Memphis intersections among the top 250 most congested locations in America. Locals know them well: The intersection of I-240 and I-55, and the intersection of I-240 and I-40; two places where ongoing construction, heavy truck traffic, and long delays are the rule. These are the "Malfunction Junctions" of Memphis. But other malfunctions come at other junctions in life. These stories explore a few of them.

The Contributors:

Daniel Reece has been writing in and about obscurity for twenty-five years. He has been published in *Memphis* magazine and two on-line publications. Daniel primarily writes novel-length fiction across all genres but occasionally dabbles in short form when called upon. He lives in Memphis with his wife, Jennifer, and daughter, Charlie. Daniel's debut novel *Knight and Daye* is available through Amazon and TouchPoint Press.

When not homeschooling, fostering, or teaching theatre, **Rae Harding** writes every spare moment she can steal. Rae was recently published in 4 Horsemen Publications' 2021 anthology Teen Angst Mix Tape Vol. 1 and received Honorable Mention in the Malice in Memphis Hit Me With Your Best Shot Contest in 2018. You can catch her on Twitter and Instagram @raehardingbooks or at raeharding.com

Rikki Boyce has turned from creating award-winning advertising to writing fiction. Contrary to what some believe, that's a huge leap. While she works towards her big break (she already has a featured story in *From a Cat's View Vol. II*), she continues to maintain her book review website at indelible-inc.com

As a Psychiatric Advanced Practice Nurse, **Kathryn Skinner** worked for twenty-one years for Methodist Hospitals of Memphis as a Nurse Counselor and Instructor in the School of Nursing and the Department of Nursing Staff Development. She has published 16 articles in the nursing literature. In retirement, she enjoys writing memoirs.

April Jones has written, read, or edited her way through dozens of fictional worlds. She spends her days convincing middleschoolers that ELA is, in fact, worth learning. When she's not writing, April spends her time traveling, learning new languages, and trying to keep her mischievous cat from eating all of her houseplants. Her debut novel is *The Curse Breaker*, and you can find her most recent short story in *Standing Defiant:Stories in the Last Brigade Universe*.

Justin Siebert is a high school science teacher, writer, and educational YouTuber in Memphis, TN, where he lives with his wife, Carol, and daughter, Alondra. His short fiction has appeared in *The Arcanist* and TLDR Press's *Beneath Strange Stars* anthology. Check out his work at justinmsiebert.com and www.youtube.com/siebertscience

Susan Hopson has always loved writing. Children's fiction and romantic short stories are her current interests. Additionally, she is developing a middle-grade fantasy novel. Her successful career in Human Resources allowed her to work on diverse assignments and live overseas. Susan currently teaches English to children online. Originally a native of Indianapolis, Susan enjoys life in Memphis with her daughter and grandson. In her spare time, she walks, reads, and bakes.

Xia L. Cox: Exciting. Enlightening. Inviting. I'm writing shit that I feel.

Printed in the USA
CPSIA information can be obtained
at www.ICGtesting.com
LVHW052321050923
757236LV00003B/285